"We take this ship!"
a bald pirate shouted.

Desperate men charged the wounded defenders.

Lying on the deck, Ryan emptied his blaster at the pirates, chilling two more before they were past him and charging the others. They clearly wanted no part of the raven-haired man with the battle-scarred face and a working blaster.

The two groups converged, each choosing a person to fight. A single blaster roared, and then it was swords, axes and knives in total blood chaos, the individual screams and curses mixing into the muted roar of mob warfare.

Weapon in hand, Ryan couldn't find anybody to chill. The people were so well mixed, the Deathlands warrior would only ace the sailors he had promised to protect. Then he noticed a movement out of the corner of his eye.

"Crew of the *Connie!*" he shouted. "Hit the deck!"

Other titles in the Deathlands saga:

JAMES AXLER

DEATH LANDS®

Savage Armada

THE SKYDARK CHRONICLES
Book I

A GOLD EAGLE BOOK FROM

WORLDWIDE®

TORONTO • NEW YORK • LONDON
AMSTERDAM • PARIS • SYDNEY • HAMBURG
STOCKHOLM • ATHENS • TOKYO • MILAN
MADRID • WARSAW • BUDAPEST • AUCKLAND

To Police Sergeant Matthew A. Mingle,
who walked that thin blue line for as long as possible

First edition March 2001

ISBN 0-373-62563-4

SAVAGE ARMADA

Let them hate, as long as they fear.
—*Accius Navius, High Priest for Tiberius the Elder,* 617 B.C.

THE DEATHLANDS SAGA

This world is their legacy, a world born in the violent nuclear spasm of 2001 that was the bitter outcome of a struggle for global dominance.

There is no real escape from this shockscape where life always hangs in the balance, vulnerable to newly demonic nature, barbarism, lawlessness.

But they are the warrior survivalists, and they endure—in the way of the lion, the hawk and the tiger, true to nature's heart despite its ruination.

Ryan Cawdor: The privileged son of an East Coast baron. Acquainted with betrayal from a tender age, he is a master of the hard realities.

Krysty Wroth: Harmony ville's own Titian-haired beauty, a woman with the strength of tempered steel. Her premonitions and Gaia powers have been fostered by her Mother Sonja.

J. B. Dix, the Armorer: Weapons master and Ryan's close ally, he, too, honed his skills traversing the Deathlands with the legendary Trader.

Doctor Theophilus Tanner: Torn from his family and a gentler life in 1896, Doc has been thrown into a future he couldn't have imagined.

Dr. Mildred Wyeth: Her father was killed by the Ku Klux Klan, but her fate is not much lighter. Restored from predark cryogenic suspension, she brings twentieth-century healing skills to a nightmare.

Jak Lauren: A true child of the wastelands, reared on adversity, loss and danger, the albino teenager is a fierce fighter and loyal friend.

Dean Cawdor: Ryan's young son by Sharona accepts the only world he knows, and yet he is the seedling bearing the promise of tomorrow.

In a world where all was lost, they are humanity's last hope....

Chapter One

Even as the swirling electronic mists began to fade,
the first shock of pain shot through his body and Ryan
Cawdor knew that something was terribly wrong with
the jump.

"Fucking hell," Ryan muttered, slumping to the
cold concrete floor of the mat-trans chamber and gagging on the taste of sour bile that filled his throat. The
big man swallowed a few times to clear his mouth.
Fireblast! They hadn't had a jump this bad in weeks.
For one terrible moment, he wondered if the machinery had malfunctioned, scrambled their insides, or
something equally awful.

But then the convulsions racking his body began
to subside, and Ryan could hear the moans and curses
of the others around him. Nobody was screaming, and
there was no smell of blood. No malfunc then, just a
rad-blasted bad jump. Dimly he could sense the others
spreading out, all instinctively trying to get away
from the source of their pain.

Time passed slowly, and Ryan finally summoned
enough strength to sit and brush the wild profusion
of black hair from his sweaty face. There was the
expected stink of sweat and puke in the air, but much
stronger than normal. Usually the life-support system

of a redoubt cleared away any unpleasant traces within minutes. The atmosphere in the underground bunkers was usually scrubbed clean and smelled with chem disinfectants. But not this time, and Ryan didn't like that.

Adjusting the patch that covered his ruined left eye, Ryan blinked his right into focus and weakly glanced about. Four, five, six, all of his friends were present, and looking as bad as the Deathlands warrior still felt.

Sprawled on the floor of the mat-trans unit, with one hand extended onto the concrete apron outside, was a tall slim man with silvery hair. Fighting for breath, the old man wore an old-fashioned frock coat, and a frilly white shirt drenched in sweat. An ebony walking stick with an elaborate silver lion's head was clenched in a twitching hand, and a monstrously huge revolver with two barrels jutted from the holster on his hip. The leather belt supporting the hand cannon was made entirely of lumpy pouches tightly buttoned shut.

"You…okay, Doc?" Ryan asked, surprised at the hoarseness of his voice.

Dr. Theophilus Tanner forced open an eye and looked vaguely about until focusing on the speaker. "Have…" He stopped to swallow, then tried again. "Have we crossed the River Styx, my good Ryan?" he asked in a deep rumbling voice.

Just then a hacking cough took Ryan and he couldn't answer for a while. Nuking hell, he thought, there was another bad smell in the air, something familiar that he couldn't identify immediately. It lay under the stink of their tortured bodies like the scum under a river of sewage. Faint, but bad. Ryan seemed to have some trouble focusing his thoughts. Another side effect of the jump? Fumbling at his side, he found a canteen and tried to force his hands to unscrew the top without spilling the water everywhere.

"We're not dead yet, you old coot," murmured a stocky black woman flat on her stomach between the two men. Slumped over a canvas bag, a wild array of dreadlocks masked her features. A sleek revolver was holstered at her hip, a battered tin canteen draped over a shoulder. As she struggled to roll onto her side, a canvas lump was exposed as a bulky backpack patched with a dozen different pieces of cloth that almost hid the small red cross.

"As always, madam," Doc rumbled softly, "I bow to your vast and profound expertise of vaunted medical knowledge."

"Stuff it," Dr. Mildred Wyeth told him.

"Ryan," she added, "what happened?"

"Just a bad jump," Ryan answered, lowering the canteen and replacing the cap. Every passing moment was pouring new strength into his body, but that odd smell was still lingering about them like flies over a corpse.

"Bad? Worst jump ever." Sitting with his back to a wall of the unit, John Barrymore Dix rubbed his pale face with both hands. He covered his features for a moment, massaging his temples. A compact Uzi lay at his side, while a S&W 12-gauge shotgun was draped across his shoulder. On the floor alongside was a canvas bag with a dull red stick of dynamite and length of bright yellow fuse peeking from under the loose flap.

Wordlessly Ryan passed over the canteen, and J.B. gratefully took the container, sipping steadily. Drink too fast and he'd only lose it again on the floor.

"Thanks," J.B. said, lowering the container, then holding it out to the others. "Any takers?"

"Here," a redheaded woman called weakly, reaching for the canteen.

Shifting position, J.B. passed it over, and Krysty Wroth drank deeply, a trickle of water flowing down either side of her full lips.

Her khaki jumpsuit was partially unbuttoned, exposing a wealth of cleavage. Draped over her strong shoulder was a bearskin coat, the fur matted from being badly cured. A Smith & Wesson revolver rode a holster near the buckle of her gun belt, the leather loops full of shiny brass.

"Thanks," Krysty said, passing the canteen back to Ryan. Already the woman was speaking normally, and she stood without trouble.

In the distant corner of the hexagonal chamber, a boy was on his hands and knees retching quietly. Nobody paid any attention to him. All the friends had gotten jump sickness at one time or another. It was the price they paid for traveling the Deathlands in the mat-trans chambers.

"What happened?" Krysty asked, her face pensive. Gently caressing her face as if stirred by secret winds, her animated hair coiled and relaxed, mirroring her anxious thoughts. "Some sort of malfunc?"

"Seems likely," Ryan said, forcing himself to stand, then leaning against the steel wall to keep from going down again.

"Least not chilled," a pale teenager said. "Or a frybrain."

"So far," Mildred corrected sternly.

Ryan frowned but said nothing.

Nodding in agreement, Jak Lauren was breathing heavily as if gathering strength for an attack. The albino teen's shoulder-length hair was the color of snow, and his strange ruby-red eyes peered out through the tangles like the spotting laser of a sniper rifle. A dozen leaf-bladed throwing knives were hidden among the folds of his clothes, and a huge .357 Magnum Colt Python revolver rested backward in a belt holster.

With fumbling fingers, J.B. retrieved a pair of wire-rimmed glasses from his shirt pocket and gently put them on.

"Where the hell are we?" he asked, staring at the drab chamber walls.

Grimacing from sore stomach muscles, Ryan moved to the door, which had a square of plain glass in its middle. He scanned the immediate area and, seeing no threat, he turned the plain knob and opened the door.

"Don't know," he replied grimly, looking into the room outside. "I never saw this redoubt before."

The domed room was made of corrugated steel, just

like the kind used on the floors of big-rig trucks, but welded together in a crazy quilt pattern as if assembled randomly from whatever was available. And across the room was a door that looked as if it had come off a submarine. That was totally wrong.

"It's not a redoubt," J.B. said grimly, retrieving his crumpled fedora from the floor. He smoothed the brim and placed the hat on his head tilted slightly backward to afford maximum visibility. "Place looks like it was thrown together."

"Fireblast," Ryan growled. "It's another bastard homemade gateway!"

"Aw, shit," Mildred said, drawing the ZKR target pistol from her belt and thumbing back the hammer.

"Homemade hellholes," Jak grunted in displeasure, his voice hoarse and raw.

Suddenly more retching noises came from across the chamber.

"Dean, are you okay?" Krysty asked, going closer to the kneeling boy.

The boy gamely nodded and slowly raised himself off the cold floor. He wobbled a bit, the heavy backpack on his shoulders obviously throwing him off balance. But he grimaced and slowly stood erect as if defying the very laws of gravity.

"I'm fine," Dean mumbled, stealing a glance at his father.

Hiding a smile, Krysty turned her back to the boy. Puberty was upon him, and the strong need to be accepted as another adult was making itself felt. But then, Dean was a battle-scarred veteran of a hundred

fights, he owned a knife, a working blaster, a pocket
full of ammo and carried more food in his backpack
than most poor bastards ate in a month. In the Deathlands, that not only made Dean a rich man, but also
a formidable opponent. He possessed a younger ver-
sion of his father's strength and speed. Dean had no
fear in a fight, and when he was fully grown, Krysty
had no doubt he would become a formidable warrior.

Taking a rag from his back pocket, Dean wiped the
sour drool from his mouth, then tossed the soiled
cloth aside. Controlling his breathing, the boy forced
his hands to start patting his clothes to make sure his
Browning Hi-Power blaster and knife were present.
He knew they were, but it was a good trait to hone.
He'd seen enough sec men jump from a height and
charge into battle, only to find their blaster gone,
fallen from its holster when the sec man had hit the
ground. As his father always said, trust nobody, not
even yourself, because one mistake, and you'd be taking the last train west. True words.

"Anybody recognize the place?" Ryan asked.

"Not I," Doc announced, nervously clicking the
lion's head on his stick and sliding out a few feet of
the steel sword hidden inside, only to slide it closed
again with a snap of his wrist.

"I've never seen steel chambers before," Krysty
added. "Looks like it was built from spare parts."

"Mebbe it was," J.B. said just as the overhead
lights flickered briefly.

The companions froze in place, watching the ceiling. The fixture had six fluorescent tubes, four dark,

and if the remaining two blew they would be in total darkness. Easy targets if attacked.

As the strobing tubes stabilized again, Ryan went to the door and closely inspected the curved oval of steel. The weld marks were plainly visible; no effort had been made to file them smooth or paint them. Ryan placed a palm against the metal, which was oddly cold. For a moment, he thought he felt a vibration in the steel, but then it was gone. As a precaution, he backed away.

"Yeah, this was thrown together fast," Ryan said thoughtfully.

"Then mebbe we should leave," Krysty suggested, her hair coiling tightly. "Who knows what's out there?"

"No need stay," Jak added, frowning. "Let's go."

A hand resting on his Uzi, J.B. turned from the strange door. "Makes sense. Let's blow, and hope for better luck next location."

"Sounds good," Dean said.

But before Ryan could respond, the flickering lights flashed brightly, then winked out completely, plunging the chamber into near total darkness.

The companions froze. Softly, from the other side of the door, came a hard metallic thump. Then another.

"Triple red!" Ryan whispered, snicking the safety off his blaster.

Quickly the others drew their weapons, then dug into their pockets and unearthed greasy candles, lighting them with predark cig lighters. The cheap butane lighters were good for thousands of lights and had cost next to nothing before skydark; now they were worth a baron's ransom.

Rummaging in her med kit, Mildred found her old battered flashlight. As she flicked the switch, the squat tube gave off only a weak yellow illumination. Cursing softly, the woman turned it off and started to squeeze the pump handle on the side to operate the tiny generator inside and recharge the miniature batteries. After a few moments, the light came back strong, the clear white light filling the chamber. However, Mildred had noticed that the batteries were holding a charge for consistently shorter periods and sadly knew that soon it would be dead.

"Save it," Ryan ordered.

Mildred grunted acknowledgment and turned off the device.

Moving quietly, Krysty and Dean anchored their candles on opposite sides of the room while the rest waited with fingers on triggers. Minutes passed in silence. Then came another metallic thump.

"Fuck this, let's go," Ryan decided, and walked into the mat-trans unit.

The companions followed close behind, leaving the candles in place in case they were attacked before the mat-trans activated. Ryan closed the door to activate the jump, but nothing happened. He hit the LD button, but it felt loose, and the swirling mists remained inactive.

"Trapped," Jak growled.

"J.B., the door," Ryan ordered, walking from the unit and taking a defensive position near the portal.

Now Mildred clicked on her flashlight and J.B. went to the door, kneeling before the wheel lock. Expertly he ran his hands along the sides and surface of the smooth metal. Then pulling some mechanical tools from his pockets, he quickly checked the jamb and locking mechanism.

"No booby traps I can find," he announced. "But who knows what's on the other side?"

Grimly Ryan nodded in agreement as he holstered the SIG-Sauer pistol and slid the Steyr SSG-70 off his shoulder. The longblaster was freshly cleaned from before the jump, its rotary mag filled with live rounds.

Working the bolt, the one-eyed man eased off the safety. Behind him, the others spread out in the short arc of a firing line, every weapon trained on the door. Another thump sounded.

"Open it," Ryan said, the longblaster held ready.

Flexing his hands, J.B. gripped the wheel, then paused, and released it. Pulling a can of oil from a pocket, he carefully dripped a few drops of the precious lub onto the stem of the wheel, then along the jamb of the door where hinges should be located.

Tucking the can away, the Armorer tightened his fingerless leather gloves, took hold and started to turn the wheel.

It refused to budge at first, then suddenly gave a scream of rusted metal and spun freely, almost out of control. The lock disengaged with a muffled thump, and J.B. quickly moved out to one side and swung the Uzi into its usual position.

Reaching out with the muzzle of the Steyr, Ryan gave the door a hard tap and it swung easily aside. Instantly a cloud of dark fumes flowed into the chamber. Covering their mouths, the companions hastily retreated into the mat-trans unit to get away from the spreading gas. As the cloud filled the chamber, it reached the candles on the wall, and they winked out instantly.

Chapter Two

The companions scrambled to find bits of cloth to use
as masks against the encroaching cloud when a familiar smell reached them and everybody relaxed.

"Shit," Jak exhaled, annoyed. "Wag exhaust."

"Inside a gateway?" Dean demanded, fighting
back a cough. The fumes were killing his throat.

"At least," J.B. said, shoving his hat farther back
on his head, "there's nobody in the next room."

"Hopefully," Mildred warned.

"Making me feel dizzy," Krysty said, touching her
temples. In response, her hair was lying limply on her
shoulders, hardly moving.

"Can't stay here," Ryan said, noticing a lack of
openings for vents or fans. "I'm on point. Let's go."

Quickly the companions prepared their weapons.
Jak eased one of his many knives loose and cocked
back the hammer on his Colt Python. Krysty checked
the load in her S&W .38 revolver, while Mildred did
the same with her Czech-made ZKR .38 target pistol.
Dean dropped the clip of his 9 mm Browning Hi-
Power to check the load, then slammed the mag back
into the grip of his semiautomatic blaster.

Meanwhile, J.B. pulled back the bolt on his Uzi
submachine gun, and reached behind to pump the ac-

tion on his S&W M-4000 shotgun. Loaded with fléchette rounds, the weapon would blow a person or creature into shreds at twenty yards.

Holding his huge LeMat steady, Doc rotated the cylinder to visually inspect the loads.

Longblaster in one hand, 9 mm pistol in the other, Ryan headed across the chamber, J.B. and Krysty flanking him. As the three entered the next room, the others waited from the doorway ready to give cover in case of trouble.

Both of his blasters sweeping for targets, Ryan stepped through the oval doorway and blinked at the harsh fumes tainting the murky atmosphere. Moving stealthily, he dimly saw a control console, some shelves to the left and a hulking collection of machinery to the right. The room continued for another few yards, then ended in another steel door exactly like the first.

"J.B., Krysty, behind the console," Ryan ordered, leveling his Steyr.

As they took the position, Ryan listened at the door for a moment, then started to turn the wheel. He struggled against the rust, finally forcing the wheel to turn, the heavy levers withdrawing from the four sides of the frame and coming free with a rain of corrosion sprinkling to the floor. As the door disengaged, Ryan pulled it aside. Raw sunlight and fresh air poured into the room, carrying the smell of a jungle.

As the fresh air blew into the gateway, it broke the cobwebs apart and stirred tiny dust devils to dance madly about the metal floor. Blinking at the harsh daylight, Ryan stepped onto a predark concrete sidewalk, tall weeds growing in the cracks. Past the sidewalk was a large expanse of bare ground, the wrecks of wags and assorted debris dotting the black soil in an irregular pattern. A telephone pole rested almost sideways amid the broken things, the remains of insulted cables dangling impotently from the rotting crossbars.

Seagulls called and circled in the sky against a dark expanse of storm clouds laced with orange and purple. Thunder rumbled softly as sheet lightning flashed in the heavens. Ryan sniffed carefully, but couldn't detect any trace of sulfur. There would be no acid rains coming for a while.

A lush jungle rose all around the metal building, colorful flowers blooming everywhere. Somewhere in the far distance, a large cat roared a challenge to the world.

Leaving the door open, Ryan turned and whistled twice, short and sharp. Soon the rest of the companions entered the small room, efficiently spreading out. Less than a minute later, they converged across the room near Ryan. Gratefully they gulped in the fresh air as the jungle breeze swirled the exhaust around and around the room, quickly dissipating the fumes.

"Nobody here," Krysty said, easing down the hammer on her S&W .38 revolver.

"Not anymore," Dean said, jerking a thumb toward the shelves.

Ryan glanced that way, then strode over. He had

missed this in the thick clouds, walking right by the poor bastard.

It was a human skeleton lying facedown on the floor, one hand extended toward the mat-trans unit. From under the tattered strips of dingy cloth, bare white bones gleamed in the reflected light from outside. There were no shoes or weapons.

As there was nothing to salvage from the bones on the floor, Ryan checked the wall shelves. But they contained only sagging cardboard boxes that had once been filled with ammo, and other assorted trash lying under a thin coating of dust. He frowned. Somebody had stored a lot of supplies here, probably getting ready for a jump, and when they departed, took everything not nailed down.

"A whitecoat," Krysty observed, identifying the style of clothing of the dead man. "Mebbe the tech who built the gateway."

"How did he die?" Dean asked, standing near the open doorway and keeping a watch on the ground outside.

Ryan noticed the boy's attention, and grunted in approval. "You see anything coming this way, just close the door," he said.

Dean nodded. "Unless it's coming fast," he agreed, crossing his arms so that the sleek Browning pistol rested on a wrist.

"I'll check those machines," J.B. said, and went to the other side of the console. He ducked and was gone from sight.

"Not see lead or arrow," Jak noted, poking among the ribs of the skeleton. "Head not bust, no club job."

"He bled to death," Ryan stated, pointing at a nearby wall. There, in plain sight now, were a couple of steel sharp spikes sticking out from the metal wall. Smeared patterns of brown went from the spikes to the floor, the trails going straight to the mutilated hands of the dead man.

Doc frowned. "Nailed him to the wall," he said. "Where he could watch the others leave."

Taking a knife from her boot, Krysty probed the brittle bones of the hands. "Crude job, center bones are all shattered," she commented. "That's how he was able to get loose. These folks obviously didn't do a lot of this."

"So he was somebody special they hated," Mildred said slowly. "Probably wanted him to starve to death, while choking in the exhaust fume, with escape only yards away."

"Lot of hate," Jak commented, taking a piece of venison jerky from a pocket and biting off a piece.

"Hate is often more powerful than love, my friend. See?" Doc espoused, tracking the dead man's progress with his ebony stick. "This stalwart chap pulled himself off the wall to escape, and died of blood loss trying to follow them."

"Her," Mildred corrected him, lifting the pelvic bone from the ancient skeleton. "This was a woman, middle-aged, good health."

"Recent?" Ryan asked bluntly. The bones looked old, but that didn't mean they were.

Placing the pelvis aside, the physician lifted the skull and unhinged the jaw to glance at the teeth. "Predark," she stated. "This is ceramic dental work, top of the line. Not old-fashioned silver inlays. From my time."

"Hey, what's that?" Krysty asked, and she brushed aside the remains of the right hand, the bones rattling as they rolled under the wall shelves.

Exposed on the floor was some sort of a symbol, written in the dead woman's blood. Two lines of different lengths were bisected by another line at an angle.

"Don't recognize that," Ryan said. "Doc?"

"Not Latin," the scholar rumbled, studying the configuration. "Nor is it from the Greek alphabet, Sanskrit or hieroglyphics. Perhaps Hebrew?"

Mildred shrugged. "Hard to say."

"Tech talk," Jak sniffed as if that settled the matter.

"Mil code," Dean suggested from the doorway.

Thoughtfully Ryan adjusted the strap of the longblaster over his shoulder. "Could be anything. Or nothing. A person can get crazy when dying from blood loss, sort of like being drunk while freezing to death."

"Nasty."

"There's no good way to die."

"Must have been mighty important for her to write in blood," Krysty said slowly, "and then lay a hand over the symbol to protect it from being smudged."

Licking the point on a stubby pencil, Mildred carefully duplicated the symbol in her yellowed notepad and slid it back into her med kit.

"Might be important," she said.

"Mebbe to her," Ryan said, turning toward the machinery. "Not us. Our concern is getting out of here."

Rising, Jak walked over to the open door and leaned against the jamb, his massive .357 Magnum Colt Python in hand. He offered the rest of the jerky to Dean, who accepted, and the two teens stood guard, chewing steadily. Edging the bare ground was a tattered wooden fence, and some rusted coils of what might have been barbed wire. On the other side was the crushed wreckage of civilian cars, and assorted junk.

"Invasion force?" Dean asked casually.

"Hell of a fight," Jak said.

"Yep," Dean agreed.

Swallowing, Jak took a deep breath. "Smells good."

"Like home?"

A frown. "Bayou swamp, not jungle." Then the albino cracked a rare smile. "But close enough."

Crossing the room, Ryan went to the hodge-podge assortment of machinery. The collection reached from the front wall to the wall of the mat-trans unit. At the front end was a pile of nuke batteries. At the other end was a coil of highly polished copper, apparently filled with lots of smaller coils inside and a single massive iron bar in the middle. What it could be he had no idea.

Dusting off his hands, J.B. rose from behind the console and started flipping switches on the control board.

"Tell me," Ryan said, coming closer.

"Damned if I know," the short man replied, turning dials. Nothing happened. "Everything here seems to be in working order, so that's not the problem."

Going to a large metal tank extending from the side of a motor, J.B. unscrewed the cap and looked inside. Then he stuck in a hand, his fingertips coming out barely moistened.

"Nuke me, we're trapped," he stated glumly.

Just then, something loudly clicked and the machinery struggled into life, spewing out black clouds of exhaust, but it stopped after only a few seconds.

Ryan scowled darkly. "Doesn't sound broken. Out of gas?"

"Yeah. Not a drop left in the fuel tank."

"The mat-trans runs on gas?" Dean asked incredulously.

"How is that possible?" Krysty asked, joining the men at the console.

Pensively J.B. removed his fedora to scratch his head, then jammed the hat back on. "Ryan was right. These folks were desperate to leave. This is the most ramshackle piece of equipment I've ever seen. I'm astonished it ever worked."

Going to the machines, J.B. said, "These nuke batteries start this big motor, which turns this modified car transmission to increase its rpm and turn this electric generator really fast so that it can feed high-voltage current into a step-up transformer, which boosts the voltage again and pours the electricity into this homemade Tesla coil until there is enough power to run the mat-trans."

"Brilliant," Doc rumbled, eagerly approaching the copper coil for inspection. "A homemade lightning bolt. Most impressive."

"Freeze!" J.B. barked, and stepped between the scholar and the machinery. "The mat-trans needs a bastard load of power to work, and while that coil doesn't have enough to send us anywhere, it's still got sufficient volts to kill you. Won't be anything left but ash and an echo."

"Indeed," Doc muttered, backing away from the predark power plant. "Thank you for the admonishment, John Barrymore."

"Be more careful, you old coot," Mildred chided.

"I will, madam." Doc smiled, displaying his oddly perfect teeth. "Next time, I shall have you touch it for me."

Once again, the motor tried to start and died.

"Homemade gateway, jerry-built power plant," Ryan growled, studying the control panel on the turbine and flipping a cutoff switch. Several weakly glowing indicators faded away into darkness. "Hell, we're lucky we ever made it here alive."

Ambling to the console, Jak went to the fuel tank and sniffed. "Only gas?" he asked pointedly. "Or shine okay?"

Alcohol, now there was a good idea. Ryan rubbed

his unshaven chin. Most wags ran on some sort of alcohol these days. Anybody could make that.

"Well?" Ryan asked.

"No, doesn't have to be gas," J.B. replied with a crooked grin. "Shine should do the job, too. This isn't a car motor, but an emergency generator. Turbine, not pistons. Designed to run on just about anything fluid that burns."

"We have this," Mildred said, hauling a glass bottle into view from her med kit.

Ryan took the Molotov cocktail and shook it gently. The brownish fluid inside the bottle frothed slightly, but didn't foam.

"Good. No soap mixed in," he said.

"This'll work fine," J.B. said as he took the bottle, but then he frowned. "Just not enough. I'd guess that we need a full gallon to recharge the system. This is less than a quart. Nowhere near what we need."

"But a good start," Doc stated confidently. "We can make the rest. Eh, my dear Jak?"

"Sure. Shine no prob. But need time. Week to turn mash. Need copper pipe for distill. Sugar no prob. Jungle got lots fruit for sweetening."

"It does not have to taste good."

"Sweetening makes to turn faster."

"Ah."

"Anybody got a better plan?" Ryan asked the group at large. "Okay then, we build a still, make shine and jump out of here in a week. Mildred, what's the food supply?"

"Three days, maybe four," she said.

"Then we'll need to go hunting," he declared. "Let's recce the local area and then make camp."

Everybody dropped their backpacks with sighs of relief, then started from the building. The last one to leave, Mildred took the chair from the console and tipped it over, sliding it underneath the oval door, jamming it open. Unlike a redoubt, the gateway didn't have a keypad lock, and she liked to make sure they always had a clear path of retreat.

Uzi cradled in his grip, J.B. stayed by the gateway as the anchor man, while the rest circled the building. As the companions moved off on patrol, Krysty went directly to the sagging fence and studied the junkyard. There was a hint of barbed wire on the posts, no more than rusted pieces of wire now. But there sure seemed to be a paved road under the piles of debris. Damage from a nuke quake? Made sense.

Starting along the perimeter in the opposite direction from the others, she could see the section of ground they were on was actually a small mesa, a column of ground thrust some ten feet or so straight up from the rest of the jungle. More nuke landscaping, but that was good news. It would be an easy climb down, but that ten feet would stop most nighttime predators. This was just about as fine a base camp as she had ever encountered. Even from this height, she could see a dozen different types of fruit hanging from the branches of the nearby trees, and the lush growth reached to the distant horizon. Very faintly Krysty caught the sounds of waves on a beach somewhere. Worst case, they could live for quite a while. As long as they found clean water.

Leading the others, Ryan strode into view from around the corner of the building and stopped upon seeing the redhead. They exchanged nods, announcing everything was fine.

Not for the first time, Ryan realized how amazingly beautiful Krysty was. Once he had found a stash of old porno mags from predark days, and none of those ancient beauties could hold a candle to the fiery redhead. Then he pushed that thought from his mind. They had work to do right now.

"See anything?" he asked, giving her shoulder a gentle squeeze.

Krysty placed her hand on top of his and squeezed back. "Not a thing, lover. No villes in sight where we could buy juice," she said, shifting her stance so that a warm thigh rested against his.

"No ruins, either," Ryan agreed, dropping his arm to go about her waist and rest on the full curves. "We're all alone for once."

"Sounds great," Mildred grumbled, holstering her piece. The physician shook out her wild tangle of beaded hair. "We've been in a lot of tough scrapes lately. Be nice to just sit and rest for a while."

"Amen to that, dear lady," Doc rumbled, resting heavily on his ebony stick. "'Ere the heart of a warrior break and die, he needs to sit sometime, and dream of nigh.'"

Biting a lip, Mildred tilted her head. "Um, Longfellow?"

"Catellus."

"Ah."

"Damn strange about all these traps," J.B. said, standing at the fence.

"Traps?" Dean asked, furrowing his brow. "Looks like junk."

The Armorer smiled. "Most things look that way after getting blown apart. There's a minefield out there."

"We're going to have a bitch of a job carving a path through," Ryan said, releasing the redhead and going to the fence. But not too close. "Hundred-year-old land mines tend to detonate whenever they feel like it."

Just then, Krysty jerked her weapon free and glanced upward.

"Something?" Jak asked, raising his hand cannon and following her gaze. But the sky was clear. Just the usual stormy clouds full of acid, sheet lightning and fiery rads.

"A shadow," she said softly. "Mebbe just a cloud."

"Mebbe not," Ryan said grimacing.

"Hot pipe!" Dean cried as he drew his blaster, pointed it at his father's head and fired. The muzzle-blast of the semiautomatic pistol warmed Ryan's cheek, and he spun with the SIG-Sauer in his fist.

Falling from the sky was a huge bird, its chest pumping blood from the bullet wound. The creature hit the ground with a feathery thump, and tried again to launch itself into the air toward Ryan, its enormous wings savagely beating the air as it screamed a high-pitched cry.

Ryan fired twice, the 9 mm Parabellum slugs slamming the colossal bird in the belly and the throat. It went quiet, and after a moment slumped lifeless.

"What is it?" J.B. demanded, going closer to the corpse. Gingerly he prodded the bird with the barrel of his Uzi.

"Condor," Mildred said grimly. "Biggest bird in the world."

"Mutie," Jak stated, easing down the hammer of his Colt Python.

Pursing his lips, Doc said, "No, indeed. It is a pure-blooded creature of nature, same as you and I. Three feet tall, eight-foot wingspan, it's the killer of the sky. In a fight with a sting-wing, or a screamer, I would put my money on this winged emperor."

Turning, Ryan studied the sky. Tiny dots were circling high above them. "Looks like they travel in flocks," he said, walking slowly toward the gateway. "Everybody move slow and walk casual to the door. Don't want to get caught in the open by these things."

"Big bastards," Jak stated, sliding out the spent brass and inserting live rounds. The empty rounds went into a pocket he buttoned shut.

"Oh, it is highly unlikely they will attack with one of their own dead on the ground," Doc stated. "Besides, birds fly in flocks, but attack alone."

"Usually," Mildred whispered, already walking toward the open doorway. "You an expert on condors?"

"No, madam, I am not."

"Then shut up."

An odd motion in the treetops caught Krysty's attention, and she started firing even before the condors hidden in the greenery launched themselves at the human prey.

"The trees!" she shouted over the discharge of her revolver.

Even as the companions turned to this new threat, the birds in the sky folded their wings and dropped straight down, their huge bodies brownish-gold blurs.

"Dive-bombers!" Mildred cursed, lifting her ZKR blaster in both hands and tracking the huge killers. Two hundred yards away, she had their speed and squeezed off a shot. A condor flipped sideways, colliding with others and breaking the mass charge.

The rest of the companions opened fire in every direction.

"Can't hit them!" Dean shouted frantically, slamming in a fresh clip. Spent brass dotted the ground around his boots, some so fresh they still contained traces of smoke. "They're too fast!"

"Don't aim at the body!" his father barked, the SIG-Sauer coughing a 9 mm death song. "Shoot at the beak! Use their speed against them!"

Dean did as ordered, and a condor died, then another, and a third. But six more took their place from the jungle trees. The supply of the winged giants seemed endless, and his ammo was dwindling rapidly.

He glanced at the doorway. More was in his back-pack, but that was fifty feet away. Might as well be on the moon.

Looping into their midst, a screaming condor flew between the companions, needle-sharp talons grab-bing for human flesh. Jak gestured and the bird hit the ground rolling, its neck stump pumping out blood by the pint.

Flicking the bird's head off his blade, the teenager grunted in satisfaction and fired his Magnum at an-other target, but kept the gore-soaked knife ready in his grip.

"Keep shifting position!" Ryan yelled, dropping a clip and slamming a fresh mag into the SIG-Sauer. "Don't give them a stable target!"

In ragged formation, the companions rotated in a circle. Disoriented by the tactic, several of the birds banked away from the group to try from a different direction. But that exposed their vulnerable underbel-lies for a critical instant, and a dozen more died in the sky.

But then the first of the mutilated bodies arrived. The booming LeMat was violently knocked from Doc's grip by a thrashing corpse, and Ryan staggered under the impact of another. As they scrambled to recover their weapons, there was a breach in the circle and the condors rushed the weak spot in the humans' defense.

The chattering Uzi spraying a wreath of hot lead, J.B. shrugged a shoulder and managed to slide the

S&W shotgun off his back. "Millie!" he shouted, tossing the blaster her way.

Holstering her ZKR, Mildred made the catch, turned and fired as fast as she could pump the action. The barrage of fléchettes tore the incoming flock apart into an explosion of feathers and blood.

Emptying half a clip, Ryan aced two more birds on the wing. One plummeted out of sight beyond the edge of the mesa, while the other hit amid the wreckage of the predark wags. It bounced off a dropping-splattered car hood to land on the ground.

"Fireblast!" Ryan cursed as feathered gobbets of flesh pelted them with stinging force. "There are too many! Run for the gateway! We'll hold them off from there!"

Breaking ranks to charge for the open doorway, the companions jumped over the twitching bodies littering the soil just as a dozen more of the feathered titans noiselessly glided around the sheet-metal building. As they soared no more than a yard off the ground, it was an eerie sight, almost nightmarish in its unnatural silence.

Yanking another round from the row of shells sewn into the strap of the shotgun, Mildred hastily thumbed it into the receiver, worked the pump and fired from the hip. The birds in the front disintegrated under the assault of fléchettes, and the rest wheeled away with uncanny speed, once again circling for another try.

For a single moment, the mesa was clear, and the companions dashed for the doorway. Piling inside, they went around the console to re-form the firing line. Nimbly Dean leaped over the skeleton on the floor, but Krysty tripped and went sprawling, losing her blaster under the shelves. Jak kicked the chair out from under the door while J.B. emptied another clip in a stuttering burst out the door. The clip ran empty, and he dropped the mag, hand scrambling to find a fresh load.

"Dark night!" he cursed, and ducked just in time to avoid being gutted by a condor flying sideways, its talons extended like a collection of curved knives.

Dean dodged low, the talons raking the air before his face, missing by less than an inch. Mildred blocked its attack with her med kit, the canvas ripping loudly, the precious supplies spilling onto the floor.

Firing a brief burst through the doorway, J.B. dropped the Uzi and shouldered the door shut. A split second later, something thumped into the steel, screaming and clawing the metal in mindless fury.

Jerking the bolt on the Steyr to free the internal mag, Ryan saw the oncoming condor just in time and swung the blaster with all of his strength to slam the bird aside. Tumbling out of control, its spine broken, the condor dropped directly onto the Tesla coil. There was a blinding flash, and a ball of ash drifted down from the air onto the floor.

Crackling through his combat boots, Ryan felt the electric discharge hit him hard. His leg muscles cramped, and every hair on his body tried to stick straight out. His kidneys convulsed, and there was a brief sensation of his skin trying to crawl away. The racking pain passed in a few moments and the Deathlands warrior gasped for breath, knowing he had escaped electrocution purely by the thickness of his boot soles.

"Mildred!" Doc bellowed from behind the console.

Ryan spun at the cry, blaster at the ready, then he balked. Doc was kneeling alongside Krysty. The woman was lying on top of the ancient skeleton, her animated hair absolutely still, a smoking hand resting on the bare metal floor.

Chapter Three

Sluggishly Krysty awakened to the odor of her own roasting flesh. Her stomach rebelled at the thought, but then she slowly realized it wasn't herself she smelled.

She was lying inside the gateway on a bedroll, a blanket folded under her head as a pillow. Right outside was a roaring bonfire. The rest of the companions were sitting around the crackling blaze while several gutted condors turned on a spit over flames. The others would cut slices off the hot birds with their knives and eat the meat right from the blade. A piece of tarp they used as a tent was on the ground, piled with fresh fruit and some odd lumpy tan sticks. A battered aluminum pot sat on a rock near the fire, its contents bubbling softly. Jak and Dean were standing guard duty again, their backs to the campfire with weapons in their hands. Neither seemed overly tense or apprehensive. The sunlight was coming from the wrong direction, but aside from that everything was quiet.

"Hey," Krysty said weakly, gamely sitting upright. Merciful Gaia, every muscle in her whole body was stiff, and her hair felt strangely numb, but aside from that she seemed to be undamaged.

Lowering a tin cup, Ryan turned in her direction

and smiled broadly. "Morning, lover. Coffee?" he asked, gesturing with the cup sloshing a little of the black brew.

"Please," she replied, rising from the nest of blankets and stumbling into the sunshine.

While Ryan poured some of the boiling water from the big pot into a collapsible U.S. Army cup, Mildred moved aside to make room for the redhead on the ground.

"Sit here," the physician said. "Feeling okay?"

"Not dead. That's good enough," Krysty said, her tongue moving awkwardly in her mouth as if it were still asleep. "Morning?"

"You slept through the night," Ryan said, opening a shiny silver envelope and sprinkling some brown crystals into the steaming water. He then carefully added a plastic pack of powdered milk and two of sugar.

Krysty accepted the cup gratefully and took a healthy swallow, regardless of the temperature. "So what happened?" she asked, savoring the warmth seeping into her stiff hands. She was feeling better by the minute, the fire driving the numbness from her limbs. "There was a condor in the gateway...." Her voice trailed off.

"Ryan aced it, but it fell on the Tesla, releasing enough voltage to melt a tank," J.B. explained, thumbing live rounds into an empty magazine. The Uzi lay nearby on a clean cloth, the blaster freshly cleaned and polished. "But the electricity went through the whole building, killing six more condors sitting on the roof. But that's what saved you, the enormous surface area dissipated the voltage enough so that you only got stunned and not fried.''

"Thank Gaia for that," Krysty said, sipping the brew with distaste. It was the usual instant coffee from an MRE pack, but there was yet an odd metallic flavor in her mouth.

"Got any toothpaste left?" she asked hopefully. "Or chewing gum?"

"All out," Mildred said. "Didn't the coffee help?"

"Not really," Krysty said honestly, placing the cup aside.

"Then try this, dear lady," Doc said offering her one of the tan sticks. "Chew it like you would gum."

The lumpy stick resembled bamboo and was as hard as a rock. Careful of breaking a tooth, Krysty chewed and sucked until the wooden tube began to soften with her saliva and a delicious sweetness filled her mouth, completely banishing the aftertaste of the electrocution.

"Sugarcane," Ryan said, hacking off another mouthful of condor. He chewed and swallowed before continuing. "We found a whole grove of the stuff. Jak says it's exactly what we need to make shine."

"What about the pipes?" Krysty asked, using her fingers to take some soft splinters from her mouth.

"Got an answer for that, too," Ryan said, tossing away the dregs of his coffee. "We got some of the coils and metal that we need from the car wrecks here. They're rusty, but salvageable."

"What are we missing? Condenser pipes?" she guessed.

"Bull's-eye. We've gotta have some copper tubing or we'll never distill alcohol clean enough to run the engine. But last night, J.B. spotted the lights from some ruins to the east. Say, ten, fifteen miles at the most. There should be plenty of copper pipes there. People used a lot of it in bathroom plumbing."

"Big," Jak stated as a fact. "Need smaller."

Mildred scrunched her face. "About the diameter of the copper pipes used for the ice-maker in a refrigerator?"

The teen nodded. "Perfect."

"But we can use bathroom plumbing if there is nothing else available," J.B. asked, pausing in his work.

"Sure. But take longer cook. Refrig better."

Picking at his teeth with a splinter of wood, Ryan grunted in annoyance. A hardware store would have exactly what they wanted, but those were almost always looted.

"So we concentrate on the better houses, or any resort hotels still standing," the Deathlands warrior decided. "Twelve feet should do us. Just remember that old copper cracks easy, so be bastard careful removing it. We can patch a small break, but nothing big."

"Excellent!" Doc beamed. "We are practically gone already."

"Hopefully. The ruins might be on another island," J.B. said, gnawing on a leg. "But we can carve out canoes to get there if necessary."

Krysty moved closer to the fire, savoring the smell of the fresh meat. "So this is an island," she said, basking her hands before the blaze. "Okay, where are we?"

Tossing aside the cleaned bone, J.B. tapped the minisextant hanging around his neck with a thumb. "Marshall Islands, in the South Pacific."

The aroma of the cooked birds was hitting the woman hard, and a wave of hunger rose from within. Sliding a knife from her belt sheath, Krysty cut away a large chunk of meat from the roasting condor. It smelled delicious and cut as easily as freshly fallen snow. She took a small bit and smiled. Mildred had once mentioned that these birds were almost extinct in her time. No wonder. They tasted wonderful.

"Been a while since we jumped off American soil," Krysty commented around a full mouth, grease on her chin.

"Still are in the U.S. America owns these islands," Ryan said, ripping open a foil packet and wiping his face with a lemon-scented towelette. Normally he saved the predark items to clean small wounds, but there was no fresh water and greasy hands on a blaster trigger would only get him aced.

"Or rather, this used to be a hunk of America," he added. "Mildred says we gave it to back to the locals sometime around 1999 or so."

"But the U.S. still has a lot of missile bases here, and a small Navy dockyard to fuel warships."

"That's wonderful," Krysty enthused. "Mebbe we can find some ammo and new boots in the warehouses."

"Possibly," J.B. said, frowning. "But there are over a thousand islands in this chain, and one of them is the most famous in the world. Bikini."

"The Bikini Atoll?" Doc gasped, dropping a half-eaten wing. "Good God in heaven, man, that was where they detonated hundreds of nuclear bombs just to test how they worked!"

"This is the area," Ryan stated, gesturing around them.

"Is the air clean?" Dean asked with a worried expression. He knew his father had to have checked already, but he couldn't help but ask anyway. Hundreds of nukes. Why would the whitecoats set off that many? It was insane.

Patiently Ryan showed the boy the tiny rad counter on his shirt. The miniature Geiger counter was silent, registering nothing more than the usual background radiation.

"This island is clean," Ryan stated, "but we better check the rads everywhere we go. Missiles bases, Navy yard, could be mighty bad out there."

"Gonna be lots of muties," J.B. added grimly, sliding the reloaded clip into the Uzi. He worked the bolt to chamber a round, then dropped the clip and worked the bolt again to eject the live round. Catching it in the air, the Armorer thumbed it back into the clip. Everything was working as smooth as silk. A man who didn't take care of his blaster was just a corpse looking for a hole, nothing more.

"That's for sure," Ryan declared, standing and retrieving his longblaster. "We get the copper, come straight back here and brewing. No exploration or looting. The sooner we leave here, the better."

INVISIBLE FROM within the thick canopy of trees, he watched as they moved, as they made odd noises and did incomprehensible things. But he knew what they were. Two-legs. It had been many moons since he last saw any of the upright animals, but he remembered the taste of their flesh with great pleasure, and the urge to leap upon them right now and feed was very strong.

Then he saw a large two-leg with only one eye lift a terrible thunder stick into view and he cringed lower among the flowery vines. Many of his kind had been killed by the sticks. They were to be avoided at any cost.

Besides, there was no need to attack the two-legs here in their nest. He knew what they would do. As silent as a cloud, the mutie turned on the branch of the banyan tree and began the long climb to the ground. Not a leaf stirred as he passed through the thick growth of vines and flowers. The two-legs would to go to the dead place as all the others did, and he could capture them there. Soon his belly would be full of their good meat, and his children would sup upon entrails and sticky brains. But the eyes he would save for the females as a special salty treat.

Oh, yes, there was no need to risk the terrible pain of the booming thunder sticks. No, he would wait and let the food come to him. Then the great feast would begin.

AFTER BREAKFAST, the companions cleaned up as best they could, using the wet naps from the MRE packs on themselves, and scrubbing the pots and cups with gravel. There was no spare water to waste on washing dishes.

"Better take everything," Ryan directed, sliding the backpack onto his shoulders. "Don't know how long we'll be gone. A day, a few days, mebbe more."

The warrior made no sign that he wasn't pleased with how light the pack felt. They were low on both ammo and food. The dead condors had helped to stretch their meager supplies, but with no way to cure the meat, the cooked birds would go rancid in a few days. At the first sign of it smelling sweet, all of the meat would have to be thrown away.

"What about this?" Mildred asked, balancing the Molotov in her palm. "Can't take it through the jungle. Could get busted, and we need every drop."

"Bury it, madam," Doc suggested, rotating the cylinder of the LeMat to check the charges. "That should be safe enough."

Brandishing a knife, Mildred went to the side of the sheet-metal building and began to dig in the rich black loam. Soon, she had a hole big enough. Dean arrived with a fistful of old rags, the tattered clothing from the skeleton. Gingerly she wrapped the glass bottle in several layers for extra protection, then covered it.

"Good enough," she declared, patting the soil smooth so no telltale lump marked the burial site.

At the front of the gateway, J.B. was busy at the closed door, stringing a piece of black wire across the jamb.

"In case of visitors," he announced, stepping back. "Anybody tries to get inside will never reach the door alive."

"Anything inside?" Ryan asked, checking his longblaster.

"A frag hidden in the light fixture. Got it angled so the shrapnel won't damage the console or the power plant."

"Good," Dean said in approval, slapping at a skeeter on his neck. He pulled away his hand and saw a tiny smear of blood on the palm. "Can't wait to leave."

"I thought you were down to your last gren? Where did you get the plas? Never mind," Krysty said, glancing at the smooth path leading from the hole in the fence to the edge of the mesa. "You were busy while I was unconscious."

Going to the hole in the fence, she saw a pathway of churned earth wandering through the piles of rubbish and rusted metal going all the way to the edge of the mesa. The treetops spread before her like an arboreal garden, disappearing into the morning mists and onward to a lone mountain in the far distance.

"Saved every land mine we could," J.B. said,

sprinkling dirt in front of the door to hide any foot-prints. "But most of the ones we dug up were just rusted lumps. Useless."

"On my hands and knees, stabbing the dirt with a knife," Doc rumbled lugubriously. "I felt like a pig hunting truffles."

"Only mushrooms don't detonate and remove your face," Mildred countered, tying a bandana around her head in lieu of a hat. The climbing sun was already raising the temperature to uncomfortable levels. "Not even in the Deathlands."

"Best way to clear a path," Ryan stated walking past the rotting fence and continuing along the churned section of ground. "Nobody got chilled. That's what matters."

Gathering at the side of the mesa, the companions looked over the land below for any possible dangers before proceeding down the ten-foot drop. The ground was steeply sloped, and slick with spongy moss. But they reached the floor of the jungle without serious mishap.

The wide trees rose above them now, dark shadows thick within their twisted branches. Thousands of leafy vines going from tree to tree blocked their view of the sky, changing the dawn into dusk. Yet colorful flowers were everywhere, making the air almost sickly sweet with thick perfume. Insects buzzed amid the foliage or crawled along the jungle carpeting. The vibrant jungle was alive with subtle noises, and it bothered the companions. It seemed unnatural to have their surroundings buzzing with so much life.

Only a few yards away, the battered hulk of an armored bank truck rose from the lush greenery, its dissolving body covered with vines and dripping with moss. The faint vestiges of a predark road were visible under the vehicle. Carefully placing each boot as if it might break through into a yawning chasm, Ryan walked closer, noticing that the tires were gone, only bare rims on the axles, and the seats inside were just a naked collection of coiled springs. Everything organic had been eaten long ago by the myriad insects, and immutable time itself.

"Might be how our dead whitecoat got here," Dean suggested.

"Or her killers," Ryan countered, his eye sweeping the foliage for any possible dangers. There was a blur of motion, and he stood with a hissing snake clenched helpless in his fist.

"Coral snake. We must be near the beach," Ryan said calmly, and whipped the creature against the side of the truck. Its spine audibly cracked from the blow, and the deadly killer went limp.

"Won't have to hunt for lunch," he said, rolling up the snake and tucking it into a pocket.

"The ruins are straight ahead," J.B. announced, checking the compass, his Uzi resting on his shoulder.

Maneuvering past the truck, Ryan brushed vines and banyan flowers out of his way with the barrel of the SIG-Sauer until reaching a wall of fronds, prickly weeds and bizarre plants with thick stems and slick with moisture. Drawing the panga from its sheath, he experimentally hacked at the dense greenery blocking the way and the plants easily parted at the touch of the razor-sharp knife.

"I'll break trail," Ryan said, holstering his blaster. "Let's go."

"You feeling up to this?" Mildred asked the redhead softly. "We could wait a day or so."

Her crimson hair moving like waves on a beach, Krysty smiled. "I'm fine," she said. "Never better."

Mildred said nothing, but privately decided to keep a close watch on the woman. She had the feeling that the electric charge had taken more out of Krysty than she wanted to admit.

Overhead, lightning flashed across the purple clouds, leaving fiery orange streaks in its wake.

Loosening the collar of his frilly shirt, Doc stayed in place until the others passed by, then he took the aft position, a gnarled hand on the grip of the deadly LeMat.

Raising his powerful arm, Ryan stepped forward and swung again with the panga. More vines fell. Tirelessly he slashed at the weeds and bushes, and was soon moving in a steady rhythm of hack, step, hack. A sweat stain spread across his back, and Ryan jerked his head to shake the perspiration from his bad eye.

Looking behind, Dean noted that the mesa was already gone from view. They would have to return quickly, or else the jungle would reclaim the path they were cutting and it'd become impossible to find the gateway again. Then he saw J.B. slash at a banyan tree with his knife, cutting a deep notch into the bark to mark the way. That would soon also heal, but not as fast as the weeds. Maybe a week or so before it was gone. More than enough.

As the day progressed, the leafy vines thinned enough to let in the sunlight, and the temperature immediately rose to intolerable levels. Panting from the humidity, Krysty stuffed her bearskin coat into her backpack, J.B. did the same with his leather jacket. Soon rivulets of salty sweat flowed down their necks, turning shirts dark and pants nearly black.

Time passed slowly, the companions saying little as they closely watched the jungle. Crossing the muddy bed of a small creek, Ryan angled around a towering pile of crumbling bricks that could have been anything in another time. In the cool shade, he paused to sip the tepid water from his canteen, then continued onward. The work was grueling, the weeds clinging to the blade of the knife, the swaying vines sometimes as hard as wood, and the impact would jar Ryan to the bone. But the man never slowed, moving with an iron strength that had kept him alive in a hundred battles.

Suddenly something large darted through the treetops, moving at incredible speed. Krysty tracked it with the muzzle of her revolver until it was gone from sight.

"Monkeys?" Doc asked, a strong finger holding down the trigger of his Civil War blaster, his other hand poised to start fanning the hammer.

"Primate of some kind," Mildred answered hesitantly, the ZKR target pistol held in both hands. "But I wouldn't want to bet the ranch on what kind."

The companions strained to hear or see anything more, the background noises of the tropical rain forest a never ending murmur. The muted call of a distant bird, the patter of moisture dribbling down the vines onto the flowers, the rustle of the huge leaves, the hum of a flying insect. They waited, but whatever had passed by was gone for the moment.

"Keep moving, it's gone," Ryan said, holstering his piece and starting to cut trail once more. But now he held the panga in his left hand, the right resting on the gun belt above the grip of the SIG-Sauer.

"Going to need fresh water soon," Mildred panted, checking her canteen. "We have enough for two, three days."

"No prob," Jak stated. A knife appeared from within his sleeve, and, grabbing a fat green vine he cut through. Clear fluid gushed from the severed stem, soon slowing to a trickle, then a steady flow of drops.

Mildred sniffed the fluid, then allowed a drop to land on the back of her hand. When there was no pain, she scratched her skin with a thumbnail and let another drop flow over the tiny wound.

"Doesn't stink, or sting," she said and lapped a little from her cupped palm. "Oh God, that's good."

The teenager shrugged. "Done before. Bayou, jungle, same thing."

As the companions trudged on, they cut the fat vines and caught the initial flow into their canteens until the containers were full, then drank directly from the gushing vines.

"Gaia, I needed that," Krysty said with a sigh, releasing a vine, the end dripping onto the ground below. Insects scurried over top of one another to gather the precious fluid, and a violent battle erupted into being beneath the tramping boots of the towering humans.

"Tasted kind of sweet," Dean commented, wiping his mouth on a forearm. "Really good."

"Lots of food, clean water," J.B. said, wiping the inside his fedora with a damp handkerchief. "We could do worse for a home than this if we can't leave."

Concentrating at his work, Ryan didn't reply. His shirt was drenched, but his arm never slowed in its machinelike destruction of the limbs and bushes. Lots of food growing wild always meant lots of predators eating the animals that ate the plants. He could think of no reason why this tropical island should be any different from a desert or the forests of the Shens. Just because they hadn't been attacked by an animal yet didn't mean they weren't close by.

The vines got fewer, the weeds thinner, easier to chop, and unexpectedly Ryan stepped out of the dense growth onto a grassy field.

"There they are," he said, lowering his throbbing arm. His fingers felt loose, the corded muscles in his arms moving under his bronzed skin, and the edge of the panga dripped green sap as if it were fresh mutie blood.

The rest of the companions walked from the greenery and spread out to savor the cool wafting over the grassy savanna. The flat field extended in every direction, only a few individual trees scattered about to break the monotony. There was a faint hint of salt in the air, and they drank in the refreshing breeze.

Directly ahead, just beyond a few low ground swells, stood the shining towers of a predark city, monoliths of glass and steel rising majestically above the rolling fields. The windows were all milky white from accumulated dirt and the sheer passage of time. But the buildings appeared intact, without nuke or fire damage.

"There's going to be more than just copper pipe to loot there," Dean said happily, then the smile faded away to be replaced by his usual serious countenance. "Canned food, new shoes, all sorts of stuff."

"We shall find out soon enough, lad," Doc said, smiling, as the group started to head that way.

But within a few yards, Ryan raised a clenched fist and the companions froze in midstep. They looked around for any possible danger and saw nothing but the grass and the distant ruins.

Ryan took another step forward, and the rad counter on his shirt began to click again. He walked a few yards more toward the ruins, and the clicking became louder and faster.

"Fireblast," he cursed, returning to the others until the noise slowed to the usual background tick, as steady as a human heartbeat. "It's hotter than Washington Hole. That was probably the glow we saw at night."

Grimacing, J.B. checked his own rad counter. The results were the same. "Not torchlight, but rad glow reflected off the glass. Aw, hell."

"Mebbe there's just a rad pit between us and the city," Krysty suggested. "We could try circling around."

Ryan shook his head. "Not with readings like this. That whole end of the island is a death zone."

"The jungle is too thick to search," Doc rumbled, twirling his stick thoughtfully.

"Take us years to even check a small section," Mildred agreed.

"Which leaves east or west," J.B. said, reaching into his backpack. Finding the longeyes, he extended the brass to its full length. Found in an antique shop, the ancient device still worked perfectly.

Finding a piece of wood on the ground, Ryan used it to clean the sticky sap off the panga before sheathing the blade.

"Okay," the Armorer said, sweeping the horizon. "I can see waves hitting breakers to our right, and some sort of rusted railroad bridge going to what seems to be another island on our left."

"Bridges," Jak growled, curling a lip. "Not trust."

"With good reason," Mildred agreed, remembering those terrible days in West Virginia. "I say we follow the shore and hope to find something useful— a wreck, maybe. Or a fishing ville."

"No, we'll head for the bridge," J.B. said, passing the telescope to Ryan. "Check it out."

The warrior adjusted the length to focus, and a faint smile came and went on his scarred face. "Bridge it is," he stated, collapsing the telescope.

"Ville on the other side?" Krysty asked, staring that way.

"Something is on the other side, that's for damn sure," he said, starting to walk. "There are a couple of big cats, cougars maybe, tied to leashes in front like guard dogs."

"Indeed," Doc said, the salty breeze rustling his long silver locks. "Then it most sincerely behooves us to discover exactly what these feline Cerebusi are protecting."

"Cerebus guarded the gates of hell," Mildred corrected.

Striding along, Doc frowned. "Too true. But let us hope for better than that, dear lady."

STIRRING FROM its nest, the mutie scampered into view and stared dumbfounded. The food was leaving! This had never happened before in its long memory. Always they came to the dead place, started moving slow, then toppled over ready to be gathered.

Wiggling his hairy body from the cool darkness of the hole under the tree, the mutie started after the two-legs, staying far behind them, darting from tree to bush. But always ready to charge at the first hint of them slowing down as the invisible sickness took them.

No food had ever escaped before! Nor would this.

Chapter Four

The companions were still a good distance from the bridge when the cats rose to their legs and started to growl.

Stopping about fifty yards away, Ryan calmly studied the animals and the bridge behind them.

The structure stretched across a channel of choppy water, with open sea on either end. The bridge itself was a box trestle, the design used for railroad tracks. However, the surface was paved, the asphalt badly cracked and dotted with deep potholes. The strutted girders were dark with corrosion, but still looked strong. Small patches of black paint still showed through the decades of rust.

"Acid rain probably helps it stay clean," Krysty commented. "I've seen it wash rust clean off steel."

"Flesh, too," Jak added without humor.

Beyond the bridge were the gutted remains of a roadway, sections of concrete visible through the windblown dirt. It meandered off out of sight into the hills of pine and bushes.

Wary of crumbling land, Ryan moved to the edge of the island and glanced into the channel. It had to have been low tide, as the shoreline mark was a good fifty feet above the surface of the choppy water, the bare rock sides of the yawning passage exposed. Schools of rainbow-colored fish darted about in the clear water, and a short way off, a glistening coral reef was heavy with the sleek shells of clams, while fat crabs scuttled about in a shallow tide pool. Whatever else, food was abundant here.

"How odd," Doc stated softly. "Those are cougars, not exactly a tropical cat. I would have more expected panthers or cheetahs."

Staring hostilely at the companions, the snarling cats were straining at the leash, padding back and forth in their desire to attack the norms. One turned its head to chew on the confining rope and released it immediately, spitting and sneezing, its pink tongue lashing madly.

"Wondered why not chew through," Jak said thoughtfully. "Now know. Chem on rope. Smart."

Ryan could see that each cougar possessed two tails, both lashing about in restrained hatred. But aside from that minor deviation, they seemed quite normal otherwise. Just big. And with lots of scars disturbing their sleek tan fur.

"Think they're here to keep out people or muties?" Dean asked, glancing back toward the steaming jungle.

"Only muties we've seen are those condors," Krysty said. "And they'd just fly over."

"Must be people, then," J.B. agreed, tilting back his hat for better visibility.

"People without blasters," Ryan said, holstering his SIG-Sauer and easing the longblaster off his shoulder. He hated to waste two live rounds on chilling chained animals, but there was clearly no way past the huge cats and onto the bridge without getting within reach of those deadly claws.

Taking a stance, he aimed the longblaster, adjusting the focus on the crosshairs to bring their faces into wire sharpness, when the beasts snapped their attention away from the companions and started to hiss, their tails motionless, fur bristling.

"Not us," Krysty said. "We're much too far away, unless they understand what a blaster can do."

"Could be," Mildred mused, moving away from the channel. If there was trouble, she didn't want to be trapped with a fifty-foot drop onto rocks at her back.

Just then the hair on the back of Ryan's neck started to stir. With battle instincts honed in a hundred fights, the man spun from the waist and fired the longblaster.

A hundred yards away, the giant spider on the ridge gave no reaction as the 7.62 mm round hit its bulbous body. It continued to scuttle down the slope, its eight hairy legs blurs of speed.

"Nuke me," Jak said, and fired the .357 Magnum Colt from his hip.

The booming handblaster blew a lance of flame from its pitted muzzle. There was a ripple in the yellow-and-black-striped fur over the massive torso, nothing more.

Dean raised his own blaster, but didn't fire; the distance was too great yet for the semiautomatic pistol. But the spider was closing in fast. There was no way to tell where its weird multifaceted eyes were looking, but the boy knew the friends were its goal. The angle of attack was too perfect. The companions were caught between the rocky channel and the cats, with the spider closing the third side of the triangle trap. Dean shot a glance at the ground, wondering if the thing did this often.

"Hurry, form a firing line, my friends!" Doc rumbled, and dropped to a knee, gripping the LeMat in both hands.

Jak and Dean went down alongside the man, Mildred and Krysty standing behind them, forming a wall of blasters. J.B. passed Mildred the shotgun, and switched the Uzi from single shot to full-auto.

"If we've got to jump," he said grimly, "stay away from the coral. It'll slice you apart like barbed wire."

"Jump, my ass. Get ready to run!" Ryan countered, and fired the Steyr twice.

The discharges echoed across the grassland, and the ropes tied to the stanchions of the bridge snapped. Instantly the freed cougars sprang forward, sprinted across the landscape with their legs pumping, backs arcing to propel them with frightening speed directly at the spider.

The insect immediately changed course and went toward the approaching animals, its mandibles loudly snapping like distant blasterfire. Staying motionless, the companions anxiously watched as the muties collided.

At first, the cats dashed around the towering spider, snapping at its legs, darting forward, only to dodge backward. The insect rushed at them again and again, only to have the guard cat nimbly avoid the rush. Then one cat stood its ground, snarling a challenge. The insect scuttled in for the kill, when the second cougar jumped on its back and started ripping out mouthfuls of hairy hide. Squealing in agony, the spider rose onto its hind legs, easily dumping the cat off its back. Tumbling through the air, the cougar landed upright on its paws and raced under the belly of the beast, while the other slashed for the multifaceted eyes with deadly claws.

But the spider countered both attacks, dropping flat on the ground, avoiding the first cat and catching the second animal underneath. Mewing in pain, the crushed cat squirmed free, one leg dragging limply behind.

"Now," Ryan said, and the companions dashed for the bridge.

With its speed gone, the second cat tried to defend its mate, but the spider rushed upon the wounded beast and caught its body in the powerful mandibles. Screaming in rage, the cat fought for freedom as the black pincers sawed into its flesh. Red blood gushed out, a leg fell off, the cougar thrashed insanely for the vulnerable face of the insect, then the pincers closed with a solid click. The animal fell away in two pieces, blood everywhere.

Both tails lashing, the other cat didn't make the same mistake, and darted among the spider's legs, just nipping here, clawing there. Thick yellow blood flow from the tiny wounds, mixing with the red on the rich soil. Soon the giant insect started to move more slowly, its legs clumsily avoiding the cat as the mandibles snapped with less force.

As the companions reached the bridge, they turned from the bloody combat and J.B. took a full minute to check for traps before waving them onward. The spider squealed and the cougar roared as they started across the ancient roadway. There were potholes everywhere, some of them going all the way through and they could see the bare steel rods set inside the concrete bed, and foamy brine below, jagged rocks and coral filling the blue Cific waters. Worse, every step they took was starting to shake the weakened structure, the vibrations mounting until it was becoming difficult to walk.

"Get off the pavement and onto the girders," Ryan directed them, heading for the side. "Can't trust this asphalt to hold!"

As they rushed to the upright support beams, the shaking bridge pavement shattered into pieces, cracks spreading outward like some terrible disease. Whole sections of asphalt plummeted away to explode into rubble on the coral and outcroppings.

"Move!" Krysty shouted, and clumsily raced along the girder to dive for the imagined safety of the next island. She landed sprawling, and rolled away to clear the area for the others, who followed close behind.

As they painfully stood on the firm ground, the

companions watched as the rest of the predark roadway broke loose and dropped into the channel until there was nothing remaining but the steel girders and struts of the trestle. On the other island, the spider triumphantly raised a struggling cougar high in the sky with its serrated mandibles, then dashed the body onto the ground, smashing it to pieces under pounding legs.

"It's going to be a bitch getting back across," Mildred stated, brushing dirt off her clothes. "The steel looks solid enough, but it'll be slick with spray without the road to block the wash from the waves."

"We can tie ropes around each other, and then to the stanchions," Doc suggested, breathing hard. "The way mountain climbers do."

"Yeah, that'll work. Good idea."

"Thank you, madam."

Checking his pockets to make sure he hadn't lost any ammo, Dean started to ask the adults why anybody would want to climb a mountain, but decided this wasn't the time or place.

"Need explosives, or more Molotovs, to handle the spider," J.B. added, adjusting his glasses. "Take most of our ammo to chill it from a distance."

Across the channel, the huge insect looked up from gutting the corpse of the cougar and stared directly at the man. If he didn't know better, J.B. would have sworn it understood what he had said. The mere thought sent a chill along his spine. Humanity's greatest weapon against the muties was their lack of intelligence. Smart muties were a nightmare.

"Keep moving. Somebody may come to check on

the noise," Ryan said, and headed off the roadway, plunging into the bushes and trees of the cool green forest.

WITH BOTH of his mouths full of meat, the spider paused in tearing off the strips of flesh, the dying cat whimpering in agony. The two-legs were gone. Had they deliberately set the cats free, to hold it at bay until they could escape? Were they that smart? It was a chilling thought.

The cougar eventually died, while the spider finished his meal. Afterward, the insect started to turn around and around, kicking a shallow depression in the soft loam. Then he nestled into the hole and began to wiggle his huge body back and forth until the loose soil covered him completely, except for a tiny slit in front of his bulging eyes.

He had food and wasn't badly hurt. The wounds would heal quickly with a full belly. So he would wait again for the two-legs to return. And this time, he wouldn't wait for them to fall or try to trap the meat. They were too quick, too clever. No, he would simply leap upon the food the second it came off the iron skeleton, crushing the leader of the pack, then killing the others at his leisure.

But for now, he would wait. The food would return. It always did.

DEEP WITHIN the forest, the companions eased their retreat only after losing sight of the bridge and the terrible thing on the other side.

Slowing to a walk, Ryan reloaded the Steyr and breathed in the cool air sweet with the rich smell of pine. He had grown up in woods like these, and they always felt like home to him. The trees were well spaced, the floor of the forest a soft cushion of needles and leaves. He recognized oak, ash and maple. How could two islands so close to each other geographically be so far apart in temperature and plant life?

"Nice." Jak inhaled, pausing to slip on his jacket. J.B. did the same with his, but Krysty didn't don her bearskin coat, luxuriating in the misty cool of the pines.

Cresting a hill and clambering through a rocky arroyo, the companions reached a small clearing in the woods and Ryan called a halt.

"We'll break here," he decided, sliding off his backpack. "Cold rations and water only. No fire. Don't know if there's anybody around here, and there's no sense advertising our presence."

"I'll take first watch," Krysty offered, and stepped away from the others to put her back to a pine tree where she had a good command of the general area.

Taking the snake from his pocket, Ryan started gutting and cleaning the reptile with a folding pocket-knife. The panga was much too big for such delicate work, reserved for big jobs of hacking through jungles and cutting throats. The curved blade was perfect for that, almost as if it had been designed for just that purpose.

"Still fresh," Ryan announced, laying out slices on a large leaf. "Help yourselves."

Doc took a piece and started chewing the tough meat. "Tastes nothing like chicken," he muttered, taking another slice.

Lowering her canteen, Mildred frowned. "I still can't get over how big that spider was," she said, sounding annoyed. "It's impossible. Just impossible."

"Saw it," Jak stated, as if that settled the discussion. Opening a self-heat can, he waited until the food was warm, then started in with a hand-carved wooden spoon, relaying the soup to his mouth with the care of a surgeon. Not a drop was wasted on the ground.

"Are you referring to the, what was it again?" Doc asked, nibbling the raw snake. The flavor was strong, but no more so than sea bass. "The inverse-square law of biology?"

"Yes!" Mildred snapped. "Muties can be utterly bizarre, any shape or color, but they always obey the laws of science. An invertebrate creature can't grow that large. It would collapse under its own weight."

"Saw a vid once in a redoubt," Dean said, unwrapping the leaves around a roasted condor leg. "Big dinosaur, lot larger than this spider."

"That was just a story," she chided gently.

He started eating. "Looked real."

"Can't get very big because it only has external bones, is that the idea?" Ryan asked, finishing off the snake.

"Yes. Exactly."

Reaching into another pocket, he unearthed a bundle of leaves and tore it open to start on some condor himself. Raw snake was good, but he preferred the taste of cooked food.

"So what if it had two?" he suggested, chewing and swallowing. "Regular bones inside, as well as that outer shell."

"Chitin," Mildred corrected automatically, then pursed her face. "Two skeletons? God help us, they could get a lot bigger than ten feet tall with two skeletons."

"Big as the vid dinosaur?" Dean queried.

"Larger."

"Hot pipe. I wouldn't want to tangle with one of those, unless we find another APC and a ton of ammo."

"Nature will out," Doc said, removing the plastic wrapper for a predark candy bar, a rare treat they found only occasionally in the military MRE packs.

"Two skeletons," Mildred repeated, pulling a gray chunk of military cheese from her med kit and cutting off slices. "What made you think of that?"

"Seemed reasonable," Ryan replied, cleaning the last of the meat off the bone. He tossed the bone away, belched and started on another.

Mildred and Doc exchanged silent glances. Ryan was the leader of the group because he was the deadliest fighter alive, and not a fool. A thinking man was ten times more dangerous than an army of fools with blasters.

Aching for a cigar, J.B. stuck a stick of minty

chewing gum in his mouth and masticated vigorously. Then taking a twig, he lifted the snake skin and inspected it carefully. "Useless," he finally decided, tossing it onto the pile of bones and rubbish. "Too small for anything. Wouldn't even make a decent belt."

A ghostly scream moved among the trees, so low they almost couldn't hear it over the gentle rustling of the leaves.

"Cougar?" Krysty asked, stepping forward, blaster in hand. Nothing was moving amid the trees nearby but a few squirrels. She looked again as one spread its arms, extending the thin membrane between its fore and hind legs, jumped and sailed away. A flying squirrel. The Earth Mother had a strange sense of humor sometimes.

"Killed lots cats," Jak answered, wiping his hands clean on the grass, then a rag. "Never heard that."

"Spider?" Dean asked.

"No vocal cords," Mildred answered, packing away the cheese and drawing her own weapon. "They can't scream. Then again, maybe a mutie can, I don't know."

The cry of anguish came again, louder this time.

"That's human," Ryan said, standing, "and it was coming from the south, not the west."

"Could be the owners of the cats," J.B. said, scooping needles and dirt onto the pile of trash. Exposed food would attract scavengers, and predators would follow.

"Only one way to find out," Ryan replied, gathering his longblaster. "Leave the packs, we'll travel faster. Two yards spread, no talking. Recce only. We find trouble, we back off."

The companions started to gather loose tree branches to toss over the bundles. When the backpacks were safely out of sight, they checked their weapons and started out with Ryan in the lead.

After a few hundred yards, the forest thinned to scrub brush, and the companions heard another cry, female this time, and something else they couldn't quite identify. Angling around a small mesa, they traveled swift and silent through a valley, following the irregular remains of a predark road. The pavement curved around the mesa, disappearing into a collapsed brick tunnel, pieces of trapped cars still sticking out from under the rubble. They could hear several people screaming now, men and women combined, plus some sharp explosions that rolled over the landscape, echoing into the distance.

"Grens?" Jak asked softly.

"Blasters," Dean said, scowling. "Don't know what kind. Odd noise."

"Those are black-powder longblasters," J.B. stated, wrinkling his nose. "I know the stink."

More weapons discharged, closely followed by screams of pain.

"This way," Ryan said, heading into the rose-bushes edging the ancient roadway.

Carefully pushing their way through the thorns, the companions exited on the side of a sloping hill overlooking a crescent-shaped lagoon. Palm trees lined the white sand shores, and a large ville of log cabins was surrounded by a stone block wall, made mostly from bricks and sidewalk slabs. A large section of the wall was smashed to pieces, and several of the cabins were on fire, the smoke masking whatever was happening on the shore. Then the wind shifted direction for a moment, exposing the beach and the lagoon.

"Look there, a ship!" Mildred whispered, pointing excitedly.

"More than that, it is a whaling schooner, madam," Doc rumbled. "A windjammer from my own time period. Somebody must have found one intact in a naval museum. By the Three Kennedys, she's a beauty! Look at that rigging. It's in perfect condition."

"Windjammer mean no motor?" Jak asked.

"None. Just sails."

"Smart," the teenager commented. "Wind free."

"And it has cannon," J.B. said, gesturing with the Uzi. "See those hatches along the gunwale? Flip those up and out come the big blasters."

"Artillery?" Dean asked worriedly. "Can they reach us up here?"

"Not black-powder cannon," Ryan answered. "They're short-range weapons, and only fire solid balls of metal. Twenty pounds each or more. We're safe at this distance."

The boy gave a low whistle. "Twenty pounds! That'd chill the spider."

J.B. nudged the boy. "Good thinking."

"Ship would need lamps," Mildred offered. "Maybe we could buy some alcohol off them."

"The solution to our problem could be right there," Krysty said, her hair waving uneasily. She wiped sweaty hands on her khaki jumpsuit to dry them.

"More likely it's fish-oil lamps, dear lady," Doc countered, checking the load in the LeMat. "But it can do no harm to ask."

"Worse comes to worst, we could sail back to the continent on a ship that large," Ryan said, rubbing his chin. "If the hull is in good condition. Let's get closer and see why they're fighting. Mebbe we can cut a deal."

"And decide which side we should take," Krysty added.

"If any."

"Winners might be grateful for our help," she reminded.

"Or they may ace us for getting in the way of a private feud," he retorted. "We recce first before doing anything else."

"Safety first, lover," Krysty agreed with a grin.

Slipping and sliding down the red clay of the hillside, the companions crawled through the bushes until reaching the stonework wall. Several bodies lay in pieces on the sandy soil, obvious victims of the blast that opened the wall. Silently they crept to the gaping hole and peeked inside.

Mutilated corpses lay everywhere in bloody disarray. Most had black holes in their chests, some with arms missing, and a few were decapitated, the heads nowhere in sight. The snow-white sand of the beach was crimson in spots from the fresh spilled blood of the bodies hacked into pieces in the shallows. Most wore plain garb of crude tan cloth, the hems only ragged threads. But prominent among the dead were men in good clothing, black boots, pants with patches, white shirts and wide leather belts. Swords lay near the corpses and what looked like crude muskets. One of the sailors had an arrow through his neck, while the other was literally cut in twain from the head down to the ax buried in his groin.

Above the tide marks, laughing men in boots and wide belts were whipping a crowd of men and women whose heavy chains shackled them ankle and neck. Other sailors moved between the prisoners roughly cutting away their clothing, leaving the people stripped naked. One man fought against the treatment and was lashed to the ground by three of the cold-hearts, until his back was a raw mass of bloody flesh hanging loose on his bones.

Oddly the clothing didn't seem to fit these cold-hearts well.

Off to the side, several young women had been stripped and waited weeping in line as the sailors cut the ropes on a woman tied to the table and shoved her to the ground. She lay there without moving, her thighs streaked with fresh blood, her face battered and bruised.

Krysty muttered a virulent curse as she helplessly

watched the next girl dragged to the table and lashed down.

A sailor ran his hands along her flanks and said something the wind carried away. The rest of the men waiting in line laughed at the comment and began to undo their belts.

Only a few dozen yards off the beach was the great wooden ship, the name *Constellation* masterfully carved into her bow. The ancient ship was fat and wide, the gunwales high above the water. A single titanic mast stood in the middle, supported by a confusing maze of ropes. A squat cabin sat on the rear deck. The vessel was colossal, maybe two hundred feet long by fifty wide. This close they could see that a section of the hull was made of greenwood planks, unlike any other part of the beautiful vessel.

"No," Mildred muttered. "Can't be."

"But it is, madam," Doc growled in barely contained rage, rubbing at the scars on his wrist. "And they're using her as a godforsaken slave galley!"

"The bastards have to die," the physician spit.

A small boat rowed to the ship, a group of the chained prisoners cowering under the watch of the coldhearts armed with huge-bore pistols. The curved hammers of their blasters were set on the side of the barrel and were bigger than a man's thumb.

"Flintlock pistols," J.B. whispered, adjusting the focus on his Navy telescope. "I'd say .75 caliber. Takes thirty seconds to a minute to reload, depending on how good they are."

"Same with the muskets on the ship," Krysty said, squinting into the distance.

Ryan took her word on the matter, knowing that her vision was sharper than most people's.

A well of laughter on the beach caught his attention. A jeering coldheart in fancy clothes was pissing on a chained man being dragged to a roaring fire.

"You can't do this!" the prisoner raged, fighting the chains on his wrists. "We are freeborn!"

The leader of the coldhearts laughed, while another backhanded the skinny man across the face.

"Not anymore," the leader said, sneering. "Hold 'em!"

The others pinned the captive as the sailor at the fire withdrew a long iron pole with a glowing red tip. The prisoner fought wildly, kicking and wiggling, but to no avail. The glowing tip was pressed to his bare right shoulder, a wisp of smoke arose from the contact and he froze, every muscle taut, eyes bulging, teeth bared from the incredible pain.

The branding iron was removed, and seared into the dead-white skin was a red symbol, an outline of a bird with wings outstretched, silhouetted by a flaming sun.

"Now you're a slave," the leader snorted, hitching up his loose-fitting pants. "Free for the taking!"

The others released the branded slave, but the man stayed on his feet, panting for breath.

"Gods of the deep, I was a fool to ever trust you bastards," the man wheezed, a rivet of drool flowing from his slack mouth. "We had a deal! You repair our ship, and we'd pay in blasters and powder. We had a deal!''

"And who'd believe a slave?'' He laughed loudly. "Even the lord baron himself can't keep track of every ship that gets storm damaged in the Thousand Islands!''

The words hit the companions hard, and they looked again at the scene before them. So the men wearing the good clothes weren't pirates raiding a ville for slaves, but were the villagers, who had stolen the ship from the sailors.

"Would have thought it was the other way around,'' Dean said quietly.

"Deal? Yeah, we had a deal. And now we don't.''

The skinny man hawked and spit into the open mouth of the slave leader. The man gagged on the spittle, almost vomiting. Then he screamed in rage, and, drawing the flintlock from his belt, awkwardly pulled back the hammer and fired. Flame and smoke exploded from the wide maw of the handblaster, the strident blast blowing away half the prisoner's head. Grayish-pink brains flowing from his smashed skull, red blood pumping from the severed neck, the lifeless body slumped to the ground.

"Any more?'' the usurper roared, brandishing the empty weapon.

"Father!'' a young man shouted, and charged from the bushes carrying a long pole with a free formed blade on the end.

The leader of the villagers turned at the cry and ducked behind another villager just in time to avoid being slashed across the throat, a spray of blood from his shield arching into the sky. A coldheart tried to use a flintlock, but it merely hissed in a misfire. Another threw a knife and it missed. The young man then threw his spear and it went completely through the coldheart at the fire, stabbing the man behind him with its unusual blade. Entrails slithering into view from between his fingers, the first man slumped over into the fire, dragging the second along with him.

Bare feet padding on the smooth sand, the young man grabbed a blaster from another coldheart when a thundering boom shook the beach, and the young man staggered backward, his right arm gone, only shattered bone and tendrils of flesh hanging from the hideous wound.

The coldhearts cheered, and yet the dying man walked onward, going straight for the nameless leader of the slavers, his whole body trembling from the incredible exertion of staying on his feet. Contemptuously the slaver pulled a pouch from his belt and began to reload the huge flintlock blaster, pouring in black powder, then ramming down a ball and wad of cloth to keep it there. The blood pumping in spurts from his wound, the young man reached the leader and raised the dagger high just as the man cocked back the hammer of the weapon and fired it point-blank. The muzzle flame engulfed the features of the captain's son, and his head shattered into bloody pieces as the solid lead miniball plowed through flesh and bone in a grisly explosion.

The coldhearts cheered, and the captives bowed their heads in complete submission.

"Any more trouble, and you'll get the same!" the leader shouted, waving his arms. "Now I want to learn how to work the great ship, and no more shit from any of you asshole sailor dungheads!"

"They can't steer the ship," Doc said softly.

"Good enough for me," J.B. grunted.

Still not liking the odds, Ryan glanced at the others. Krysty and Doc nodded, Mildred cocked back the hammer on her revolver, Dean jacked the slide on his semiautomatic, Jak gestured and a knife dropped into his palm. He agreed with their decision.

Standing into plain view, Ryan started to shoot.

Chapter Five

Doc was a heartbeat behind Ryan. Leveling the LeMat, the scholar walked onto the beach firing his blaster. The .44-caliber hand cannon thundered flame and smoke, and a coldheart left the ground, flying backward for a yard before landing sprawled on the ground, his chest an ugly mess of bones and organs.

The chained sailors stared in wonder, while the shocked coldhearts hastily tried to draw their weapons. A few clumsily attempted to reload the flintlock longblasters, ripping open pouches of black powder that spilled onto the beach and was carried away by the blue waves.

Firing with every step, Doc strode among the slavers, bodies bursting from the impact of the soft-lead miniballs. Mental images of his own time of captivity flashed before his eyes, and the gentle scholar killed with ruthless satisfaction.

Meanwhile, the other companions opened fire from behind the cover of the broken wall, but J.B. stepped into view and triggered a spray of 9 mm Parabellum rounds at the slavers on the beach. Caught in the act of loading blasters, their riddled bodies tumbled into the surf, but amazingly the chattering of the submachine gun froze everybody into a tableau. Then the captives wildly cheered, and the coldhearts dropped to their knees.

Switching the selector pin to the shotgun chamber on his pistol, Doc paused at the bizarre surrender. What had just happened here?

"Rapidfires! It's the lord baron's sec men!" a slaver cried, dropping his flintlock. "Forgive us, masters!"

"W-w-we didn't know this ville was under your protection!" another said, cringing in the bloody sand. "I humbly beg pardon for our actions."

"Sirs! We are freeborn!" a chained man shouted, raising a fist in spite of the heavy links. "They branded us as slaves to sell!"

"So it would seem," Ryan said in a low and dangerous voice. The Deathlands warrior was starting to understand what was happening. The locals had black-powder weapons, while the sec men of the baron in charge had automatic blasters. "Release the prisoners by order of the lord baron!"

Hesitantly the slavers started to obey, but many were whispering among themselves as they fiddled with the locks. The surf carried away most of the conversation, but Ryan still heard a few words.

"...so where are they?"

"No tattoos anywhere..."

"Are they really...?"

Taking advantage of the temporary peace, Krysty went to the table and cut the bound girl free. Weeping her thanks, the teen joined the other young women, clutching each other in terror. Krysty moved behind the table for protection, and with her hands out of sight, quickly reloaded her revolver. Doc joined her, his hands purging the spent chambers of the LeMat and reloading.

"How long?" he whispered.

"Any moment," she whispered.

The sea breeze shifted the thinning smoke from the burning houses in the ville away from the beach, leaving them all in clear sight.

"Shit," Jak muttered, leaning against the broken wall.

As the chains came off the sailors, the men fell upon the corpses, retrieving their clothes and weapons. Dean and Mildred meandered close by and took position near the roaring fire.

Lining the gunwale of the ship, men stood with flintlocks in their hands, uncertain of what was happening on shore. Removing a half-spent clip to insert a full mag, J.B. noted the stubby black barrels of cannons now jutting from the side of the sailing ship. Ryan had played a good turn, but the slavers were getting wise, and the situation was turning bad fast.

Summoning some courage, a large bald slaver walked from the crowd and directly addressed Ryan. "Sir," he began respectfully, "are you...are you sec men of the lord baron?"

"Yes," Ryan lied.

"Then where are your tattoos of rank?" The bald man seemed suspicious, his vision flicking from weapon to weapon, the avarice in his gaze painfully obvious.

Nothing more needed to be said. Ryan knew he was caught, and with blinding speed opened fire. Crying out in surprise, three coldhearts dropped to the ground wounded. The fourth staggered, but managed to discharge his muzzle-loading pistol. Even as he fired back, killing the man, Ryan felt an angry buzz by his ear and then a hot trickle. He touched the side of his head and the palm came away red. Fireblast! He nearly bought the farm.

Instantly the rest of the companions cut loose at their chosen targets and a score of slavers fell, gushing blood.

Screaming in rage, the half-naked sailors joined the fray, firing blasters with remarkable speed. More slavers fell, their numbers reduced to a few dozen. Then the sailors charged at their captors with drawn knives and hot branding irons. Every remaining flintlock discharged, blowing clouds of dark gray smoke over the combatants, the screams of pain and yells of rage mixing into the muted roar of battle. In seconds, the battle went hand to hand, and the companions could no longer find easy targets.

Trying to run into the forest, a coldheart raced directly into the reach of the raped young women. He was twice their size and armed, but all ten of the teens leaped upon the man in bestial rage, clawing at his face with their nails. He fell shrieking and didn't stop for quite a while.

Ryan killed another two, then switched to the Steyr. He was out of loaded ammo clips for the handblaster. Blood was everywhere, the black smoke of discharged weapons mixing with the smoke of the burning houses in the ville until visibility was reduced to mere feet. Trying to listen for the sounds of the surf, Ryan moved for the beach. Unless these villagers were fools, they would start for the ship any time now, and he planned to be there waiting for them.

Smashing a man in the face with his LeMat, Doc tried to fire and found a sticky red wad of hair caught on the hammer. Holstering the piece, he unsheathed his sword and lunged at a man, stabbing him through the neck. The man was motionless from the pain, unable to use the weapon in his hand. As Doc savagely pulled the blade loose, he twisted the handle, forcing the wound to widen. Gurgling horribly, the slaver dropped, his hand clutching at the mortal wound, trying to staunch the crimson flow of life with dirty fingers.

Reaching the shoreline, Ryan saw the men on the ship scurrying about madly. A flintlock fired, and the anchor chain suddenly rattled through a hole in the gunwale, sinking into the sea.

"Bosun, look! They're trying to steal the ship!" a sailor cried out, pulling an ax from the split skull of a prone villager.

"What? We'll be trapped here forever!" a burly man snapped, grabbing a leather pouch of black powder from the belt of a corpse and reloading a flintlock pistol. He fired at the ship, but the miniball only hit the wooden side, doing no appreciable damage.

"It's too far!" the bosun raged, stuffing the pistol

into his belt. "Bones of God, who's got a fucking longblaster!"

"What do you mean trapped?" Ryan demanded, walking around the piles of corpses. "Isn't there any other way off this island?"

"Hell's bells, no! Why do you think they wanted the *Connie* so bad?"

"Fireblast. Where are their boats?" Ryan demanded as he dropped a spent clip and shoved it into a pocket. He pulled a fresh magazine from the pouch at his belt and slipped it into the handle of the sleek blaster.

"On the ship, sec man," a bearded sailor said, sneering, cradling a broken arm. The brand on his shoulder was bleeding freely, but it didn't seem to bother the big man much.

Ryan glowered. "I meant the boats of the ville!"

"Over here!" a woman cried, and limped for a clump of weeds on the shore of a small inlet.

Whistling sharply three times, Ryan raced after her with the rest of the companions, except Doc, following close behind. Reaching the reeds, they found a crude dock made of stones simply piled on top of one another, without mortar or any other filler. But floating in the still water were two long dugout canoes, lashed together with stout bamboo poles into a single vessel.

"An outrigger," Mildred said as they climbed on board.

"Row!" Ryan ordered, shoving the craft away from the dock.

Oars bending and threatening to break, the companions put their backs into the task and the nimble craft leaped forward over the crashing waves toward the *Constellation*. Standing amid the reeds, the young woman silently watched them go, then turned her back to slowly walk away.

A wave crashed over the outrigger, almost swamping the boat, but they leaned against the swell and stayed afloat. Looming before them, the *Constellation* rose from the sea like a wooden cliff, imposing and indestructible. On the shore, the fighting had slowed to a few scattered gunshots and the steady thumping of an ax slamming into meat. Then Doc appeared from among the fighters, his gory sword stabbing here and slashing there. In the crow's nest, a villager looked down in shock at the approaching outrigger and reached for the rope attached to a warning bell. Rocking against the waves, Ryan fired the Steyr, and the man fell backward with most of his face gone.

"J.B., keep these stupes off us for a minute," Ryan ordered, rowing with one hand, the other holding the SIG-Sauer and blowing flame at the men on the deck.

Nodding, the Armorer released his oar, pulled a large gren from his munitions bag and began to unwrap the tape around the old-fashioned lever handle.

"Fireblast! That the reload?" Ryan asked, pulling the top of the SIG-Sauer along his pant leg to jack the slide and clear a jam. There was more ammo for the Steyr in his backpack, but only a few loose rounds for the longblaster in his pocket, with no time for reloading the magazine.

The Armorer nodded grimly. The gren was an old World War II model called a pineapple. Normally the two-pound gren was filled with gunpowder, but that had lost its ginger over the decades and wouldn't explode anymore. So J.B. had replaced the dead gunpowder with C-4 plas-ex. Problem was, the old-style gren held six times more plas than a modern lightweight gren, and nobody could throw it far enough to survive the explosion. J.B. had been saving the bomb for a special job, and this was it.

"Now!" Ryan shouted, and the companions stopped rowing to duck.

In a lofting arch, J.B. threw the gren over the gunwale.

There was a shout from the main deck, then a strident fireball erupted, blowing pieces of deck and bodies into the sky. A dozen men fell from the rigging, plummeting to the deck with horrible thumps.

"Head for the bow!" Ryan directed, sliding the longblaster over a shoulder. "Stay away from the bastard sides! Those cannon will cut us into mincemeat!"

At the shout, another face appeared over the gunwale and aimed a crossbow at them. Releasing her oar, Mildred triggered the shotgun and the man went flying out of sight, the iron quarrel slamming into the deck of the outrigger, missing Krysty by a scant inch.

"Thanks," she grunted.

"No prob."

Reaching the side of the vessel, Ryan grabbed the muzzle of the cannon and hauled himself off the outrigger canoe. As he peeked inside the ship, he saw the gunners jerk in reaction to his presence and claw for weapons. The SIG-Sauer coughed a song a death, and the slavers dropped where they stood.

Bracing his shoulder against the side of the ship, Ryan grabbed the cannon with his free hand and started to push. It took all of his strength, but the cast-iron weapon slowly moved along its recoil track until there was enough space for him to wiggle through and enter the gun room.

A match flared from the dark end of the room. Ryan dropped and rolled as flintlocks boomed and miniballs loudly ricocheted off the iron cannon.

From within a pool of darkness, he waited for his eye to adjust to the low light, then backtracked the muskets and emptied half the clip. Grunts announced lethal hits, then he spun about, firing twice more in the opposite direction.

Standing in a stairwell, a fat man struggling to load a musket dropped the weapon in surprise as a 9 mm round only nicked his arm. Shifting position, Ryan dropped the spent clip and slapped in a fresh mag while the coldheart raced to ram the cloth wad down the barrel of his blaster and finish the reloading process. Both men clicked back hammers at the same time, and fired. Ryan proved to be the better marksman.

Quickly making sure the rest of the cannon deck was clear, Ryan tossed some rope out the cannon hole and stood guard while the rest of the companions climbed inside. Moving up the stairwell, they found only pieces of men, gore trickling down the steps leaving a grisly trail.

Reaching the main deck, the companions paused, listening for any voices, then charged out and spread apart as they searched for cover. The entire deck was smashed, pieces of planks jutting wildly from the tremendous explosion. Small fires burned here and there, and in the deck was a gaping hole large enough to drop a tank through. Teeth and slick stains told of several kills. A wounded man sat with his back to the mast, a belt tied tight around the oozing stump of his left leg.

"Ya fucking shitters!" he screamed, and fired both of the flintlocks in his hands. Even before the smoke of the double discharge cleared, he tossed the weapons aside and drew another set from his belt, clicking back the spring-driven hammers.

"Kill ya all!" he spit, reddish foam at the corners of his mouth.

J.B. threw his hat at the man, and as he shifted the aim of his weapons, Ryan fired. The slaver slammed backward against the mast, cracking his head. Slumped over, blood dribbling from his slack mouth, the man struggled to raise the blasters once more.

Ryan fired again and ended the matter.

Staying low, the companions studied the ship from their safe locations. Nobody else was in sight, on the deck or in the rigging above. The bow was piled with rope, and the quarterdeck was a full story above the main deck. The steering wheel would be on top, the captain's cabin and chart room underneath.

Rocking to the motion of the sea, the huge ship creaked gently as the evening tide carried it farther and farther away from the island.

"Not like," Jak said, scowling. An easy victory usually meant they had missed something important.

"Agreed," Ryan said, brushing back his hair. "J.B., Mildred, check the bunk room for survivors. Krysty and Dean, take the hold. Make sure they haven't done anything to sink the ship. Jak, with me," Ryan commanded, and started sprinting along the long deck of the battered vessel.

Everybody moved with a purpose.

Staying alert, the two men headed for the quarterdeck, using as cover one of the low turnstiles that rotated to lift the heavy anchor chains. Going to the door of the cabin, Ryan covered the teen as he stayed flat against the wall and pushed at the door. It swung open on oily hinges.

Diving inside, Ryan hit the floor and saw that the room was empty. The bed was a blood-stained mess, the table smashed, the honeycomb of holes that formed the chart locker empty. Every map was gone.

Exiting the cabin, Jak assumed guard, while Ryan walked past the companionway that led to the top of the quarterdeck. As he passed, a shot rang out, and Ryan jerked aside, hearing the whine of the passing bullet. He hit the deck and rolled to safety away from the steps.

Masked by the shadow of the mainsail, Jak tilted his head and gave Ryan a nod. He had expected an ambush, yet that was no flintlock, but a predark revolver. Rushing the man between reloads wouldn't work this time.

"Wanna try again, slave!" a man shouted in laughter. "Lots more where that came from. Ya got any more a dem bombs?"

"Don't need any more," Ryan shouted. "You're the last man alive."

Another shot and more laughter. "Bullshit! Every stud in the ville is with their baron! Ya couldn't have chilled sixty this fast. Ain't possible!"

"Then call for help, Baron. Go ahead, do it!"

A minute passed with only the sounds of the sea and the creaking ship.

"Shitfire. Okay, let's cut a deal!" the man shouted from the quarterdeck. There was a motion near the companionway and a revolver hit the wood planks, skittering along to drop down the hole in the deck.

"I'm unarmed," the baron shouted. "But move slow, or we all go ta hell!"

In the shadows, Jak asked a silent question, and Ryan grimaced. Unfortunately it didn't sound like bravado. The local baron had seized a fully armed gunship, and taken its crew prisoner, so he was no fool. The man had something in his favor, and Ryan could guess what it was.

The tip of the SIG-Sauer blaster leading the way, Ryan proceeded up the stairs until reaching the top deck. Standing behind the wheel was a big man, bleeding profusely from the cheek, his jawline stitched with tiny splinters. He was dressed in rolltop boots marred by fire, torn pants and a gore-stained shirt. An empty bandolier was draped across his chest, a MAC-10 machine pistol hanging over a shoulder. One hairy-knuckled hand was lashed to the tiller, the other held a sputtering torch held above an open barrel full of dark grainy material.

"This is black powder," he said. "Got a fuse in its belly leading down to the powder room. One touch of this torch, and the ocean gets a new hole in it. Follow?"

"Understood," Ryan said, lowering his blaster, but not holstering the piece. "You got a name?"

"Baron Tucholka. You?"

"Ryan. Looks like we got a standoff here. You don't want us to leave, and we can't let you stay."

"Fuck that," the baron snarled, as a wave broke over the bow of the ship. "Get off my ship!"

"No," Ryan said, and swung the SIG-Sauer toward the man.

Another wave hit the ship as Tucholka lowered the torch toward the open keg. "I'll give ya to three to drop the blaster," the baron snarled. "Then I'll—"

Ryan fired before the man could finish the threat. The pitch torch flew from his grip and hit the gunwale, going over the side. But some of the burning resin had been knocked loose by the impact of the bullet, and glowing sparks floated toward the black powder. Backing away in terror, Tucholka fought to free his bound hand, and Ryan could only stare as the burning pitch fell through the air, tumbling and turning.

Chapter Six

The first glowing droplet of pitch winked out before landing in the explosives, but the second hit the edge of the keg and teetered. Ryan fired, and blew away a fist-sized chunk of the keg, which skittered across the deck for yards.

Ryan felt his muscles relax as the danger passed. If that had gone inside, there wouldn't have been enough remaining of the whole ship to stuff into a spent brass casing.

Bound to the wheel, Tucholka was still tearing at the rope around his wrist. Ryan stood and leveled the pistol at the fat man.

"No, wait!" he cried. "I know something important about this boat!"

"Ship," Ryan corrected, and fired again.

The body slumped over the wheel, the weight dragging the spoked rim clockwise. Obediently the *Constellation* started heading to the right, straight for the breakers.

"Fireblast!" he cursed, and grabbed the huge mechanism with both hands, fighting to correct their course backward. The ship didn't respond, and they continued straight on for the deadly pink coral. The irregular surface glistened in the salty spray like a wall of daggers.

Suddenly Jak was alongside Ryan and slashed with a knife. The dead baron slipped from the cut ropes and rolled over the side, splashing into the briny deep.

"Take the left side," Ryan grunted, and the two men struggled to try to regain control of the mammoth runaway. The wheel moved as if the baron were still attached; every direction they pushed in, pushed right back.

"We're fighting the sails!" Ryan cursed, his boots slipping on the blood. "Not going to make it!"

"Idea!" Jak growled. Reaching out with a leg, he hooked the top of the black-powder barrel and dragged it close. Shoving it under the grips, the wooden handhold jammed tight on the weakened wood, and the teenager let go his grip.

"Get the others," he panted, and jumped down the companionway, landing heavily on the deck below.

"Hey," Krysty hailed from a hatchway in the damaged deck. "Nobody else on board. She's all clear."

"Gonna crash," Jak barked. "Help Ryan at wheel!"

The redhead glanced at Ryan holding on to the giant wheel, and hurried forward without saying a word.

"What can we do?" J.B. asked, tucking his glasses into a pocket for safekeeping.

"Dunno," Jak said, his hands clenching and unclenching helplessly at his sides. "Only room for two at wheel."

Above them was a labyrinthine maze of ropes and pulleys going in every possible direction.

"Pull the wrong one and we hit the breakers!"

"Know that!"

Mildred went to the gunwale and held the railing while she tried to see where they were headed with the spray blurring her vision. "Son of a bitch!" she shouted. "That coral will rip the guts out of this ship."

"We'll sink like a rock."

"Drop the sail!" Dean shouted, going to the port gunwale. He released the ropes around a belaying pin. The twisted hemp shot away free, disappearing into the complex rigging.

Jak drew a knife. "Come on."

"Don't!" Dean ordered, pulling another pin. It took both hands, but the boy managed the task. A small sail at the distant front of the ship sagged, but didn't drop. "We'll need them to get off the island! Just set them loose, and drop the big sail!"

Jak joined Dean, J.B. and Mildred going to the other side of the huge vessel. As fast as possible, they pulled out the belaying pins and untied knots. At first nothing happened; the ship stayed true on its course for the breakers. Another sail loosened in its stays, then sagged and finally fell to the deck in a loud rush of salt-stiff canvas. Mildred dived for the deck as the jib boom disengaged and swept across the deck. She heard it swoosh overhead and then slam into the quarterdeck, knocking away the companionway, the smashed wood shotgunning overboard.

The waves fought every turn, and Ryan found he could only alter their direction in tiny increments. Ryan and Krysty didn't seem to notice their near extermination, all of their concentration on the stubborn wheel and the approaching coral.

Knuckles white from the strain, the man and woman fought side by side to overcome the wind and the tide. Then in a deafening rustle, the main sail collapsed, nearly smashing Jak under its awesome weight.

"Thank Gaia!" Krysty shouted, as the strain noticeably lessened.

Ryan didn't waste any breath on words. He stayed at his position, fighting to steer the lumbering giant back toward the lagoon and calm waters. Slowly, every so slowly, the *Constellation* moved past the coral outcropping. However, once they cleared the array of breakers, the pull of the evening tide eased, the whitecaps stopped cresting and the ship now slowly obeyed them like a well-trained plow horse.

"Got no anchor!" Krysty reminded.

"Sandbar!" Ryan shot back. "Hold on!"

Everybody grabbed something solid, and the ship shuddered as its bow plowed into the underwater ridge of sand. There was a moment or two of rocking back and forth, the stays and jib creaking loudly, then the ship went still in its earthen berth.

Releasing the wheel, Ryan flexed his hands, trying to get some feeling back into his fingers. He had once killed a cougar by grabbing its front legs and pulling them apart to break its chest wide open, and that had been easier than this.

"Anybody hurt?" Krysty shouted over the quarterdeck railing.

"Alive and undamaged," Mildred shouted back, rubbing a sore shoulder.

"Speak for yourself," Dean said sullenly, inspecting his chafed hands. The skin was gone from his palms in spots, the flesh raw and oozing.

Jak took a glance. "Not chill ya," he decided.

"Yeah, I know," the boy snapped irritably. "But it stings."

J.B. glanced at the towering pile of canvas forming a gray mountain on the deck. Had to be a ton, maybe two of the material. Anybody caught underneath it would have been squashed flat.

"Could have been worse," he said, pulling out his glasses and checking them for damage.

Tying off the wheel so the rudder wouldn't get damaged from the random slapping waves, Ryan went to the railing. Krysty stood there like a queen of the sea, her wild red hair blowing in the breeze.

"Company coming," she said bluntly.

Hawking to clear his throat, Ryan spit over the side and studied the beach. There was no sign of any live slavers. The sailors were scavenging among dead, taking boots and blasters, occasionally kicking a corpse. However, at the creek, Doc and some of the better-dressed sailors were climbing into an outrigger and setting into the surf. All of them were heavily armed.

"Doc doesn't look like a hostage," J.B. said, wiping his face and tucking on his glasses.

"He's not," Ryan said. "And that buys us some leverage. Jak, let them on board. Everybody else, stay close. We need to show a united front. We're a crew, just like them."

"Gotcha," Krysty said, and jumped down the main deck, only bending her knees slightly to absorb the impact.

"Leverage for what?" Mildred asked. "What are we bargaining for?"

Ryan said nothing, but checked the clip in his blaster to make sure it was fully loaded. In a few minutes, the outrigger full of sailors reached the side of the *Constellation* where there was a gap in the gunwale.

"Ahoy!" a short man at the front of the boat called out. "We're coming aboard!"

"That you, Adam?" Ryan shouted down from the deck, arms crossed, hands dangling near the SIG-Sauer.

Doc raised an eyebrow in puzzlement, then remembered their old code. If one of the companions was with strangers, calling him "Adam" was asking if it was a trap. Answer the name, and the companions would cut loose with every weapon they had, hopefully catching the enemy off guard. Any name with a *B* meant leave immediately, and so on. It was something they had cooked up on board the *Leviathan*, sadly destroyed some time ago.

"Clear as crystal, Charlie!" he shouted back though cupped hands.

Ryan nodded at the all-clear code. Good. Maybe they could cut a deal with these sailors yet. He really didn't want to chill them and take the ship, but that was his only other option.

Going to the hole, Jak kicked over a coiled rope ladder that appeared to be for just such a purpose. The first of the sailors climbed on board with ease and surveyed the destruction with a dour expression.

"Any of them alive?" the sailor demanded. He was a short man, with a barrel chest and arms like a gorilla. The handles of knives jutted from each rolltop boot, and two pistols rested in his wide leather belt. His shirt had a bloody bullet hole in the chest, obviously taken off a fallen comrade.

"Alive? Not anymore," Ryan replied gruffly. "How about ashore?"

The man grinned. "As you say, Blackie, not anymore."

"Ryan," the Deathlands warrior stated coldly.

"Bosun Jones," the little man replied. "Bosun Jackson Carter Jones, commander of the *Constellation.*"

"A bosun in charge of this goliath?" Mildred asked suspiciously.

As more sailors climbed aboard, Jones frowned. "Guess I bloody well have to be. All the officers are dead. I'm the only rank left."

Just then, Doc rose into view, his ebony swordstick stuck into his belt. "By the Three Kennedys, that was brilliant! Dropping the sails and ramming the bar. Ingenious!''

Ryan merely grunted, knowing the question could tell the man way too much about them. Dangerous.

''Why didn't you just drop anchor?'' Jones asked.

''They shot it loose,'' Ryan replied. ''Or didn't you see that?''

''Yeah, I saw. So what about the sea anchor?''

The ship had two? Ryan lied, ''Jammed.''

''Is it now?'' a burly sailor demanded, his nose broken, a bare sword in his three-fingered grip.

''You have my permission to go see for yourself,'' Ryan said calmly.

''Permission?'' Jones roared. ''This is my ship, lubber, and I give the orders around here.'' He stabbed himself in the chest with a thumb. ''Me and only me!''

As the rest of the crew came on board, they formed a surly mob behind Captain Jones. Their brands still leaking blood, they looked exhausted, but grimly ready to back any play of the small commander.

''Was your ship,'' Ryan stated, resting a hand on his blaster. ''It's ours now.''

The companions drew their weapons just as the sailors did the same. For a few moments, nobody breathed for fear of starting the point-blank shooting. Ryan prepared to move fast. At this range, the .75-caliber miniballs would literally blow him in two. Heart or head shots were too chancy. He'd have to hit the blasters themselves as the bosun drew.

''Jus' give the word, Cap,'' a tall man growled.

"Belay that," Jones snapped, and the men eased their stance. But callused hands were never far from their assortment of weapons.

"You set us free on the beach," the captain muttered, "so we owe you our lives. Then ya saved the *Connie* from the slavers, so we owe you half the cargo. Put them together, and much as I hate to say it, you want to stake a claim on the *Connie* I have to agree, on my oath I do."

"Bosun!" a sailor shouted in shock. "Ya giving away the *Connie*?"

Jones turned on the taller man, and he backed away. "That's 'captain' to you, O'Malley. And if I say die, you say how-often-sir, natch?"

"Yeah, I understand, Captain," the man mumbled, lowering his gaze.

Turning, the short man scowled darkly at the companions, then spoke to Ryan directly. "Say she's your ship. What's the deal? We work as crew or get marooned?"

"No," Ryan said, cutting the air with his hand. "We came here by accident and only want to leave."

"Soon as possible," J.B. added bluntly.

Captain Jones snorted. "Ship broken, eh? Waddaya need, wood, canvas, rope? Got plenty of that. Take what ya want."

"We need shine," Ryan said, resting a boot on a layered fold of canvas. "Couple of gallons of wine would do, even beer, or some copper pipe to make our own. Get us that, and the *Connie* is yours."

The sailors murmured among themselves while

Jones chewed over the amazing request, his face going through a variety of expressions.

"Any alcohol or juice in the lanterns?" Dean asked, gesturing at a hanging lamp.

"Juice in a lamp, boy? Don't be daft. It's fish oil," Jones said as if it were obvious. "Smells bad down below, but gives good light. Got lots, if that's any help."

Jak shook his head. "No way."

"Shine to fix a ship," Jones said, cracking his knuckles. "Black dust, we've got nothing like that on board. Drunk sailors fall overboard. Now the ville had plenty, that's what they gave us to celebrate finishing the work. We drank every drop and woke up in chains. More fools we for trusting villagers. If ya don't walk wood, then ya ain't worth spit, as Captain Fallon used ta say. God rest him."

After a moment, Jones continued. "Now Lord Baron Kinnison has got lots of predark machines, some of them even work. He'd have that copper ya need. But I can't take no man there. Oh, I thought about it. There's a powerful reward for outlanders. But once he knows ya got rapidfires, he'll skin ya alive to find out where they come from! And I can't risk the lives of any man who saved my crew. That's the first thing I'm paying you back. Your lives."

"Mebbe we could reason with him," Krysty asked. "Cut a deal."

"With the lord bastard?" A sailor laughed, then abruptly stopped to grasp his ribs. "Better chance of arguing cold to fire," he finished, wheezing for breath.

Mildred knew the man had broken ribs, possibly a punctured lung from the sound of his breathing. But she could do nothing until some sort of treaty had been negotiated. Politics was always getting in the way of medicine.

"No, can't take ya there," Jones went on, crossing his arms, displaying a wealth of crude tattoos. "Got plenty of shine at our home port, Cold Harbor ville. Shine so strong it'll knock the stink off a mutie. Probably make your other eye fall out."

Instantly Ryan felt the red anger well from within, the unbridled urge to chill everybody. But then he saw the sailor holding back a grin, and forced himself to be calm. Fireblast, the runt had been testing him! In spite of himself, Ryan was starting to like the man. He was hard and direct. Somebody they could trust, for a while, at least.

"If that's what melted you down to this size, pee-wee," Ryan shot back, "then it'll do."

Jones sputtered in rage while the other sailors burst into laughter. The short captain grabbed the curved butt of a flintlock, paused, slowly took his hand away and reluctantly cracked a grin. "Okay, Ryan, you want shine, then by God, I'll drown ya in it! We'll take ya to our home port, pack the hold with the oldest shine, best in town, steal it from the gaudy house if needs be and take ya back here. Then you're on your own and we're quits. Fair steven to the nine. Agreed?"

Ryan wasn't sure what that last phrase meant, had to be something local, but the tone carried the ring of truth.

"Deal," Ryan said, and he held out his hand.

However, Captain Jones raised a hand to stop him. "Not so fast," he said quickly. "There's something I need from you folks in return. Gimme an oath you'll fight alongside us in case of trouble. These villagers caught us asleep. But there's pirate ships out there that raid these islands. Sleek windjammers armed with our own cannons. We're big, but they're fast. Those fancy rapidfires might make them think twice, mebbe go try some other ship." The new captain spit in his own palm, then held it out. "That's the deal. Shine and two trips, for your blasters at our backs, both ways and in port. Deal?"

"Fair steven," Ryan said, repeating the earlier phrase, and saw the reactions in their faces. The trade was sealed.

Just then, a lone seagull flew by cawing for its mate. The companions flinched at the sight of the bird, reaching for their blasters, and Jones surreptitiously noted the fact. Obviously they had tangled with the condors of Spider Island. That had to be where their ship was moored. How interesting.

"What should we do first, sir?" a sailor asked, holding a dirty rag to his shoulder. "Check the hull for leaks? She hit that sandbar awful hard."

"I can do that. It's you sons of bitches I'm worried about," Jones stated, looking over the crew. "Where's Danvers?"

"The healer tried to run," a big man said. When speaking, he displayed a lot of missing teeth. "The locals gut shot him."

"Blasted coward," Jones growled. "Served him right. Okay, O'Malley, you're the new healer."

"Me?" the sailor asked, startled.

"You. Get busy binding wounds."

"Aye, aye, skipper," O'Malley said hesitantly.

"I'm a healer," Mildred said, patting her med kit. "Best you'll ever find."

Jones scowled at the stocky outlander with her bizarre hairdo. "Then get to work, woman! My crew is bleeding while we jaw."

"I'll need a private room to sterilize," Mildred said. "Some of those wounds are deep and will need stitches, maybe even minor surgery. I want the captain's cabin as sick bay."

Jones glanced at the quarterdeck and noted the stairs were gone. It had to have been a hell of a fight, he realized. These outlanders were good.

"Do whatever you want, take whatever you need," he said wearily.

"Mildred, I'll start boiling water and ripping any clean cloth I can find," Krysty offered, starting to reach for her backpack. Gaia, those were in the bushes behind the ville. "Where's the galley?"

"Boiling water?" a sailor grunted, a knife jutting from his thigh. "We're not making soup."

"Shut up! Don't walk or touch the knife. You two, carry that man," Mildred ordered, starting off across the long deck and around the huge mound of the downed mainsail. She had no intention of trying to explain the existence of germs to these sailors. They never would believe her. Few did these days. "The rest of you, follow me."

Grumbling among themselves, the survivors did as they were ordered and limped along behind, leaving a crimson trail of footsteps in their wake.

"Meet you in ten," Krysty said, going for the open hatch that led belowdecks.

"Hurry," Mildred shouted over a shoulder, already rummaging through her meager supplies. No sulfur, no alcohol, no ether—it was going to be bare-handed surgery once more. May God help the men, but she would save as many as possible.

Knowing he would never see some of those men alive again, Captain Jones watched the wounded men hobble off, then turned and addressed the rest of the crew. "Okay, the rest of you swabs get back to work! Bust open the ship's stores, and take all the lead and powder ya want. Reload those blasters, boys. We'll never get caught unarmed again, by God!

"After that, I want Curtis in the nest and keep a sharp eye for incoming ships," Jones directed, his fists placed on his hips. Short on stature, the runt was still every inch a captain.

"Yes, sir!"

"Daniels, man the wheel. Baltier, take one of the outlanders and search the lower decks for any stowaways. Don't want any surprises once we're at sea."

"Ya wanna talk to anybody we find, skipper?" the

tattooed man asked, testing the edge of a long curved knife on a callused thumb.

The captain scowled. "Feed them to the fish."

"We already checked below," Ryan said, scratching at his bloody ear. Then he forced himself to stop before the scab came off and it started to bleed again. "Ship is clear."

"Did ya? Good," Jones grunted. "Then check the mainsail, Baltier. We're not going anywhere without that."

"Aye, sir," the man said, and began to examine the chest-high folds of canvas.

"I'll help," Dean offered, and rushed to assist.

"Good lad!" Jones shouted, then added softly. "Blind Christ, I'm reduced to using brats. Hope that healer is good, Ryan, 'cause we're powerfully short on crew and will need every man alive to get off this stinking rock."

"Pray tell, sir, what about the girls?" Doc asked, glancing at shore. The women were moving among the dead, using knives on the dead men to settle accounts. The ragged bits of flesh they hacked off were tossed into the crackling fire and raised a wretched cloud of dank smoke.

"Eh?" Jones frowned, confused for a moment by the change of topics. "They were to be a gift to the baron. He's looking for a new wife. Ain't no good now. Kinnison likes them young and fresh. But you want one, go ahead, she's yours."

"Indeed I do not!" Doc rumbled, offended. He angrily thumped his stick on the deck. "Do I seem a pedophile? You misconstrued my meaning entirely!"

"Did I now," Jones said, unsure if he was being insulted or not.

"Make crew," Jak explained, tucking thumbs into his belt.

The captain stared at the teenager and the old man. "Women?"

"You need hands," J.B. stated, pointing a finger at the man, then jerking a thumb at the ville. "They each have two."

"Aye, and a lot more," Jones said, scratching at the throbbing scar on his shoulder. The numbness of the branding was wearing off, and it was starting to itch bad. "Hey silverhair, Doc is it? You were the one that stayed on shore. Go take the outrigger and offer them the deal. Any women who signs the ship articles will be crew, and treated as such. My word."

"Done, sir," Doc stated, and headed for the breach in the gunwale where the canoe was moored.

"Good news, skipper! The main looks fine," Baltier reported, while hoisting a stiff layer. "Nothing much wrong here, just some bullet holes and… Shitfire!"

In a soft rumble, the canvas slipped from his grip and slid into the gaping hole in the deck, the ropes trailing behind lashing about madly. It piled in the hold, almost reaching the deck.

"Rad me, that's thirty feet wide!" Jones erupted, walking around the yawning pit, his stubby legs moving briskly. "Thirty! What the hell did you bastards fire on my darling ship, a nuke?"

"Close enough," J.B. said, tilting back his fedora. "But it chilled most of the slavers."

"I'll say. Gren?"

"Plas."

"Know anything about cannons?"

"Some," the Armorer admitted hesitantly. "Want me to help work with the blaster crew?"

"You are the blaster crew," Jones said gruffly. "The rest got aced."

"All of them?"

"Every man."

"Fireblast! This is why you wanted us on board so much," Ryan growled, advancing on the smaller man. "You've got no trained gunners. This ship would have been defenseless at sea!"

The captain shrugged. "Said I wanted those rapidfire blasters on my side, and that was no lie. Besides, I knew you only needed to cut a deal 'cause none of you could sail a ship."

"That obvious, eh?" J.B. asked, clearly annoyed.

"Shit, yes." Jones stabbed a finger at Ryan. "So remember that without us you're marooned."

"And you'd be chilled," Ryan reminded bluntly.

"Mebbe," Captain Jones grunted at the veiled threat. "But I want to ride the ass of the evening tide out of here, so ya better get busy at your work. There's lot to do and little time." Then, turning his back on the armed companions, he walked away shouting orders to the sailors.

Chapter Seven

Skipping over the ocean waves, the PT boat angled around the conning tower of a sunken aircraft carrier and headed for the narrow passage into the calm bay.

The water was choppy around the island, the natural banks of the landmass reaching out to sea and almost completing a circle. The entry into the harbor was tight, barely twenty feet across, and made even smaller by the piles of concrete and brick from pre-dark ruins, along with the occasional smashed wreck of a submerged vessel. Some were rotting wood, others rusting hulks of exploded metal, and a small handful were space-age polymers, still as clean and bright as the day they had come from the injection molding.

Stout bunkers stood on either side of the harbor's passage, their sloping concrete walls proof to primitive cannonballs and musket rounds. Grim sec men stood guard within, oily M-16 rifles slung over their shoulders. A rectangular metal box rose in their midst, its honeycombed interior jammed with sleek fat tubes, their pointed tips barely protruding into view.

As the PT boat slowed to enter the pass, a lieutenant walked into view and raised a closed fist. Standing on the bridge of the fighting ship, a tall man with black hair copied the motion, then snapped the fist to his chest, then slashed an open palm down to his side.

"Let them pass!" the lieutenant shouted to the men inside the bunker, then faced the other structure and tapped the stock of his longblaster with two fingers spread wide. The sec men across the water nodded in understanding, and went back inside their bunker and out of the ocean spray.

The predark military craft slid through the passageway, its aft funnels blowing black smoke into the air, the heavy beat of its engines audible over the crashing of the waves. The tall officer on the deck glanced at the guards in passing, then turned his back to them as the boat reached open water again, and increased its speed.

"Think he found them?" a sec man asked around the dangling cig in his mouth. The smoke was greenish, like the tobacco, but he drew in the pungent fumes with obvious pleasure.

The lieutenant took the kelp cig and pulled a deep drag himself before giving it back.

"Don't really care," the officer muttered, buttoning his heavy coat a little tighter. "I was hoping the shitter would die this time."

The deck throbbing beneath his polished boots as the PT boat moved easily into the vast calm harbor, Lieutenant Craig Brandon closely studied the defensive bunkers hidden along the curving shore, and noted the holstered blasters of the muscular fisherman working the nets of a small trawler. A stone castle stood on a distant mountaintop, its imposing array of

Firebird rockets undetectable in the manicured gardens, the beachfront dock busy with ships and men.

Everything seemed in order, which slightly displeased the officer. As the sec chief for Baron Kinnison, it was his job to always make sure no pirate fleet or attacking armada could break through and reach the baron. Perfection bothered the man, and he made a mental note to offer some of the slaves a full pardon from the saltpeter mines if they would attack the island ville. He'd take them out to sea, give the fools some blasters and knives, and watch how his sec men handled the assault. It would be interesting. And if the slaves decided to try to run, well, that would be a good test of the weapons and crew on board PT 264. For every slave who escaped alive, the whole crew would receive ten lashes. For every slave aced, and their blaster recovered, an hour in the gaudy house. Private level.

"Fuel," Brandon said to the man at the wheel.

Both hands on the till, the sec man checked a gauge set amid the predark control panel. Most of the gauges and dials didn't work, but the important ones did: engine temperature, engine pressure, speed and compass. What else did a sailor need?

"Ain't touched a drop, sir," the pilot reported crisply. "Only used wood the whole trip."

Already knowing the answer, Brandon grunted in acknowledgment. He just liked to keep the men alert. Coal oil gave the boilers twice the heat of wood, which translated as twice the pressure and speed. However, wood was cheap and squeezing shale for the few precious drops of oil was a long and slow process. He was determined to never waste a single ounce.

Ahead of PT 264, several large sailing ships floated a hundred yards from the docks, prizes won in battle with the renegades to the south. Now the booty served both as items to be sold to villes that needed to increase their fleets, and as physical protection for the vulnerable dockyards.

Maneuvering through the picket line of vessels, the wooden giants became lost in the billowing exhaust plumes of the squat PT boat. Now the vast green expanse of Maturo Island filled his view, and Brandon reached over to tug on a thick rope, giving two short blasts on the shrill steam whistle to inform the shoreline Firebird batteries they were approaching. Standard regs from the baron. Nobody approached without notice, or else they were blown from the water before reaching the dock. The man was insane, but no fool. Many had tried to take Maturo Island, but none ever reached the shore, much less the Castle Kinnison.

"Home." The pilot smiled.

"Pay attention to that buoy, and do your job," the lieutenant snapped irritably.

"Aye, sir!" the pilot replied, hiding his annoyance. The bastard never seemed to relax or enjoy anything.

Leaning forward, the pilot shouted into a bamboo tube going down into the deck. "Engine room, give me back spin. Half speed."

"Back at half, aye, sir!" a muffled voice shouted back.

There was some heavy mechanical clunks from belowdecks, and then the PT boat noticeably slowed as the propellers began to spin counterclockwise, killing their momentum.

With practiced ease, the deadly warship coasted to the pier and came to an easy halt alongside the concrete-and-green-wood dock.

"All stop," Brandon ordered, rising from his chair.

As the crew of PT 264 hurried about, tossing mooring lines to the dockside crew, Brandon hopped off the metal boat and strode quickly along the workers. The nets were neatly folded, a few old slaves repairing rips, and the smell of fish guts was thick in the air, as it should be. If the baron depended entirely upon the villes for food, the sec men of Maturo Island would soon find themselves starved into submission and chained with the rest of the slaves, to toil in the nitrate mines until they died of the white cough. Brandon would rather eat his blaster than let that happen.

Fifteen more PT boats were docked at the piers, with six more out on patrol. Every boat was similarly armed with machine guns and torpedo tubes, but only the 264 also sported a rank of Firebirds.

"Morning, sir! How goes the pirate hunt, sir?" a sec man asked as the frowning officer walked by.

With a snarl, Brandon backhanded the sec man. "Never ask me the baron's business!" he barked, and marched away.

"Son of a bitch," the sec man muttered, rising to his feet. He rubbed his hand across his mouth, and it came away streaked with red. "Guess the pirate won this trip."

"Bad for us," a corporal answered, a hand resting on the shoulder strap of his M-16. "Now Old Iron Ass will make us parade and shit so he won't feel bad."

"We need a new sec chief," the first man growled softly, touching the fishbone dagger sheathed on his belt.

"Just let me know if you decide to challenge the man," the corporal said. "I could use your boots."

"Fuck you, too," he grumbled sullenly.

"Yeah, pal. Any time."

The crowd of workers, sec men and slaves parting before him, Brandon reached dry land and stood for a moment, savoring the feeling of it not moving under his boots. He hated the sea, but that was part of the job. So be it.

With a toothless grin, a hunchback slave harnessed to a rickshaw bowed before the officer, inviting him to climb on the wheeled cart. Needing the exercise, Brandon pushed aside the old woman and strode through the warehouses and cannon bunkers, enjoying the feeling of stretching his legs.

He glanced toward the distant green hills, seeing the dark areas of burned earth where some stupe bastard had made a mistake and a storehouse of black powder had exploded, leveling hundreds of trees and chilling dozens of slaves and sec men. But much more importantly, the fatal mistakes reduced their supply of ammo. Lead was salvaged from the predark ruins—lots of it there—and slaves made more slaves all by themselves. But flash was a major problem. There was only one major source of that, and it didn't belong to Kinnison.

Reaching a tall flight of stairs cut into the very granite of the mountain, he started to climb at an easy lope. A hundred slaves had died cutting the staircase, and fifty more while decorating it with fancy designs. But that was only fitting for the man who ruled the thousand known islands of the entire world. Once, an outlander found on the beach had claimed to come from the mainland. Brandon shot him in the face on the spot. Such foolish talk could make others think of leaving, undermine the power of the barons and their sec men. Absolutely intolerable.

At the top of the stairs, the lieutenant walked slowly across fields of manicured lawns edged with flowering gardens. Sec men saluted as he passed.

Passing a splashing fountain, Brandon headed straight for the front door of the baron's castle. It used to be a post office building, but its thick walls and lack of windows made it a perfect fortress. The glass door had long ago been replaced by thick wood bound by straps of iron. Three of the four doors were closed, the open doorway guarded by an armed sec man standing stiffly at attention.

"Morning, Private," Brandon said as he tried to enter, but the young sec man stood his ground and didn't move.

"Halt!" the teenager ordered, and snapped the bolt on his longblaster. "Password, sir!"

Contemptuously, Brandon sneered at the youngster. "You know who I am and what I do to idiots who annoy me. Now get out of the way!"

The sec man paled, but swung the barrel of the Weatherby .30-06 rifle toward the sec chief. "Password or die," he said calmly. "Your choice."

The two stared at each other, then the lieutenant made a move for the pistol at his side. Instantly the guard shifted his aim and fired. The holster jerked, a ragged scar in the polished leather where the round had plowed through.

"Next one goes in your face," the teenager stated, sweat dripping off his cheeks and dampening his shirt.

Suddenly a squad of sec men raced into view carrying a wide assortment of weapons.

"Excellent." Brandon smiled, easing his stance. "Good response time and fine shooting, Sergeant."

"Private, sir."

"Not anymore," Brandon said. "Nor are you working for internal sec. You're with me now, a private guard for the baron himself. I need a new XO on the boat, and I think you'll do."

"Me, sir? Thank you, sir!"

"What's your name, son?"

"Hannigan, sir. Thor Hannigan."

"Meet me down at the dock, slip 2, PT 264. We'll talk later, Sergeant Hannigan."

"Aye, sir!"

"The rest of you men are dismissed!" Brandon shouted.

Relaxing, the other sec men shouldered their weapons and walked back to their assigned posts. Beaming a smile, Brandon tried to get past the boy, and the longblaster was shoved into his face again.

"Nice try. Password or die," Hannigan said low and dangerous. His finger was already putting pressure on the trigger, and any attempt to knock the blaster aside would only set it off.

In cold fury, the lieutenant stared at the man, then slowly nodded. "Excellent," he said. "Black dust, I'll take you on as crew! The password is broken sword."

"Pass, sir," Hannigan said, lowering his weapon to port arms.

Watching his step, Brandon walked inside, then turned. "Don't forget to pick up that spent brass," he said, gesturing vaguely at the spent round on the ground.

Hannigan sneered. "That's for privates, not me."

"Good man," he grunted. "You'll go far."

Proceeding down the main corridor, Brandon went past the dining hall, the armory and then the soundproof doors to the dungeon. Whimpering and the thump of metal on flesh could be heard softly from within. Soundproof, his ass. Damn door needed repairs again. Too many near escapes had damaged the jamb once more. When would the men learn to cut the hamstrings of prisoners so they couldn't run, even if they got free from the shackles? Time for more beatings.

Stopping before the entrance to the throne room,

the lieutenant smoothed his hair and made sure the flap on his holster was buttoned down tight before entering. The baron had more rules on sec than he did.

He knocked on the sheet metal covering the door, and an old woman pushed the heavy portal aside and let him enter.

"How is he?" Brandon asked, glancing around the huge room. The baron was holding court over some people from another island who were trying to buy more black powder.

"Bad, sir," the woman muttered softly. "Wife nineteen gave him another girl."

"Black dust! Did he let this one live?"

She shook her head. "Threw it into the sea himself."

Brandon heard the shift from a person to a thing. He couldn't blame her. The woman was trained to deliver children, not murder newborns. But the baron was set on getting a son to replace him when death finally came, or claimed that he would take them all to hell when he died. Nobody doubted the threat.

On a raised wooden platform, an obscene pile of flesh sat in an armless throne, wads of mottled flesh hanging over either side of the chair. Slaves stood attendant on both sides, with armed sec men in the corners, and a large crowd of people standing patiently before the pulsating mound of fat as he nosily guzzled from a cup of wine made from a spent 120 mm artillery round.

Baron Maxwell Kinnison was beyond repulsive.

His hard piggy eyes were sunk deep in a pool of fat, and a tremendous belly flopped over his gunbelt and quivered upon his unseen lap. His clothing was a mixture of Navy uniforms and bedsheets, and the checkered grips of predark revolvers jutted from his clothing in several locations. Hair grew in irregular tufts in his otherwise bald head, his face was a mass of open sores and the fingers of both hands were wrapped in strips of cloth stained black and yellow from the dried blood and pus.

His disease was called the red death. Some old healer once called it by the fancy name of leprosy. Kinnison was dying by pieces, and only massive amounts of jolt and alcohol helped him dull the pain enough to stay coherent. Any remaining sanity had disappeared years earlier. However, he was still the only person alive who knew the secret formula for making black powder, which was the very heart of their power over the lesser islands. No matter how many people wanted him aced, that secret had to be pried from the bloated whale first, no matter what the cost.

Snorting for air through his tiny nose, the baron took a whole chicken from the bowl of roasted birds alongside his throne and started to rip the skin off the white meat with jagged yellow teeth.

"My lord," Brandon said, advancing and snapping off a salute.

"Report," the baron mumbled, his mouth overflowing with food. Bits of bird fell to add to the vast collection of stains on his embroidered tunic.

"Pirates attacked another convoy headed for the western islands. I sank two, but couldn't find their hidden docks."

"Some escaped?" Kinnison shouted, bits of food spraying from his mouth. "Unsatisfactory, Lieutenant!"

"Indeed it is, my baron. Also the payment ship from Cold Harbor ville is extremely late. Almost two weeks behind schedule. I checked with their baron, and it seems that ship did sail on time. I found no evidence of trickery on their part."

"Better not," the baron muttered, tearing off another mouthful.

"My lord, there was a bad storm," a slim man suggested. "Mebbe a sea mutie got them. It has happened before."

Brandon scowled at the man, but kept his peace. Griffin was the baron's personal healer. He was always scrubbed clean, from his pointed beard to his soft leather moccasins. His clothing was plain, almost nondescript, and if he was armed, the blaster was nowhere in sight.

Swallowing the partially chewed meat, Baron Kinnison tossed away the half-eaten bird and picked up a fresh one. "That is a possibility, Griffin," he said, nibbling on the capon. "Or they may only be damaged and trying to make repairs on some uninhabited island along the route. How many do they normally pass, Lieutenant?"

"Twenty-four," Brandon replied, "if they follow the undersea rivers to make good speed."

"Too many to check." Kinnison frowned, then winced as if in pain. Reaching quickly into a pocket, he withdrew a vial and sprinkled a pinch of white powder into his brass mug of wine. He drained the container, the excess flowing over the rim and down his wattled cheeks.

"Better." He sighed in relief, then resoundingly belched and extended the mug. "More!"

Nervous slaves rushed forward to fill the brass mug from sealed glass bottles, and a terrified slave was forced at gunpoint to sip from the cup before the baron drank once more.

Politely most of the people in the throne room glanced away from the sight of their baron quaffing so huge a dose of jolt. As if on cue, a slave who was serving food to the visitors cast aside his plastic tray and shoved over a man from an island ville, the man's silvery belt knife now in his bony grasp.

"Die, pig!" the slave screamed, charging the throne, the steel blade raised high for a killing stroke.

With blinding speed, Brandon pulled his weapon, but Griffin was standing in the line of fire. Damn the man! As the lieutenant tried to get around the obstruction, the armed guards in the room reacted instantly, the cross fire of their longblasters chilling two slaves and hitting the running man twice before he made it to the steps that led to the throne. Bleeding profusely, the slave staggered onward, then screamed in fury as he lunged forward with the knife.

Still sipping wine, Baron Kinnison calmly drew a sleek blue revolver from within the voluminous folds of his tunic and shot the assassin directly in the face, the flame from the barrel engulfing his features.

Gore went everywhere, as human debris blew across the chamber. The shocked crowd could only stare as the mutilated body slumped toward the floor. Then Kinnison's revolver spoke twice more, blasting away chunks of the would-be killer before the corpse hit the granite floor. A bare foot twitched once, and the corpse stopped moving.

Taking aim, Kinnison fired three more times into the body, then tossed the empty blaster aside, only to pull another into view. "Griffin!" he bellowed.

"Yes, my lord?" the man asked, rushing closer. He knew the baron wasn't hurt, and asking would only anger the man more than he was. If that was possible.

"What ville was this man from?"

"Blackstone, on the Island of Flowers."

As the pain began to ease, Kinnison set aside his mug and scowled. Blackstone, what a useless place, only good for slaves, some meat animals and not much else. An island covered with flowers, few crops and no ruins or minerals. Even the fishing was bad.

"Triple the amount of their tribute for black powder over the next two seasons," he stated, tucking away the snub-nosed .44 Magnum pistol. The blaster had no range at all, but for targets under a yard away it was devastating. "If they claim to be unable to pay, fine. Tell them they're cut off for five seasons. When the ville falls, I'm sure the new baron will be much more accommodating."

"At once, my lord! And the body?"

"Throw it to the dogs."

Griffin bowed. "As you order, sir. Guards!" Two sec men stepped forward, took the arms of the dead slave and hauled him away. In their wake, slaves arrived with wet rags and started to wash away the blood.

"I'm so pleased you are not hurt, Baron Kinnison," a man said politely from the attending crowd. "And if I may take this opportunity, Tiger Shark ville is being constantly attacked by jungle muties and we are desperate for more black powder. Now we can offer you three ships of grain and fruit, instead of the usual two. But not until next year, so I was wondering—"

"Silence!" the baron roared, pounding a fist on the table full of food. "Your audience is over. Come back tomorrow."

Begging forgiveness, the group daintily stepped over the sticky trail on the floor on their retreat. When the last of them had departed, a sergeant bolted the door shut.

"Whiny bastards," Kinnison growled, reaching for another chicken. Then he stayed his hand, and incredibly lifted his imposing bulk from the throne.

"Come with me, Lieutenant," he commanded, waddling across the room with tiny scraps of food falling off his stained clothing.

Marching very slowly alongside his baron, Brandon followed the sweating fat man into a smaller room. Here the walls were lined with longblasters, hand cannons and even rapidfires. Covering an entire wall was a detailed painting of the Marshall Islands, every known landmass, island and atoll clearly noted. Some sections of the wall map were raised higher than others, layers upon layers of corrections lifting the features until it was almost a contoured relief map.

Casting a glance to his left, Kinnison frowned at a framed map of the archipelago, the ancient paper brittle and yellow. The two bore so little in common that the predark map was almost useless. How many new islands had risen during the nukestorm of skydark, while so many more disappeared beneath the boiling waters? There were no indications of any active volcanoes on the old map, yet now the volcanoes were the secret source of his power. The only known source of sulfur in the entire chain of islands.

"My world," the baron said softly.

"The whole world," Brandon corrected him. He felt allowed to speak such now that they were alone in the war room.

"Brandon, I have four wars going on in the western and southern islands," Kinnison said, tracing the areas on the wall with a bandaged finger. Flecks of dried blood marked the painted surface. "And the sea muties are rising early to the east. We lose those villes, and it's no beef and fewer slaves until we find some more fools to go live there again."

"We need more flash," the lieutenant suggested. "And aside from Cold Harbor, the only other source is Forbidden Island."

The baron stared at the small crescent island to the

south of his domain. On the old map, it bore another name, but that meant nothing to him here in the present. "You volunteering to go there?" he asked, slightly amused.

"Fuck no," the lieutenant replied curtly. Then hastily he added, "Sir."

The baron allowed the discourtesy because he felt the same way. Nothing imaginable could ever force him to set foot on that rad-blasted hellhole.

"Didn't think you were that stupe," he admonished. "I have enough flash for a while, but the mills must have more, and soon."

"Can't risk using any of our own stores," Brandon said, thinking aloud. "It would weaken our defenses too much, and the pirates are getting bolder every day. At least we don't have any muties to fight on our home island."

"Not since my father slaughtered them twenty seasons ago," Kinnison agreed. The hairless giants with forked tongues were immune to fire and possessed inhuman strength. Incredible fighters, the last to die had sent his father on the last train west and made him the ruler of the world.

"I don't like this," Kinnison muttered. "Cold Harbor loses a ship just when we need their flash the most. This could be a trick of some kind. Weaken us, catch us off guard."

Reluctantly Brandon was forced to agree. "We could send a single ship to Cold Harbor and report to their baron that we found the wreckage of their cargo ship. We chilled the pirates who sank it, and now want our original shipment. Plus a bounty for the pirates."

"They can't refuse that," Kinnison stated, moving to the only chair in the room and gratefully sitting down. His leg was hurting again. "Yes, very good. We'll go with your plan."

"I'll need reinforcements," Brandon stated. "In case they refuse to pay or outright resist. One ship, far from home, and some coldhearts could night-creep us and steal the entire vessel."

Kinnison stopped massaging his sore leg. "Refuse!" he roared, his face contorting into a feral mask. "Refuse one of my sec men?"

"Or they could plead poverty," Brandon suggested hastily. The baron was becoming more and more violent. Perhaps the rot was spreading to his brain. That wouldn't be good. "You know the same old stories, that shipment was all they could spare, blah, blah, starving children, boo-hoo. Might even be true, but what do we care? Pay or die. That's the law."

"Blasted people might even be working with the pirates. They have a base somewhere, why not Cold Harbor?"

"That's true, sir."

"All right, take a couple of the windjammers and—" The baron scowled. "No, can't take any chances. Better take an armada, ten of the PT boats, fully armed with rapidfires, torps and Firebirds. Hide the fleet on a nearby island, and then go in alone to ask about the tribute. If they apologize and pay, take the flash and come home."

"If not?"

Kinnison sneered. "Then level the ville and put everybody in chains to work the mines. Afterward, ace the men and bring me the rest alive. The brats will become slaves, and I'll choose a new bitch to fuck."

The baron grinned lustfully. "Mebbe I'll finally get a son if I seed enough of the women."

Hiding his emotions, Brandon was pleased. The sec men would have the pick of the sluts once the fat bastard was exhausted. And the women would do anything the sec men asked, anything at all, to avoid the terrible bed of the baron.

"I'll leave on the morning tide," Brandon said, giving a salute. "I would like to sleep in a bed that doesn't move for one night."

"Acceptable," the baron said leniently. As with any valuable animal, a good master had to know when to beat his dog and when to pet. Too much one way and it became useless; too much the other, and it would turn and attack. "But I want you to leave before dawn, and return by the end of the week. I need that flash, Lieutenant. Get it, and do not fail me."

"Have I ever, sir?"

"Not yet," Kinnison grunted. "Which is why you're still alive."

Brandon said nothing aloud, but his eyes were smoldering pools of hatred as he marched from the room and down the long corridor of the predark castle.

Chapter Eight

With Mildred and Krysty setting up sick bay, and Dean helping to raise the sails, J.B. stayed on the *Constellation* to cover Ryan, Jak and Doc with his Uzi while they retrieved their backpacks. The three men on shore then did a recce of the ville with some of the sailors from the ship to make sure that none of the slavers was still alive. None had survived the wrath of the women prisoners. Body parts lay strewed along the beach, the crabs scuttling among the dead, dragging everything they could into the shoals. High above, hungry scream-wings circled the ville, waiting until it was clear for them to join the bloody feast.

Suddenly there was a motion in the sky, and the scream-wings were gone, clutched in the beaks of golden condors. Then they were gone from sight.

Knowing the women would sooner believe Doc before the young sailors, Ryan had Doc invite the females on board as crew. Cowering in the empty houses, most of them laughed wildly at the suggestion and declared their intention to stay and make the deserted ville their own. The few who decided to board the ship, did so hesitantly, as if afraid to disobey.

Once they were back on board the *Constellation*, Captain Jones had O'Malley free the sea anchor and started to shout incomprehensible orders to Daniels at the wheel. The crew dashed about pulling on ropes and climbing like monkeys in the complex rigging above. Soon the great ship was moving away from the shore, then past the breakers and into the open sea. Now the mainsail was raised, the yards of patched canvas billowing taut as it caught the wind and the ship lurched forward with renewed speed, the waves breaking into white spray across her bow.

Standing at the port-side gunwale, the three men watched as the lush tropical island receded. Now the second island with its vine-covered mesa rose into view above the forests of the lower woody atoll.

"Any sign of the gateway?" Doc asked softly, glancing behind them.

"None," Ryan replied, squinting. "Nor the bridge."

"Good," Jak grunted. "Others not find."

"Hey!" Krysty shouted from the other side of the ship.

They waited as she rushed across the deck to rejoin the companions. "It just occurred to me," she said, breathing normally as if the one-hundred-foot dash had been nothing. "If that short circuit ran through the whole building, it might have blown the comps!"

"Don't know much about comps, but we have to hope for the best. Mebbe it just affected the fuses. And there usually is a full replacement set underneath the console. The comps will be fine."

Krysty exhaled in relief.

Standing motionless at the gunwale, J.B. didn't join

the conversation, concentrating on his work. Carefully aligning the half mirror of the minisextant, he tried to focus on the tropical sun hidden in the roiling storm clouds overhead.

"Got that location down yet?" Ryan asked as the green island vanished into the distance.

Lowering the predark device, J.B. nodded and used a pencil stub to carefully write some figures on a small scrap of paper that he slipped into the sweat-band of his fedora. "Shot the sun twice, just to make sure," he said confidently. "I could find this place in a hurricane."

"Hope so," Ryan said, rocking gently to the rhythm of the swell. "That trail we cut is already growing back. Stay away too long, and we'll have to level the whole bastard jungle to find it again.

"Accurate to a hundred feet," J.B. boasted, patting the sextant. "I'll get us back. No prob."

"Good."

Gazing into the ocean, Doc muttered softly, "It is odd how often I encounter this ship in my travels."

"What mean?" Jak asked, puzzled, a loose strand of white hair moving across his scarred face. Annoyed, the teen tucked it behind an ear. "Been here before?"

"Oh, yes, indeed, my friend. Emily and I once took a summer vacation on this very ship," Doc whispered, lost in memory. "Or was that when Ryan and I escaped from that burning redoubt?"

Ryan snapped his head toward the man. They had never escaped from any redoubt in a windjammer, just the two of them. Doc had to have slipped into his madness again.

"Sure is warm," Ryan said in forced casualness.

"Cold, so cold..." Doc muttered, hugging himself. Then he shook like a dog coming in from the rain. "Actually, my dear Ryan, it is rather warm. But from the angle of the sun at its azimuth, I would estimate it is summer here at the equator. Do you not agree?"

Curling a lip, Ryan muttered something in assent and turned away. Fireblast! It was damn near impossible to get any accurate info from Doc when he kept weaving the past, present and future in the same sentence. Then the Deathlands warrior gave a shrug and dismissed the matter. Doc would eventually snap out of it.

"Better check those cannons now," J.B. said, hoisting his munitions bag.

"Let's go," Ryan said, and they headed for the nearest hatchway leading belowdecks.

Far across the damaged deck, Captain Jones climbed down from the quarterdeck and addressed the waiting group of nervous women.

"All right, ladies, the captain is dead, so I'm in charge now," Jones said, jerking a thumb. "The starboard barrel has the ship's articles. Cut a finger, put a thumbprint on a clean page and you're crew. Get me? Now move smartly. There's a lot to do."

Several of the women were obviously confused, as there were barrels on either side of the short man.

"It's a test," a tall woman said, a split lip slurring

her speech. "Port has four letters, same as the word left."

"So starboard is right," another said, her battered face brightening in understanding. "That's easy!"

Captain Jones merely harrumphed as the women went to the correct barrel and helped each other cut fingers and seal their prints in the massive tome.

"Done," the tall woman said, closing the volume. "What next, skipper?"

Skipper, eh? "Now get outta those clothes," Jones said, and saw the terror fill their eyes. "Blood of the sea, ya stupid bitches! Think I had you mark the book for a laugh? Ya idiots! Should chop ya into chum and feed you to the fish! I meant go to the aft quarters and put on some pants! Can't climb rigging in a skirt, can ya? Huh? And trim that long hair, or tie it off! Get that caught in a pulley, and it'll come out by the roots."

Jones touched a bald spot at the back of his head. "Hurts like a mutie's kiss, too," he stated with a half smile.

"Captain, sir, where is the a...where do we go?" a busty teenager asked, a barely closed wound crossing a face that had once been beautiful. She would carry the scar for life with no way to ever hide it from sight. She had bitten a slaver when he forced himself into her mouth. She drew blood, but hadn't removed his cock. The furious man had slashed her face and tied her to the table to take his revenge. But in the fighting she had found the man and castrated him. He died screaming, and long after he was chilled she had continued stabbing and cutting, all the while muttering curses.

"Down this hatch, and all the way in the back," the tall woman explained again, pointing a hand. "There will be a storage room there for pieces of canvas to patch the sails. Thank you for the privacy, Captain."

Jones merely grunted and studied the big blonde. Her knuckles were raw from a fistfight, a tooth was missing where her lip was split and bruises bloomed everywhere she showed skin. It had to have taken six of them to haul her to the table, he bet.

"And stop at the table. Each take a knife and blaster from the quartermaster!" Jones added hastily. "No swab goes unarmed on the *Connie!*"

"We get weapons?" a brunette asked nasally, her pert nose smashed flat from a dying slaver's club.

The big blonde started for the table. "Don't be stupe, girl. We're crew now. Step lively there!"

His arm in a sling, the skinny sailor behind the table started to talk about the pieces on display, but caught a head shake from the captain and stood there mutely as they looked over the blasters. A plump red-head stared at the collection in awe, then grabbed a blaster at random and walked away with it hugged to her ample chest. The blonde went next, passing over several shiny flintlocks to choose an older weapon, massive and thick, almost Parkerized by age.

"You!" Jones snapped. "Got a name?"

"Abagail," she replied, cocking back the hammer and dry firing the blaster. The heavy hammer

slammed down, the piece of flint scraping the steel
spur and spraying sparks into the pan where the black
powder should have been.

"Why'd ya choose that one?" he asked more politely.

"The rest have been repaired," she said knowingly. "This is the only reliable piece. But then, these
are the leftovers. Your real crew took the choice blasters first. Which is fair. How do you know we
wouldn't shoot off a tit, and then faint?"

The quartermaster roared in laughter, while the
short captain walked closer to the woman and removed the leather bag of shot and powder tied to his
belt.

"Best we got," Jones stated, tossing it over. She
made the catch with one hand. "Know what a bosun
is?"

She nodded.

"Good, 'cause you're in charge of these newbies.
One of them falls off the ship and drowns, gets tangled in the rigging and hangs, it's your fault. Get
me?"

"Aye, aye, sir."

"So take charge, bosun."

Abagail stepped behind the table and waved the
next girl over.

"Let me see your hands," she commanded. "Bah,
too small. Take this pocket blaster. Gonna have to
make your own bullets. Know how to do that?"

"Yes, ma'am," she answered. "I did that for my
brother, a sec man."

"Good enough. Then show the others who don't. Next!"

In a few minutes, the women were armed and trundling down the starboard that led into the ship's interior. The quartermaster put the last few blasters into a wooden box, each separated by a layer of cloth, and carried his burden back to the ship's armory.

"Hey, bosun!" he said, lifting the heavy box with ease, the muscles rippling on his thick arms.

"Yeah?" Abagail demanded, braced for a reprimand. In the ville, she had been little more than a gift for the baron. Things could be a lot different out here.

"Good job." He grinned and started across the rolling deck with the swagger all seafarers affect to maintain their balance on a moving ship.

"That it was," Jones muttered in frank approval. "Wife of a sec man? Sister, mebbe?"

"Close enough," she replied, busy with her weapon. Locking the pan cover in place to protect the powder in her loaded blaster, she tucked the hogleg of iron and wood into the ropes around her waist serving as a belt. "My father built the wall for Baron Langford."

The captain raised an eyebrow. "Old Stony? You're his spawn? Then you should know blasters. He was the best gunsmith Cold Harbor ever had."

"So they say," Abagail said, not impressed. She had heard it all before many times.

"Better be telling the truth. Lie to me and you'll get ten lashes," he stated coldly, taking her lack of reaction the wrong way. "Just like any other member of the crew. Remember that!"

"Fair enough, Captain," Abagail replied, standing proudly. "And if anybody bothers my girls, I'll blow their balls off." In a smooth move, she drew the blaster and pointed it between his legs.

The short man stared at the towering blonde. "Threatening the captain?"

"Sure," she said, cocking back the hammer.

His face underwent a variety of expressions, then Jones burst into laughter. "You're kin of Stone," Jones said. "You'll do fine. Should have taken ya on as crew years ago."

Easing down the hammer, Abagail tucked away the blaster and openly regarded the burly officer. Then without a word, she turned and started toward the hatch after the women. For some reason, Abagail caught herself putting a bit more hip movement into her walk than usual.

"Aye, mighty fine," Jones added very softly.

Just then, an anguished cry sounded from the nearby sick bay, and a pale sweaty man stumbled into view, holding a wet cloth to his shoulder.

"Let's see it!" another sailor demanded.

Gulping air, the first exposed the fresh wound.

"Nuke me," the other gushed. "Looks like a bullet wound! Nobody could ever tell ya got branded there. It's all lopsided, and four times too big."

"That was the idea," Mildred stated from the open doorway, a leather apron covering her from neck to knees. "Come on," she demanded, waving the red-hot poker in her hand. "You're the last. Doesn't hurt as bad as it looks."

"Oh, yes, it does," the second man muttered out of the side of his mouth. "But better than steel around your ankles."

"Aye, that's a fact," the last sailor agreed. Removing his shirt, the burly man swallowed hard and walked into the sick bay as if heading for the gallows.

Jones flinched in memory of the healer covering his bleeding scar with finely ground black powder and setting it afire. The pain drove him to his knees, but the blistered scar now perfectly resembled an old war wound. The brand of a slave was gone forever.

ON THE WINDBLOWN CREST of a sandy atoll, two men stayed low in the middle of a clump of dying bushes. Once a week they dragged more shrubbery to the top of the atoll, and even watered it from canteens, but the shrubs wouldn't take root in the bare sand and grow. This was the best spot in a hundred miles, but they needed the coverage to do their job.

"Hey, looky there," the older man muttered, adjusting the focus on his broken half of a binoc.

"Where?" the other asked, squinting at the calm sea.

"East by nor'east, boy. Here, look!" he said excitedly, offering the broken optical to the other.

The young man scanned for a while, then beamed a wide smile. "Well, fuck me twice," he cackled in astonishment. "It's the *Constellation*! Been missing for a month. What do you think?"

"She's damaged," the older man agreed. "And that's green wood on the starboard side."

"She's been damaged and repaired."

"Aye."

He swept the decks of the distant vessel. For an unnerving moment, a woman with red hair seemed to stare right back at him, but then she turned and continued to talk with some big stud with only one eyeball. "Not many crew showing. Must have been a bad fight."

"Riding low, too. Hold is full of something."

"Ain't listing from water in the bilge," he stated knowingly. "Heading south for home port."

Softly, sheet lighting flashed and rumbled in the stormy sky overhead.

"Then she's coming back from visiting the lord baron."

The older man stood, not caring if the crew of the damaged ship saw him now. "Aye, coming back from Maturo ville with a full load of black powder. What else can you trade for there?"

The young man licked dry lips. "Enough ammo for a fleet of ships! Let's take her."

"Aye, lad, we will. Let's go." Kicking the dying bushes aside, the older man started down the sloped side of the mushroom-shaped atoll, sliding down the sand on the seat of his patched pants, until dropping off the edge into the sea. The other man splashed into the water right behind, and the two began their short swim to the tropical island only a hundred feet away.

Hidden in the cool shadows of the pines and palm

trees, big men armed with flintlock blasters stood abruptly at the sight of the two swimmers and rushed to meet the sentries on the smooth sands of the golden beach. Helping the swimmers onto land, the guards escorted them through the woods and into a large clearing.

A dozen more men sat around a pool of spring water, sharpening weapons, smoking green cigs or whittling on bits of wood. A bound man was hanging upside down from a tree branch, while two pirates took turns punching the moaning captive. Another slave knelt by a campfire, feeding it twigs in a steady procession so that the fire remained even and didn't burn the seafood stew in the bubbling cook pot. His hands trembled with hunger, but he didn't eat until offered the dregs in the pot by his masters.

"Captain Draco, a ship!" the older pirate shouted, stumbling across the encampment. "A ship, sir!"

Situated under a piece of canvas stretched between some trees in the manner of a crude tent, lay a large man with his boots removed. A nearly empty bottle of shine rested on the grass nearby, and a sword protruded from the ground within easy reach.

"A ripe fat one!" the other sentry added eagerly, stopping before the captain.

Slowly opening his eyes, the captain sleepily raised his head. He was tall and heavily muscled, his rugged face a network of scars, a dead-white, marled eye staring blindly at the world. His clothes were badly stained with sweat, but were without patches. A huge revolver, not a flintlock, was tucked into a gun belt draped across his chest so that the holster rode directly before his heart.

"You two again? This better not be another trawler," the captain growled menacingly. "We already have enough dried fish to last a month."

"No, sir! Large ship, no escorts," the younger man panted, dripping water. "Looks to be the *Constellation*."

"The Cold Harbor ship?" Draco asked, his interest increasing. Quickly he sat up and pulled on his boots.

"Aye, sir! Fore an' aft rigging, yellow stripe, ten cannons side, gotta be her, skipper. And she's damaged, running heavy in the water."

"Sinking?" a lieutenant demanded, striding closer. The big man carried a rusty iron fire ax in his right hand as if it belonged there, the green-wood handle wrapped with strips of leather for a sure grip. Matching flintlocks rode in a wide belt. His face was heavily pockmarked by old acne scars, and long greasy hair twisted into a thick ponytail dangled down his back.

His soaked clothing sticking to his skinny form, the young sentry violently shook his head. "No, sir. Must be cargo."

Standing, the captain buckled a belt about his waist made of only ammo pouches. "Heading north or south?" he snapped.

"South, sir," the old sentry replied smartly.

The two men exchanged looks. Could it be? The *Constellation,* damaged and heavy with cargo, coming back from the lord baron at Maturo ville. The fat bitch had to have a full hold of black powder. As rich a prize as they had ever heard.

"Enough powder to last a lifetime," Lieutenant Giles murmured eagerly, twirling the ax by its handle. The wide blade was rusty and deeply nicked, but the dire weapon still moved as if it were a living part of the man.

"Powder enough to buy us another ship," Captain Draco agreed, checking his blasters. "Good work, lads. Stay here and watch the camp. You've earned a rest. Lieutenant, call the crew."

"Aye, aye, skipper. Heads up, scum!" the big man bellowed, brandishing the ax. "We've got a rich ship to raid before the sun sets!"

"Fresh clothes!" one man cried in delight.

"Ammo!" another added grimly.

"More slaves!" Another grinned lustfully.

"To the *Delta Blue*!" Draco shouted, then headed into the woods away from the ocean.

Shouting in unison, the motley crew of pirates swarmed through the trees and onto the beach of a small lagoon. A rumbling waterfall fed the small expanse, mixing freshwater with salt, a deadly combination to everything aquatic except for a few plants and the all pervasive crabs. The shoreline was hard-packed clay, and floating into the swirling waters was a long sleek ship, three masts rising from her sloped hull, and a double row of cannons bristling along her patchwork hull. With every battle came repairs, un-painted green wood mixing with seasoned timbers taken from the very enemy vessel that caused the damage. The beaten and battered pirate ship looked as if it were about to fall apart and sink at any minute. But the *Delta Blue* was the second-deadliest ship in the entire pirate armada. Only the *Langolier* was faster and carried more cannon. Even the lord baron's men went out of their way to avoid her oversize thirty-pound cannons.

Captain Draco walked among the men streaming up the gangplank that led to his vessel. A grandfather had rescued the clipper ship from a predark museum and had lovingly rebuilt it by hand, using tools found in another section of the museum. It had taken him and a host of others almost a year to complete the job, and nearly another to knock down the wall and drag the vessel the six miles to the ocean. But it gave him a way off the stinking island and into the freedom of the ocean. Only to discover that he was trapped in the archipelago chain, the currents and the sea muties refusing anybody exodus to the North American continent. One jungle prison exchanged for another. It drove the man insane, and he slit his own throat. But his wife took command, then her sons, and the Draco family lived on.

Within minutes, the anchor was lifted on a rattling chain, and then first sail rose into the rigging. The sleek vessel caught the gentle breeze and started to ease out of the lagoon and into the salty sea, going faster and faster as the second sail was raised, and finally the mainsail, billowing as it shoved the vessel onward with remarkable speed.

A man in the crow's nest pointed to the south, Captain Draco bellowed orders, Lieutenant Giles cleaned his ax blade on a sleeve and the *Delta Blue* swiftly headed for its next victim.

Back on the shore, the soaked sentries lay in the warm sunlight to dry and to bask in their good fortune of being on watch when the treasure ship had sailed by their atoll. Soon the talk of the tired men became peppered with yawns, and gradually they drifted into a light sleep.

A slow hour passed, then two, and finally the slave sitting by the campfire dared to move. Rising from his kneeling position, he quietly went to a nearby tree. Brushing away some sand, he uncovered a flat piece of shale. Lifting it carefully, he exposed a shallow hole filled with a canvas bag. Untying the stiff twine that held the bag closed, he pulled out a double-barreled flintlock, plus a screw-top jar of shot and powder. Tears started to run down his face as he loaded the ungainly blaster and slid the two pieces of used flint into the receivers. It had taken him weeks to sharpen the worn rocks by rubbing them with a broken piece of granite stolen from the bilge of the pirate ship, but it had been worth the effort. The flint was perfectly shaped, twin stone daggers.

Standing erect for the first time in months, he painfully limped over to a pit in the ground. The smell was horrible, stomach twisting, but he refused to retch and wake the sleeping men. There was only one way off this island, and he would never have another chance.

"Honey?" he whispered, his throat scraped raw by

the first words spoken in months. The masters didn't like chatty property, and his back bore the scars of their displeasure.

From within the reeking depths of the sewage pit, a mutilated thing turned its ruined face to the open sky, and in a barely audible voice, croaked a plea for death. The masters also didn't tolerate escape attempts, and there were many punishments hellishly worse than simple rape and torture.

The tears started anew as he lowered the blaster and cocked back the first hammer. "With all of my love, wife," he murmured, then fired. The voice from the pit stopped begging instantly.

On the beach, the sentries jumped erect, weapons at the ready.

"What the fuck was that?"

"Over there!"

Quickly the slave turned the blaster around, cocked the second hammer and placed the hot barrel into his mouth. It tasted bitter and metallic, and he thought briefly of the first day he saw his beloved wife. Then he pulled the trigger.

As his head exploded, the sentries stopped in their tracks.

"How the fuck are we gonna explain this to Draco?" the younger sec man shouted furiously. "That captain is going to lash us for days over letting two slaves escape. With a blaster yet!"

"Aye, Giles will do us personally," the older man said, his face a grim mask. "Only one explanation I can think of that might work. A slim chance, but all there is.''

"Yeah?" the other asked hopefully. "What is it?"

"That I was patrolling the island when you fell asleep and let the slave steal a blaster."

"What?" the teenager shouted. "Gonna blame it on me?"

"No choice," the older man said in a flat voice, and slashed out with his knife. Gushing blood, the teenager reeled backward, his head almost completely severed from his body. Clutching at his neck, the dying youth stumbled about, then slipped and fell, tumbling into the spring, the red spreading out until tinting the entire pool.

"Sorry, my son." The man sighed, sheathing the blade. "But it was you or me."

Only yards away, the bound slave hanging from a tree branch began to shake, convulsing as he wildly thrashed in his bonds. For the hundredth time, he mentally relived that terrible night when he sold his own brother and his wife into slavery to purchase a blaster—only to also be taken into chains by the laughing pirates.

Silently the traitor began to cry as he realized nobody with a blaster was ever coming to set him free, and he would pay for that cowardly crime forever.

Chapter Nine

"Mr. Daniels! Steady as she goes," Captain Jones shouted from the main deck, through cupped hands.

Never releasing the wheel, Daniels nodded. "Aye, sir! Steady on course!"

"Follow this heading for another fifty miles. Then go ten degrees due east."

Startled, the sailor stared through the spokes of the wheel. "Fifty miles, sir?"

"We're heading for the river. Only way we're going to get our *Connie* back home."

Daniels swallowed hard. "Aye, skipper. Fifty it be."

Giving the man a casual salute, Jones walked past the mainsail and tugged on the ropes to make sure they were properly secured. Then he went to the cargo hatch to check that the lid was bolted tight. It was a four-deck drop from the main deck into the hold where they stored cargo, and he didn't want some damn fool peeking in for a look and getting chilled.

Satisfied for the moment, Jones went past the winches to the ragged hole in the ship's deck. Dressed in loose clothing, Abagail was directing the women to nail down strips of old tarpaulin across the opening, sealing it closed. The work was progressing nicely, so Jones saw no reason to interfere. Some skippers wanted to watch over everything like a chicken on an egg, which Jones though was triple stupe. Train sailors to only do as they were told, and in a real emergency they'd pause before acting and maybe sink the ship. Slaves and bootlickers should have no part in a crew. It took brains and balls to sail the seas. Jones paused, and mentally changed that to brains and heart.

Going to the farthest point away from their work, he looked down at the lower level of the ship. Smashed debris covered the gun deck, busted slats and bits of canvas everywhere. Working with brooms and shovels, Ryan and his friends were busy clearing away the trash, tossing the odd body part out the gun hatches and into the sea. Even their healer was helping.

"Ahoy, gun deck!" he shouted over the steady creaking of the pounding of the hammers. A ship was never silent, any more than a ville full of people. "What's your status!"

Hefting a shovel full of miscellaneous wreckage, Ryan glanced directly upward at the man. "Bad," he bellowed in reply. "Best come down and see!"

Jones frowned. That wasn't what he had wanted to hear. Going to the nearest hatchway, the captain followed the companionway to the gun deck, nearly breaking his neck when he tripped on a missing step. Working his trapped boot loose, he stomped through an open hatchway in sour humor. Twisted remains of iron hinges in the jamb still supported broken bits of planks. It had to have been a hell of a blast.

"What's the problem?" he demanded gruffly, glancing around. "The cannons look fine."

"Made of solid cast iron, of course they're undamaged," J.B. agreed, stepping out of a firing troth. "Need thermite to harm these blasters. And we got plenty of cannonballs, and rope for fuse."

Impatiently Ryan interrupted. "Most of the powder barrels were crushed by the concussion. We're lucky they didn't detonate and blow the ship into kindling."

The captain felt a surge of helplessness and forced it under control. Without her cannon for protection, an attacker would simply sail in close and fire a broadside that would tear them apart.

"No luck involved. Black Harry never kept the barrels near each other for just that reason," Jones growled, hooking thumbs into his belt. "Okay, how much we got left?"

"Roughly two hundred pounds," J.B. said solemnly. "Mebbe a little less."

The sailor was stunned. "Two hundred! Shitfire, man, that's not enough to load every cannon once!" Desperate, Jones gestured at the dirty floor. "Can we salvage any of this?"

"Not mixed with all this sawdust, sea salt, blood, brains and other crap," Krysty stated, leaning on her broom. "Be easier to make new."

"If only we could," the captain growled, his fists clenched.

The companions exchanged glances. J.B. started to speak, and Ryan cut him off with an abrupt hand gesture.

"Fucking black powder," the Deathlands warrior said in a consoling manner, hoping for a reaction.

"Fucking lord baron is more like it!" Jones spit furiously. "That fat son of a bitch guards the secret like his own balls! I once heard some asshole tried to sneak on to Maturo Island to steal the formula. The lord baron tortured him to death over a full year. A year!"

"Diabolical," Doc rumbled, clearly disgusted.

"Advertising," Mildred retorted hotly. "He did it as a warning to others."

"Aye, that it was. Good one, too. Not a soul has tried since."

"And what if somebody discovered the formula and started making their own?" Krysty asked casually.

Chewing a lip, J.B. remained stoically silent.

"Make your own black powder," Jones breathed a few times before speaking. "Not worth the risk. Lord baron catch ya, it'd be the Arena."

This the companions understood. They had often been forced to fight in gladiatorial-type games for the amusement of barons or warlords.

"Not afraid of death," Ryan countered gruffly.

"You should be," the captain said softly, then shuddered.

Krysty felt her hair tighten protectively. What could possibly be worse than one solid year of bloody torture?

"Chill them," Jak stated bluntly.

The captain sneered. "Don't ya think folks have

tried? Years ago, some of the pirates and a few villes combined to send a fleet to Maturo Island. Fuckers didn't even reach dry land before getting chilled. The lord bastard has got steel boats called Peteys that don't need wind and move faster than eels. And fancy rapidfires like yours, only much bigger. Plus, those triple-damn Firebirds!''

"Describe it," Ryan ordered.

Jones bristled at the command, then decided he was being a fool. The more these outlanders knew, the better they could protect the *Connie*.

"It's like an arrow," he stated, "only with flame coming outta its ass. And when it hits something hard, she blows like a keg of powder."

"LAW rocket?" J.B. guessed.

Ryan scowled. "Mebbe, but more likely a black-powder rocket with some sort of payload. A green, mebbe."

"Those would strike like thunderbolts from Zeus against men armed with muskets," Mildred said, as a great feeling of weariness filled her soul. In the Deathlands, starving men fought over a can of beans. Here in the Pacific, food was plentiful, and still they fought. It was madness beyond her understanding.

"Tell me about those steel boats," Ryan said, kneeling on the deck. He drew his knife and scratched a crude outline of a battleship in the dark wood. "Anything like this?"

Sticking a green cig into his mouth, Jones made no effort to light his smoke as he studied the picture.

"Sort of," he said, then drew a knife and started

adding to the outline. "Only not so many cannons, and they got chimneys in aft, always smoking. Only good point about the Peteys is that ya can see them coming for miles, what with all the black ash and smoke, and that frigging loud whistle."

J.B. muttered a curse, and Ryan agreed. Peteys? Steam-powered PT boats. The killers of the first great war. Would have been better if the lord baron had a working battleship. At least they could dodge out of the way of one of those behemoths, but not the smaller, faster, patrol transport boats. Long ago in a well-stocked redoubt, Ryan had watched a predark vid of a tiny PT sinking an aircraft carrier a hundred times its size. The *Constellation* would never have a chance against one of those sleek war machines, no matter how bad shape it was in. There went any chance of the companions trying to steal fuel from the crafts. Best to avoid those Peteys completely.

"Why not leave the islands?" Krysty asked, her green eyes wide with curiosity.

"Currents fight ya," Jones stated. "Can't get more than a hundred miles past the last island before ya gotta turn back."

Then the short man hawked and spit, his right hand making some sort of a symbol in the air. "Besides, there be muties in the deeps that can swallow a whole ship, masts and all."

"Balderdash," Doc rumbled in disbelief. Every sailor throughout recorded history told tales of behemoths from the sea that ate ships. None of the stories were true. Then he recalled the double-boned spider from the gateway island.

"What do they look like?" he asked anxiously, suddenly very aware that less than a foot of wooden planks was all that stood between the companions and the cold blue sea.

"Captain!" a sailor interrupted from above.

Everybody looked upward to see an anxious face staring down at them from the partially covered hole in the deck.

"Report!" Jones barked, getting off his knees.

"There's a ship on the horizon coming our way!"

The captain frowned. "In these waters? What heading?"

"East, southeast!"

"Nuke me!" Jones spit, and pulled out his blaster to check the load. Then he took off at a run. "Everybody topside!"

Grabbing their own blasters, the companions rushed to the main deck. Most of the crew was lining the starboard railing, squinting into the horizon.

"Due west!" a bald man shouted while pointing. "Three-masted schooner!"

Going to the gunwale, Jones placed a varnished bamboo tube to his eye, pulling a smaller length of tube from out of the big one. J.B. stood alongside the man and pulled out his brass Navy telescope. The designs were almost identical.

"Can't focus," Jones said, extending the makeshift scope to its full length.

"Got her!" J.B. announced out of the side of his

mouth. "Big ship, lots of cannon." He lowered the
scope. "The gun hatches are open. They're ready to
shoot."

"Any flag flying?"

"None. Name on the bow is *Delta Blue*."

"Pirates," a sailor growled hatefully, and pulled a
flintlock from his belt. "Stinking coldhearts."

"Can we outrun them?" Mildred asked, clutching
the railing with both hands. Both of the ships were
bobbing on the waves, and the sight was making her
a little nauseous.

Irritably Jones lowered his bamboo scope and com-
pacted it with a slap. "Run? Impossible! We're bigger
and fully laden. They have three sails to our one.
They'll reach pistol range in short order, and then
they'll board and storm us."

"Aren't they going to use their cannons?" Dean
asked.

"Don't want to sink us, lad. They want the ship,
its cargo and us in chains. Cannons be the thing they
use if we try to escape."

"Go faster," Jak said, aiming his .357 Magnum at
the enemy vessel, but held off firing. The range was
too great for his revolver. "Dump cargo."

"That would take hours. They'll reach us in only
minutes."

Abagail put a hand on Jones's shoulder, and he
covered her hand with his.

"I'll scuttle the *Connie* and take us all to go see
Davey before I ever go back in chains," he muttered
in a voice of ice.

"Give me liberty, or give me death," Doc said softly.

Suddenly the pirate vessel veered to the south to bring it broadside to the *Constellation*, and a line of flashes dotted its side.

"Down!" Ryan shouted, and hit the deck.

Everybody went prone, and a heartbeat later iron balls whistled over the deck.

"That was a warning shot," Jones fumed, standing again. "The shitters think we'll try to bargain or plead our way out."

He turned to the companions. "Okay, outlanders, time to find out if you're any good."

Without a word Ryan slid the Steyr rifle off his shoulder. Working the bolt, he focused the cross of the scope on the other ship and swept the deck, looking for targets. Through the hatches he saw gunners busy with the cannons. On deck, sailors raced about with nets and leg irons. Standing on the quarterdeck was a man with a gun belt draped over his chest like a bandolier. Behind the wheel was a big ugly man, an ax tucked into his belt. Either could be the captain.

Ryan chose the man with the blaster. Gauging the crosswinds, he began to sway with the movement of the ships, then laid the crosshairs of the longblaster on the man's face, shifted his aim into the wind and below, then fired.

The report echoed between the ships, skipping across the waves, and the target doubled over, clutching his gut. Ryan fired again, and the man at the wheel lurched backwards, spraying blood into the air.

Out of control, the ship swung with the wind, and veered away from the *Constellation* just as the pirate cannons bellowed again. The balls splashed harmlessly into the ocean.

The mixed crew of the *Constellation* shouted in victory and waved their weapons. Two hundred yards away on the pirate ship, the men shouted in anger and waved their weapons.

"Now they know we mean business," Jones said, obviously pleased. "Okay, swabs, prime your blasters and grab a blade! You there, master gunner, give me six cannons with solid shot on my command. No more and sooner! Aim to hit amidships! Only got ten shots, gotta make every one count. Get going!"

"On my way!" J.B. said, tossing Mildred the shotgun. She made the catch and he took off at a run. "Doc, Dean, with me!" The adult and teen followed close behind.

Grimly Mildred slid a fresh cartridge from the loops on the shoulder strap and fed it into the belly of the S&W M-4000. Not buckshot, but the stainless-steel slivers called fléchettes. Just let the pirates get close, and they'd think they stepped into a meat grinder.

"Ready on the deck...aim...mind the pan flash...fire!" Jones bellowed, and a dozen sailors discharged their flintlock muskets. Puffs of smoke on the enemy ship showed where the .75 miniballs impacted, but not a pirate fell.

In response, a flight of arrows from the *Delta Blue* arched into the sky, then plummeted to hit all over the *Constellation,* mostly only punching holes in the taut sails.

Then Ryan shot again, and a lantern shattered, starting a small fire. The archers rushed to extinguish the blaze.

"Good shot," Jones said, pouring black powder into his musket.

Ryan said nothing and jacked a fresh round into his weapon.

The pirate cannons bellowed flame and smoke, and another volley of cannonballs whistled over the deck. But much lower. Caught loading her blaster, the busty redhead gave half a scream as she was hit directly in the stomach. Blood vomited from mouth, and both arms and legs broke off from the brutal collision. The torso went sliding across the deck, leaving a crimson wake and went over the side of the ship.

"Susie!" the scarred girl shouted, reaching out an arm as if to help her friend.

Abagail grabbed the girl by the arm and shook her hard. "Forget the dead! Now start shooting straight unless you want to know the feel of the pirates' table under your ass!"

The girl went white with fear, but her hands moved, purging the spent flintlock, filling the pan, ramming home the shot and cloth. Cocking the hammer, she aimed, fired and started the long process all over again.

Estimating the range at 150 yards, Ryan started levering rounds at the pirates. The man in the crow's nest clutched his face and fell, spiraling to the deck.

The acne-scarred man flinched as a spoke on the wheel exploded into splinters, but he never let go and continued doggedly for the *Constellation*. Ryan aced three more men on the open deck, but it seemed to make no difference. Another pirate was already climbing into the crow's nest, shouting orders to the crew below.

The rest of the companions stood with blasters ready, waiting for the other ship to get closer so they could shoot.

"Ace them!" Ryan shouted, and the others cut loose, the barrage of rounds startling the pirates and chilling several.

"We need a bastard bazooka," he cursed, jacking out the spent magazine and shoving it into a pocket. Searching his belt, he found another rotary clip of five rounds and slid it into the open breech of the hot weapon.

"Satchel charge," Jak added, thumbing fresh rounds into his .357 Colt revolver.

Shotgun slung over a shoulder, Mildred did the same with her Czech-made ZKR .38 target pistol.

"Ready...fire!" Jones shouted, and the crew shot their muskets once more.

As the crew of the *Constellation* reloaded, only two archers on the *Delta Blue* unleashed arrows, then the pirates fired their longblasters. Rounds hummed by and a rope parted, but nobody was hit. However, the three-masted ship was much closer, and gaining every minute.

A sharp whistle sounded from below, and Jones stuck his head over the railing.

"We're ready!" J.B. shouted out the hatch directly below.

"Then fire!" the captain shouted, raising his face to glare at the pursuing vessel.

The *Constellation* shook from the volley of her cannons, dark smoke stretching across the waters. On the pirate ship, a water barrel exploded, several pirates reeled covered with splinters and a large section of front gunwale was torn away. A pirate fell missing a leg, and was dragged to safety by his crew mates.

"Too high!" Jones shouted, slamming a fist onto the railing. The broadside had done little damage. "And use chain this time!"

"CHAIN?" Doc asked, swabbing out a hot cannon to quench any lingering sparks inside. He withdrew the wet bundle of rags and stroked in the dry rags to remove any excess moisture.

"You'll see," J.B. grunted, carefully scooping handfuls of black powder into another cannon. Jones was a crafty devil. "Load these two! We've got to conserve."

When Doc and Dean had done their jobs and retreated to a safe distance, J.B. used a piece of burning rope on the end of a pole to touch off the fuses. The three cannons roared in a neat line, the black smoke of the discharge blocking their view for a few moments. As it cleared away, the companions saw a dozen ropes dangling loose, sliced completely through by the whirling length of heavy chain spinning across the ship. A lot of men on deck were missing, and aft mast slowly cracked and toppled over into the sea, taking five men caught in the rigging along with it into a watery grave.

The pirate ship was crippled, but still moving closer.

"Again!" J.B. shouted, and the sequence was repeated. A huge tear appeared in the forward sail, and a gaping hole was punched in the side of the *Delta Blue,* a good ten feet above the waterline.

"By the Three Kennedys, we missed!" Doc raged, baring his teeth. "Just a tad lower and she'd be sinking like a rock!"

"Once more should do it!" Dean panted, hauling a ball to an unused cannon. It was faster to load a cold cannon then to swab out a hot one.

"With what?" J.B. cursed, casting aside the pole. "That was it for black powder. There's nothing left in the barrels. Now we go up on deck and dig in with the rest."

"I have two pounds of black powder," Doc said, patting the ammo pouch on his belt. "Any good?"

"Useless. Wouldn't get a twelve-pound ball halfway."

Dean muttered darkly and went to the nearest open hatch. Pulling out his Browning semiautomatic blaster, he aimed at the pirates.

"Dean, no!" Doc shouted in warning.

The boy frowned. "Why not?" he demanded. "Might get one of them."

"Firing from a cannon port would mean we are out of powder," Doc explained. "And that means we are defenseless…but are we really defenseless?"

"What's the plan?" J.B. demanded, extending the wire stock of the Uzi for better stability.

"C-4, my good man. Do we have any left?"

"Dark night, we do!" J.B. said, easing the safety back on the Uzi, and rummaging in the munitions bag hanging from his shoulder. With a cry of triumph, the Armorer extracted a grayish rectangle of what looked like oily clay. "A full block. That might be enough."

"Start cutting," Doc rumbled, going to an open hatch and triggering the LeMat in a deafening discharge. "We'll do the rest."

As J.B. got busy with a knife, Dean's face suddenly brightened in understanding, and the boy joined the silver-haired man at a portal, banging away steadily with his Browning.

THE ROW OF CANNONS on the *Delta Blue* thundered again, and the *Constellation* trembled as something slammed into her sides.

"Grapeshot!" a sailor cried, glancing over the gunwale. "Got holes in us from stem to stern."

"Above the water level?" Jones demanded, casting aside his longblaster and pulling two blasters from his belt.

"Aye, sir!"

"Then fuck it. Keep firing!"

The girl with the broken nose said, "Captain, I'm out of powder."

"Aye, sir. Me, too," another sailor added.

"Any more?" Abagail demanded, kneeling behind the gunwale to stay out of sight while she checked the powder bags of the dead. Nothing. Lots of shot and wadding, but every grain of powder had been used.

"That was it," the captain stated, cocking back the hammers of his huge pistols. "We lost too much chilling those slavers."

Another girl fired her weapon, then turned. "That was the last for me," she said. "What now?"

Abagail drew a knife and yanked the belt off a corpse, started lashing the blade to the end of her musket. "Make spears!" she shouted, tightening the strap with a vengeance.

The cannons of the *Delta Blue* were pulled inside the ship for loading. Knowing he had a few moments in the clear, Ryan stood and placed his shots with care, not willing to waste a single round. He had more ammo in the backpack, but not a whole lot more. He hadn't planned on any extended firefights. Again and again, the Deathlands warrior tried for the pilot, but the ace man was now hiding behind a corpse lashed to the wheel as protection. Worked, too. And the gunners working the cannons were much too well protected behind the stout oak bulkheads. Every minute, the *Delta Blue* was edging steadily closer to the ship. Every move made by the pilot at the wheel of the *Connie* was countered by the pirates. There was no escaping from the big blasters of the small ship.

The pitted muzzles of the black cannons emerged

once more, and Ryan ducked only moments before the twenty pounders roared a full salvo. A rain of lead pellets hit the ship, the masts rippling with a thousand tiny holes.

"Grapeshot again." Krysty scowled.

"Aye, trying to slow us down," Jones growled, raising his blasters, then lowering them again. If they had lots of powder, he would have risked a few wild shots, but not now.

"It's working," Mildred said, firing her ZKR in a two-handed grip. Wounded in the shoulder, a pirate spun about while firing his blaster and chilled one of his own crewmates.

Suddenly there was a loud crackle of blasterfire from below.

"What the fuck are they doing?" Jones screamed, tilting his head toward the noise. "Don't they know that'll only draw the pirates in quicker?"

"Yes, they do. Wondered how long it would take them to think of it," Ryan said, shouldering the Steyr and drawing the SIG-Sauer. Short-range and silent, it was a close-quarters combat weapon, but carried more rounds and loaded faster than the longblaster.

"Think of what?" Jones barked, furious. "They've sealed our fate!"

"Saved our ass is more like it," Krysty corrected, then paused, for the first time noticing the trickle of red going down the sleeve of her jumpsuit. Testing her shoulder, she found a sore area, the fabric black with her blood. Her fingers moved, and the blood didn't spurt out from a torn artery, so it was only a

flesh wound, nothing serious. Mildred could patch it
later. If they lived through this.

Panga knife in one hand, blaster in the other, Ryan
went behind a water barrel. Drawing a bowie knife,
Krysty did the same at a yard-high coil of rope. Brandishing the shotgun and revolver, Mildred took a firing position behind a turnstile used for raising the sea
anchor.

"Everybody take cover!" Ryan shouted, as the pirate cannons spoke again, showering them with more
grapeshot. "And get away from the railing! Far
away!"

Suddenly Jones understood. So that was the plan.
By Davey, it might work at that! "O'Malley, Daniels,
get axes up here on the double!" he ordered. Then
filled his lungs with air and bellowed, "Prepare to
repel boarders!"

The crew of the *Constellation* rushed to obey.

GORE COATED the deck of the *Delta Blue,* a corpse
was burning by a hatchway, dropped weapons lay
scattered about, pieces of the smashed gunwale and
barrels everywhere. It looked as if they had already
lost the battle, and not in the process of winning.

"Captain Draco!" a sailor said, saluting crisply.
"The master gunner says they're firing from the cannon ports!"

Holding a bloody bandage around his belly, Draco
sneered. "Out of ammo, eh? Good. Giles, cut in
close. We'll seize the ship and capture the crew
alive!"

Half of his shirt soaked red, Giles merely nodded, and spun the wheel rapidly. The nimble schooner angled sharply for the lumbering giant.

"Prepare to board and storm!" a bosun cried, drawing a sword and a flintlock.

USING EXTREME CARE, but moving quickly, J.B. hesitantly moved the knife blade to the quarter mark on the block, then to the third. This was a dangerous gamble. Too little and a cannon ball wouldn't penetrate the hull of the pirate ship. Too much and the cannons would burst.

Slicing the block apart, he sheathed the blade and went to the nearest cannon. Grabbing the ropes, he strained to pull the half-ton blaster away from the firing port and finally got it clear.

"Stop shooting and help me," he panted from the exertion, then knelt and shoved a stave under the carriage slide to hold it motionless.

Moving fast, Doc and Dean tucked away their blasters and ran to give the man assistance.

"Load the middle three!" J.B. ordered, fiddling with a timing pencil. "Two balls each!"

Two each? There was no time for questions, so Doc went to the left, Dean the right. Lugging iron balls, they came waddling back to see J.B. toss a block of plas-ex down the muzzle of the second cannon and move on to the third.

"Move faster!" J.B. urged them, stabbing the cube with a timing pencil and breaking it off at the shortest mark. Then he tossed the wad of plas-ex down the barrel. "We got two minutes!"

"These are solid iron, sir," Doc reminded him, lugging a dull gray ball to the mouth of the first weapon and rolling it inside.

Dean did the same thing, and as they moved to the second cannon, J.B. started pushing the first forward until its muzzle was sticking out the gun port. In moments, the three cannons were fully loaded and in position. The fighting above was louder than ever, the pirate ship only fifty yards away, and closing.

Moving to the farthest end of the deck, J.B. took refuge behind a cold cannon and removed his glasses, tucking them into his shirt pocket.

"One minute," he panted, checking his wrist chron. "Brace yourself. This is going to be loud."

Joining the Armorer at his sanctuary, Doc and Dean crouched behind the half-ton cannon, then covered their ears and opened their mouths to prevent going deaf from the concussion. None of them knew if this trick would actually work, but it was the best chance they had.

"What happens if the cannons can't contain the blast?" Dean asked.

"We die. Forty seconds," J.B. read off. "Thirty-five, thirty..."

Chapter Ten

At nightmarish speed, the two ships headed toward each other on a collision course.

On the quarterdeck, O'Malley was hurriedly tying off the wheel so he could join the defenders on the deck.

"What the fuck are ya doing?" a girl said, from the main deck, holding open the door to the captain's quarters while others hauled out an oak wardrobe and heavy wooden chairs.

"If we keep the ship on course, then all we gotta worry about is fighting," he replied over his shoulder, awkwardly climbing down to the deck. He landed on his boots and turned. "We let the *Connie* run free, and she might swing away and them slam back against the pirates, sinking both ships."

"So we cut the wheel loose if we're losing," she stated grimly, releasing the door as the last piece of furniture was hauled away.

Checking his weapons, O'Malley scowled at the teenager. "Too chancy," he stated. "We go to the bilge, open the petcock valves and flood the hold. No pirate son of a bitch is ever gonna walk the wood of this ship!"

She nodded, then jerked and slumped to the deck,

blood gushing from the hideous wound in her throat. O'Malley knelt by her side, trying to think of a way to staunch the hole when the teen gurgled meaningless sounds, violently trembled and went still.

"Calm waters and safe harbors, little one," O'Malley said softly as he took her knife and duckfoot blaster. The pilot tucked them into his belt and raced to join the rest of the crew at the starboard gunwale.

Now less than thirty yards from the deck of the *Delta Blue*, pirates irregularly fired at the *Connie* while a dozen men stood twirling grappling hooks around in circles above their heads at the end of long ropes. The coldhearts looked eager, almost excited, but none of them spoke or laughed or shouted. The rigging was full of men with knives in their teeth, a scarred man with a marled eye was shouting orders and the ugly pilot stood defiant at his post, safe behind the bullet-riddled corpse lashed to the wheel.

On the *Constellation*, the companions were crouched below the gunwale, along with anybody else who had a loaded blaster. The rest of the mixed crew frantically moved things to form a barricade across the deck, tables, water barrels, lifeboats, spare sails, anything that could offer any protection. Even the girls knew that the fighting had to remain on the main deck, or else the ship was lost. Here they had room to maneuver. In the tight confines of the hold, they would be easily captured.

Holding her makeshift spear, Abagail made sure she still had the extra knife in her boot. She still hurt, fore and aft, from the gang rape by the slavers, and had no intention of ever being captured alive again. One quick slice to the right side of her neck where that big vein was, and she'd be aced in less than a minute. Most of the other girls were also carrying spare knives, and quite a few of the men, too. Their expressions were even fiercer than those of the girls.

"On my mark, now!" Ryan barked, and the companions stood, firing their weapons in volley.

The decks of the vessels were almost level, the *Connie* riding low with her heavy load of cargo. The range was thirty yards, and the fusillade of rounds caught the pirates by surprise. Jak's big-bore .357 threw thunder at the coldhearts, the hollowpoint rounds ripping away chunks of the other ship's railing. A pirate screamed, his hand missing fingers, and another spun away with most of his face gone.

Her red hair tightly coiled at her nape, Krysty shot her Smith & Wesson in a two-handed grip, the .38 revolver clearing the gunwale of pirates as they ducked for cover. Only a few stood to fight back, one pirate raising a flintlock and firing, but the weapon only fizzled, the pan improperly filled. Krysty caught him in the shoulder, and he dropped the blaster.

The ships were twenty yards away, the distance narrowing fast.

Archers released a flight of arrows, but nobody was hit. Aiming and firing as fast as he could, Ryan chilled three of them before the rest dived for cover. A sailor on the *Constellation* threw an ax that only reached halfway before falling into the water.

Pumping and shooting, Mildred cut loose with the shotgun, aiming at the men in the rigging. Several fell and dropped to the deck; one only made it halfway before getting tangled in the ropes and dangling help-lessly by a foot. But there were a lot more remaining, and even as she slid fresh cartridges into the blaster, more coldhearts raced out of a hatchway—big men armed with axes and swords. The boarding party.

Slapping in a fresh clip, Ryan emptied the SIG-Sauer at the fresh troops, concentrating on head shots. Even if he didn't get a clean chill, at least they'd be partially blinded by the blood in their eyes. Jak went for the captain with the weird eye, Mildred fanned the rigging again, Krysty concentrated on the pirates lin-ing the railing.

Casting aside his musket, a man turned and ran from the rapidly firing blasters of the companions. That seemed to rattle the rest, but then the captain cut down the coward with a sword slash to the belly. Screaming in agony, the pirate tried to hold in his slippery intestines, and failed miserably, dying as his guts spilled onto the deck through his fingers. Nobody else broke ranks.

Suddenly the *Delta Blue* was too close, the heavily armed schooner gliding sideways toward the lumber-ing *Constellation.*

"Here they come!" Captain Jones shouted, wrap-ping an arm around the damaged mast for support.

In a strident crunch of smashing wood, the vessels violently slammed together, knocking everyone not braced sprawling to the deck. Loose items skittered underfoot, planks splintered and rigging snapped, the ropes flailing about like living whips.

Even as the crew of the *Constellation* got back on its feet, a dozen grappling hooks sailed into the air and landed on the deck, scraping back to the gunwales, catching on planks and bodies along the way. One sailor shrieked as the hooks ripped into his body, pinning him to the gunwale. Jak threw a knife and cut the rope, freeing the man, but the sailor stayed moaning on the deck, the iron hook deeply embedded into his chest. Another hook got caught on the canvas and ripped it free, exposing the hole in the deck.

Timbers creaked in protest as slaves in chains operated winches that tightened the lines drawing the two vessels closer until their gunwales touched.

"Charge!" a pirate bellowed, jumping from his ship onto the deck of the *Constellation*. He landed in a crouch, knife and blaster at the ready.

From behind, the wounded sailor pinned by the grappling hook stabbed the invader in the calf with his knife. Crying out in pain, the pirate turned and kicked the hook. The sailor started to convulse and abruptly died.

Shouting a war cry, the coldhearts swarmed onto the battered vessel, waving swords and handblasters, as the pirates in the rigging swung across to land on the spars of the *Connie*.

Ryan spent half a clip at the enemies above, then was forced to deal with the men charging along the deck. Krysty shot one pirate in the face and kicked another between the legs. A coldheart caught Jak reloading and triumphantly grabbed the teenager by the collar, then shrieked as his hand came away minus fingers, the hidden razors now gleaming with fresh blood. Jak gestured and a knife appeared in his hand. He slashed the cringing man across the throat, then fired the Colt Python wildly into the oncoming mob.

Coldhearts dropped on them from above, and Mildred cleared a path with four fast rounds from the shotgun, the stainless-steel fléchettes tearing the invaders apart. A dozen pirates fell, tripping those behind, and the companions went around the hole in the deck, retreating to the barricade.

In retaliation, the invaders quickly formed a ragged line and triggered their flintlocks, most of the blasters discharging, the miniballs hitting the barricade with hard slaps. As Ryan and the others climbed over the pile of furniture and assorted wreckage, Jones and Daniels gave cover by firing all four of their hand cannons, the dense clouds of acrid smoke making it temporarily impossible for anybody to see a target.

One pirate inadvertently found the hole in the deck, and he shouted all the way down to the gun deck and abruptly stopped making noise.

As the rest of the invaders reached the barricade, the companions fell back and the women rose to thrust their crude spears into the enemy. Bearded faces registered shock as the knives found flesh, then brutally twisted sideways, opening the wounds, and blood spurted everywhere. With only his ear missing, one pirate grabbed the spear wielded by Abagail and raised an ax high overhead. Snarling in rage, Jones placed the muzzle of his last blaster against the man's face and shot the coldheart from behind. The second man fell with his chest blown open, but the first man dropped the ax, his hair now in flames from the muzzle-blast. The heavy blade hit the deck, going inches into the hard wood. Ignoring the burning man, Abagail stabbed out again and again with her spear, as Jones pulled the ax free and started chopping at any arm bearing a tattoo.

"Down!" Ryan commanded, and the crew hastily got out of the way.

The companions cut loose with all of their weapons in a single volley, clearing the barricade and driving the pirates back.

In the brief pause, the crew of the *Constellation* snatched blasters from the dead and dying, hastily reloaded and sent the stolen lead right back to the pirates. For one glorious moment, the deck of the ship was clear of invaders, but on the *Delta Blue,* a second wave was forming, the chained slaves held in front as human shields.

"What do we do?" a girl asked, blood streaked across her face.

"It's them or us," Abagail answered resolutely, cutting an ammo pouch off a supine pirate. He moaned softly, and she stabbed him in the chest until he stopped.

"What the fuck is taking so long?" Jones demanded, tucking a loaded blaster into his belt and starting on the next.

"Any sec now," Ryan muttered, aiming the SIG-

Sauer, but not firing yet, as the haggard slaves began to stiffly climb over the gunwale dragging their heavy chains.

ON THE GUN DECK, the pirate painfully stood, his right arm hanging at an unnatural angle. Grunting at the pain, he glanced around and was relieved to find this deck of the ship empty. Not a soul was in sight, the line of cannons unattended.

He sighed in relief, and then the middle cannon thunderously erupted, lifting off the tracks even as it sent the hot iron out the gunport. Propelled by the block of C-4, the double load of shot smashed through the hull of the *Delta Blue* and punched out the other side of the vessel.

Split lengthwise, the broken cannon slammed into the pirate standing agog on the gun deck, crushing him flat. Then the second cannon stridently exploded, its lead balls going down into the belly of the enemy ship, punching through the deck and into the powder magazine. Instantly the black powder detonated from the crushing impact, sending flame and shrapnel everywhere. The last cannon spoke deafeningly, the massive wad of iron chains spinning through the wounded ship, cracking timbers and making the thick wooden column of the main mast wobble as it started to break loose.

A hundred feet behind the last cannon on the port side of the *Constellation*, J.B., Doc and Dean lay sprawled on the deck from the triple concussion, fingers feebly twitching, faces slack and pale.

ON THE *DELTA BLUE* a pirate in the crow's nest howled as the damaged mast loudly cracked in two and hurtled downward, taking the rigging with it.

In the middle of shouting orders, Captain Draco glanced upward at the terrible noise and disappeared in the avalanche of ropes and broken spars. Top-heavy, the mast tipped over the side of the ship and slipped into the choppy water, dragging everything along behind. Still attached by a hundred ropes, the bow mast broke free of its predark stanchions and swept across the deck, smashing into pirates and slaves alike. Planks ripping apart, the deck collapsed and the aft mast toppled over, heading for the quarterdeck.

As the mast descended, Giles brandished a defiant fist, then exploded as the tower of wood squashed him flat and crashed onto the wheel, driving the captain's cabin in the ship, the aft windows spraying outward like a sparkling shotgun blast. Rolling over the deck, the mast followed the others and dragged even more into the cold depths, bringing death to the sailors and blessed freedom to the chained slaves.

On the *Constellation,* the boarding party of wounded pirates turned to stare at the vessel. The side of the ship caved inward, flailing men spilling into the churning sea. Sunlight was visible from the other side of the enemy ship. The craft was holed all the way through, and burning out of control.

Bright lights came from within the dying ship as the fallen lanterns set fire to the wood and orange flames licked upward from every hatch and port. The flames increased to a roaring inferno, and the crew of the *Constellation* cheered as something inside the pirate vessel detonated again, spreading the conflagration even more.

"Cut those mooring lines!" Jones bellowed, racing for the gunwale with his ax. "Get her away from us!"

But it was too late. A larger explosion shook the *Delta Blue,* blowing corpses and cannon out both sides, then the whole world seemed to shake as the main powder magazine ignited and she blew apart into kindling, wreckage rising on a column of smoke and fire into the air.

"Hit the deck!" Jones roared, diving for wood, and the *Constellation* violently shuddered from the arrival of the heavy shrapnel.

An anchor plowed into the bow, ripping away most of the forecastle, and O'Malley was blown overboard with a splintered plank driven completely through his chest.

"She's…gone," a pirate whispered, staring at the flotsam sinking into the churning ocean. The surface was littered with bits and pieces, most of them sinking as they became waterlogged.

"We're trapped," another snarled, raising his blaster.

"Then we take this ship!" a bald pirate shouted, and the desperate men charged the wounded defenders.

Lying on the deck, Ryan emptied his blaster at the pirates, chilling two more before they were past him and charging the others. They clearly wanted no part

of the raven-haired man with the battle-scarred face
and a working blaster.

The two groups converged, each choosing a person
to fight. A single blaster roared, and then it was
swords, axes and knives in total bloody chaos, the
individual screams and curses mixing into the muted
roar of mob warfare.

Weapon in hand, Ryan couldn't find anybody to
chill. The people were so well mixed the Deathlands
warrior would only ace the sailors he'd promised to
protect. Then he noticed a movement out of the corner
of his good eye, and saw a chance.

"Crew of the *Connie!*" he bellowed. "Hit the
deck!"

The private name of the ship caught their attention,
then sailors and girls reluctantly did as ordered. The
pirates stood above the supine crew, confused by the
sudden halt to the battle.

"Ya surrendering?" a burly man asked

In reply, J.B. triggered the Uzi from a hatchway.
On full-auto, the stuttering stream of 9 mm Parabellum rounds tore through the stationary men, mowing
them down. Slapping in his last clip, Ryan started to
fire, and the rest of the companions cut loose with
their weapons. Then thunder was heard above the
crackle of gunfire, and Doc appeared at a hatchway
recklessly fanning the LeMat, the barrage of .44 miniballs slamming through one pirate and chilling the
one behind him. Then Dean was at his side, the sleek
Browning steadily banging.

Caught in the withering cross fire, the pirates were

slaughtered and soon the last man fell, bleeding from a dozen wounds. An odd peace reigned over the bedraggled vessel, the crackling of the burning pirate ship the only sound.

"Any more?" a girl asked, struggling to her feet. There was a blistered wound on her thigh from a blaster that missed, a bad slash across her bare shoulder, but the ax in her grip was smeared with red blood and pinkish brains.

"We beat them," a sailor said in disbelief. Then he shouted, "We beat them!"

Standing amid the score of dead, the rest of the survivors raggedly cheered.

"Outlanders did," Abagail retorted weakly. "Took ya long enough."

Ryan started to hotly reply when he was cut off by the captain.

"Shut the fuck up, everybody," Jones commanded, holding his side. With every breath, he could feel the broken bones grind against each other. "Somebody go check the starboard hull!"

As he was the closest, Ryan went to the railing and glanced over the side. Then cursed. There were several large holes in the side of the ship below the waterline, the waves flowing into the hold, barrels and wicker baskets floating out in a yellowish cloud.

"We've been damaged," he reported, now noticing that the deck was listing slightly, spent brass and other small loose items starting to slide across the planks.

Favoring a leg, Jones hobbled over to the railing

and studied the damage. "Can't patch that," he announced bitterly. "The ribs of the *Connie* are busted clean through. Bastard shrapnel from the explosion. Must have been hit by one of their cannons, maybe a couple. Nuking hell!"

"Orders, sir?" Daniels asked after a few moments. He had waited for O'Malley to ask, but then recalled that he was pilot and chief of the crew now.

Silently Captain Jones looked over the valiant craft, every plank, every rope known to him. There wasn't an inch of the vessel he hadn't stood watch on, helped repair or scrubbed clean.

"Abandon ship," he said softly.

Chapter Eleven

The sky was slowly turning purple with the approach of night, the ever present storm clouds thinning enough to allow the moon and stars to shine upon the small tropical island.

At the lee of a wide smooth beach was a crude dock of tree trunks and piles of stone. Beyond was a ramshackle ville, its protective wall live bamboo woven with tree vines. A living barrier with lovely blossoms on the outside, hell flowers that spit deadly spores and pulsed with acid-based sap.

The thick smell of fish stew wafted from the bamboo huts, mixing with the reek of animal dung in the dirt streets. The houses were of bamboo with thatched roofs, looking exactly the same as they had for a thousand years.

Lard torches crackled before the wood barracks of the sec men and the small gaudy house. The smooth clean light of alcohol lanterns shone brightly through the glass windows of Baron Somers's brick fortress, the predark police station now his armed bunker inside the walls of Namu ville. But it had been a long time since there had been any fighting in the poor fishing ville. Only a hundred people lived in the squalor, with less than a dozen slaves. There was nothing to attract pirates or raiders from another ville. The lord baron chilled the seagoing coldhearts at every chance, but didn't really care if one ville attacked another. The strongest should live, the weak die. That was his law, and none openly dared to disagree.

High on a hill overlooking the dirt ville was a natural cleft in the side of the mountain. The ground was bare, the red clay resisting even the jungle. A rickety predark house was slowly collapsing under the weight of age, the windows long gone, the interior a death trap of rotting floorboards and tiny hell flowers growing in the corners and cracks.

Water flowed freely from a crack in the granite face of the hillside, splashing along a gully in the dirt, past a cold cook fire and then down into the jungle below. The area was densely ringed with pungi sticks, the sharpened bamboo rising a full yard in height, offering a stubborn defense against the big cats that prowled the jungle, mutie snakes and the much more dangerous men from the ville.

Across the cleft was a squat predark structure with one side door and an odd wall that could be lifted by two strong men. The ancient two-car garage was artfully covered with vines in layers so thick it was almost invisible amid the lush greenery of the jungle edging the clearing.

Soft sounds came from the building, a grinding, some cursing and finally a muffled roar.

"Yes, sulfur is part of black powder," a man cried in delight, backing away from his worktable and waving at the expanding cloud of bitter smoke. "By Socrates, I'll discover the formula yet!"

Walking over to a pool table, the felt removed to make clothing ages ago, Wof Nikon wiped a grimy arm across his forehead and threw some water on his face from the slightly cracked bowl of a birdbath, managing to sluice off most of the black residue from his body. Next the man gargled with a brew in a coconut shell that was freshwater and seawater mixed with lime juice. It helped cut the taste of the acrid smoke.

Sitting quietly in the corner was a woman of indeterminate age, her feet bare, and her full breasts nearly spilling from the tight confines of a tattered dress, a cascade of long hair masking her features. Her small hands were busy with a fish-bone needle and a short piece of thread, trying to patch a rip in a badly stained shirt.

"You!" Wof barked in command.

The young woman hastily placed aside her needlework and ran to the rock stove and began striking flint to steel to start the dinner fire. An old pot rested in the rusty grill of the stove, assorted fish bits and some fruits mixed together in water.

"Over here," he ordered gruffly.

Leaving the stove, she fell to her knees before him, her head bowed in submission.

"Rise and strip."

Silently the slave did as she was told, untying the knotted shoulder straps. Her thin clothing fell in a whisper to the cracked concrete floor. The girl stood with head bowed, hands folded, waiting for the next command.

Moving closer, Wof ran cruel hands over her breasts, pinching the tender nipples hard, then slapping her firm buttocks. Breathing heavily, the man opened his pants and placed her warm hands on his cock.

"Service me," he said throatily, already hard with anticipation. "Every inch, girl. Front and back."

Going to her knees, the girl fought back a wave of nausea from what she had to do. But being here was her choice, even if it was a form of hell she had never known existed.

Tenderly stroking his thighs, she cupped his manhood gently and began to use her tongue and full lips to arouse her master.

Minutes ticked away, and Wof was drenched in sweat, savagely thrusting his hips at her when the side door to the garage burst open and armed sec men rushed inside.

Startled for a moment, Wof tried to grab his flintlock pistols on the worktable. But now the slave adamantly refused to let him go, her hands and teeth holding the man in the warm, moist trap of her bruised mouth.

"Dirty traitor!" a sec man growled, and slammed the wooden stock of a longblaster into the man's chest.

Ribs cracked from the blow, and Wof staggered away from the kneeling young woman and fell backward over a low stool.

"What is this?" he demanded, scrambling to his feet and drawing up his pants. "I ain't done nothing. Leave me alone!"

"Shut the fuck up," a sec man growled, brandishing a flintlock. More sec men grabbed both of Wof's arms and twisted them cruelly behind his back until he was helpless in their grip.

"Baron, spare me!" he cried out, trembling in fear.

"Silence," Baron Somers said calmly, going to the worktable and inspecting the items on display. The crude instruments were mostly carved wood and bone, only some small items made of metal or plastic. There were lots of powders and oils in jars and bottles, but nothing he could identify. However, the mere fact it was a chem workshop of some kind was enough. More than enough, actually.

"So it's true," Somers stated grimly. "You've violated the lord baron's law by trying to make black powder."

Wof's eyes rolled about in terror. "But I was only—"

"Silence!" Baron Somers commanded, slapping the man across the face. "Drag this scum to the ville."

Brutally grabbing his hair, the sec men departed with their prisoner, leaving the door wide open and the naked slave sitting patiently on the cold concrete.

All the way down the hill, Wof fought every inch of the way. He kicked at the boots of the sec men and snapped at their hands. They tried to put shackles on him and by sheer luck, Wof managed to butt one sec man in the stomach with his forehead. The man doubled over in pain, and the rest of the sec men began to savagely beat Wof with blasters and fists.

"Cease that immediately!" the baron shouted, knocking away their weapons. "How can we torture a dead man?"

The sec men backed off the bloody man, and galvanized by sheer terror, Wof unexpectedly broke loose and charged wildly for the nearby cliff. The river below was full of rocks and rapids, if the fall didn't chill him. But anything was better than torture. He had never harmed a soul. How could this be happening to him?

Leaves and branches tore at his clothes as he sprinted in blind panic, and Wof nearly reached the cliff when he abruptly jerked to a halt and painfully hit the ground. In horror, he saw the chain shackled around his ankle. A slave's chain.

"No!" he howled, wildly slamming the chain with a rock, digging in his heels to still try to escape.

Walking slowly, the sec men gathered around, rough hands grabbing from every direction, and Wof was hauled back down the winding trail to the ville. The wooden gate in the bamboo wall was wide open, crackling torches lining the street. The center of the ville was full of people, most of whom he knew, friends, enemies, neighbors and kin. The area was brightly lit by alcohol lanterns held by strange sec men, and in the middle of them was a granite column, some sort of predark memorial for fallen men in some distant war. It was a totem of great power and the pride of the poor ville. Ancient words had been carved into the stone, but they were too faint to read even by daylight. The column was also the ville execution site.

Weeping for mercy, Wof was hoisted by his wrists and armpits until he was suspended off the ground. Then more chains were added until he was stretched as taut as ship rigging and completely unable to move in any direction.

"Please," he whimpered. "Oh please…"

Smoking a green cigar, Lieutenant Brandon walked to the prisoner and ground out the red glowing end in his right eye. Wof shrieked pitifully.

"Gag this fool," the sec chief ordered.

Grim-faced guards forced a thick wad of leather into Wof's mouth and wrapped lengths of leather straps around his head to keep it in place.

Sucking air through his nose, Wof tried to speak, to plead for clemency, but the leather wad blocked any attempt to make noise.

"I must thank you for reporting this crime," Brandon said to the local baron.

"Anything for my great friend, Lord Baron Kinnison," Somers said, trying to make the words sound sincere.

The crowd waited, hanging on every word spoken by the sec man, their lives hanging in the balance of the casual conversation. In the crowd, a baby began to cry and was forcibly hushed.

"I can see the loyalty in your face," Brandon lied,

"so I have decided there will be no punishment on this ville for the acts of one man."

Women began to cry with relief and men allowed themselves to breathe once more. They would be allowed to live.

"However, for a crime this great," Brandon continued, lifting a pair of pliers from a table, "I feel it only proper that the punishment should be done by your own people."

"Of course," Somers replied, unable to meet the pleading eyes of his cousin lashed to the stone column. "My idea exactly. Sergeant, strip the prisoner."

Wof raged against the chains, but could hardly move as the burly sec man cut away every item of clothing until the man was nude.

"Castrate him," Brandon said, licking his lips, a tremor of excitement in his voice.

The sergeant cupped the prisoner's genitals and lowered the knife. "I'll do it quick, my friend," he whispered.

Thanking the man in his heart, even while cursing his name, Wof closed his eyes and braced for the coming torments. Maybe he would go insane. Yes! He'd seen it happen before. Prisoners singing songs and laughing while they were being taken apart like a blaster for cleaning.

The knife began to cut, white-hot pain shooting through his groin, when unexpectedly Brandon called a halt to the gory proceedings.

"Trying to escape again, eh?" the lieutenant commented, lifting a curved blade in the lantern light.

"We need to remove the eyelids so he can see everything that happens."

Some of his men walked to a table into the clearing, carried it forward and placed it before Brandon. It was filled with little knives and a mound of leather pouches.

"But work like that is no job for a sec man," the officer continued, "so we shall pay the reward of one full ounce of black powder for an act of torture."

The people in the crowd whispered among themselves in shock, and even the baron was perplexed. Why such a high price for a simple chilling? It made no sense.

Clumsily an old man stomped forward, a chunk of intricately carved wood strapped to the stump of his left leg. He paused before the table, then dared to look at the tall officer. Brandon gave a nod, and the old man chose a knife. Going to the column, he grabbed Wof's right eyelid with a thumb and forefinger, then began to cut away the tender flesh.

Rivulets of crimson trickled down Wof's anguished face as he thrashed against the bounds, his face twisted feral from the pain. It was over in a moment, and the old man placed the tiny piece of flesh between the knives and mound of pouches.

"Clean job, well done," Brandon complimented him, passing over a leather sack.

Suspiciously the one-legged man opened the pouch to check inside, then flashed a toothless grin. This would keep him warm and fed for a month!

"Can I do another?" he asked hopefully, hugging the precious ammo.

Brandon stared at the wizened oldster, then burst into laughter. "What a greedy little bastard! Stand aside and let others show their loyalty. If none steps forward, you may do so again. Often as you like."

"Thank you, sir," he gushed, bobbing his head like a parrot. "Hail to the lord baron!"

"Enough," Brandon said, waving him away. "Who's next?"

Suddenly Somers understood what was happening and glowered in suppressed fury. The bastard was stealing his people away right in front of him! His mind whirled with some way to turn this to his advantage and failed. That fat bastard on Maturo had won another battle without firing a shot. Curse him to hell.

Avarice on his features, a teenager forced his way from the crowd, and a reeking fisherman was next. Then more, even some of the local baron's own troops. The pile of flesh grew one bloody gobbet at a time, and soon every hand in the ville was smeared with fresh blood.

Brandon was pleased. Tortured by his own kin. Now the locals would never trust one another again, and would watch for any signs of research or science. This island would offer no more trouble to the lord baron for years.

Finally the ragged body on the stone column went limp, and gore ceased to flow from the endless cuts. A single eye stared from the skinless face, and what remained more resembled a decaying carcass than anything born human.

"Satisfied?" Baron Somers asked gruffly.

"Not quite," Brandon said, placing aside a cup of wine. "There is the still the matter of his workshop."

Somers grunted. "We'll burn it, of course."

"No need," said the officer, raising a fist high overhead, then opening it twice.

Immediately there were flashes from the PT boats moored at the dock, and moments later a flurry of screaming objects trailing fire whooshed by overhead, their contrails bathing the ville in bloodred light. Moving almost faster than vision could follow, the Firebirds zigzagged over the jungle, climbing toward the cleft in the hill. Then they separated, one going directly for the predark bungalow, the other for the disguised garage.

The double explosions shook the landscape, merging into a huge fireball that rose on a glowing mushroom cloud into the sky. The people of the ville cowered at the sight, even the baron looking ill at ease, his sec men shuffling their feet nervously. Armed with blaster and knives, this was something beyond their comprehension. Many heard tales of what a Firebird could do, but the sight of that mushroom cloud, the ancient symbol of skydark, was more intimidating than any beating or verbal threat.

Watching their reactions, Brandon raised his hand again, and two more rockets streaked by to finish the job of removing the secret workshop from the face of the island. As the concussions faded away, the top of

the hill was sliding down over the wound, and the
tress were burning for dozens of yards in every direction.

"Now I'm satisfied," Brandon said smugly, then
turned to address the baron directly. "However, I expect no more unpleasantness, or else I will be forced
to return and use...extreme measures of justice."

"Fair steven," Somers said, managing to smile,
forcing his hands to stay at his sides and away from
his blasters. That any man could talk to him in such
a way, inside his own ville, was maddening, intolerable. Yet he had no choice but to obey. He was bound
to life even as Wof had been shackled to the stone.

"Anything for my good friend Baron Kinnison,"
he added in feigned politeness.

"That is Lord Baron Kinnison!" the lieutenant
snapped. "And don't you forget it again!"

A furious sec man standing next to the baron
started forward, and Somers held him back with a
gesture. With those triple-damn boats in the cove, the
Maturo sec man was untouchable. "Yes, of course,"
Somers spoke coldly. "Lord Baron Kinnison."

Glancing at the corpse, Brandon saw it was now
covered with a black coat of crawling flies. "Burn
that," he ordered, then turned and walked casually
from the ville.

Moving quickly, his sec men claimed the few remaining bags of black powder, folded the card table
and followed quickly after their chief. Behind them,
Baron Somers started calling for wood, and a pile
began to build around Wof's tattered remains.

Wary of the dark shadows in the bushes, Brandon strolled back to the dock, a hand always on his blaster. Never trust others was his first rule of survival.

Reaching the piles of stones that served as a dock, the lieutenant noted that the green lantern hanging from the tide pylon had been extinguished. Good.

PT 264 was rocking in the waves, tugging against the mooring lines, wisps of smoke rising from the flue as the crew in the hold stoked the boiler as a preparation to departing. On the stone dock, Thor stood with his Weatherby resting on a shoulder, closely watching a slim girl kneeling on the hard stones, hands folded, head bowed, her long hair falling down to hide her face.

"That the one?" Brandon asked, stopping a few feet away. The rest of the sec men moved around him to haul the table and other items aboard the boat.

"Think so," the sergeant answered. "Ain't said a word yet."

The lieutenant went to the slave and nudged her with his boot. "Stand," he commanded.

The female rose like dawn, and the officer saw that her eyes were as green as the summer sea, her face a flawless pearl. Beautiful seemed inadequate a word, and he had trouble speaking for a few moments.

"You set the lantern, girl?" he asked, much more polite than was usual.

She nodded vigorously, pointing at the lantern then herself.

"How did you know a green light was the way to signal us there was a traitor in the ville?"

Timidly she lifted her skirts until it was obvious there was nothing under the thin clothing.

"A gaudy slut, eh? Yeah, we make sure they all know that. Teach them one at a time."

The slave violently shook her head.

"Okay, used to be." The man smiled benignly. "Why ain't you talking? Somebody cut out your tongue?"

She touched her throat and gestured outward, her hands falling by her sides.

Oh, a simp. She never had been able to talk.

"Well, you did us a favor," Brandon said, snapping his fingers, "and the lord baron always pays his debts."

Thor placed a heavy leather bag in the officer's hand, and he passed it over to the girl.

"Two pounds of powder, one blaster, with bullet mold, ten rounds, two flints," he recited. "You find anybody else doing science, and I'll pay the same again."

Incredibly she offered him the bag back and touched the brand on her bare satiny shoulder.

"Your freedom?" He laughed scornfully. "Have to do more than find a traitor for that, girl!"

As if waiting for those words, the slave pressed her warm body against the officer and cupped his face to passionately kiss him, her small hands teasingly moving across his body, invoking responses the man had never felt before with a willing partner. The sergeant chuckled softly at the sight, but never turned away, his grip firm on the loaded longblaster.

Minutes passed, and when the couple was forced to break apart for air, she nuzzled his cheek, her forked tongue encircling his ear, flickering inside and out.

Gasping at the sight, Thor worked the bolt on his weapon and aimed it in her direction. Equally shocked, Brandon grabbed the woman by the arms and pushed her away for a better view. Wantonly, she writhed to be against him again. He squeezed until she stopped moving, then looked hard into her eyes. There was no doubt that she was a mutie, but unlike anything he had ever encountered before. He felt drunk with lust. The urge to take her right there in front of the troops almost drove him mad.

"Okay, freedom," Brandon huskily agreed. "Come with us to Cold Harbor ville and right afterward I'll—"

At the name of the ville the slave fought to get loose of his grip, terror distorting her features. Her nails raked across his face, leaving bloody furrows.

"Bitch!" he cursed and threw her to the dock. The girl fell to the deck, kneeling before the sec man in a fetal position.

"Stupid, slut! I would have set you free!" Brandon spit furiously, touching his cheek. "Didn't I just prove we pay our debts? How dare you strike a sec man of the lord baron!"

Cowering in submission, she started to crawl away,

and he planted a boot on her back, crushing her to the stones.

"Oh no, you're mine now. You'll go where I go, and obey my every order, or die ten times worse than your last owner! Get me?"

Dumbly she nodded, cowering behind her supple hands.

"Get on the boat," Brandon snapped. "And you'll show me what that fancy tongue of yours can really do tonight in my bunk. Then the rest of the crew, too, if it amuses me!"

Limping, the girl awkwardly climbed onto the PT boat, the laughing sailors roughly shoving her out of the way as they loosened the mooring lines and got ready to leave. Sec men of the lord baron rarely stayed on shore. The risk of getting aced in a night-creep by the locals was too great.

Cowering in the corner of the angled wheelhouse, the slave watched carefully as the norms got their wood-burning vessel under way and started steaming away from shore.

Receding into the distance, a conflagration raged freely on the jungle hillside, while a much smaller blaze licked fiery tongues skyward from the middle of the ville.

"Finally I'm going home," she whispered softly, luxuriating in speaking again. "And the lord baron will pay."

A passing sec man snapped his head toward her, and she opened her dress to display her golden breasts. He smirked and went back to coiling the ropes, already thinking of what he'd do to the mutie if he got the chance.

For a moment there, the sailor could have sworn she said something, but that was impossible. Muties were too dumb for talk. It had to have been the wind. Yeah, that was it. Just the wind. Dumb slut.

GROWING DARKNESS covered the calm sea, broken only by the faint silvery moonlight and the dim yellow light of fish-oil lanterns on the sinking ship. The *Delta Blue* had quickly and quietly gone to her grave, the cold sea consuming the wild blaze raging over the shattered pirate ship. Slowly sinking, the victorious *Constellation* was alone in the middle of the ocean, surrounded by a bobbing corona of wreckage and bodies.

Knowing their valiant ship was doomed, the crew had blocked the holes in her hull with the sacks of dried fish to slow the rushing water, then chopped holes in the opposite side of the ship to make her sink level and buy them precious minutes to gather supplies. Unfortunately it was soon discovered that most of the lifeboats used to build the barricade had been badly damaged in the firefight. Lolling belly up, the skiffs were half-submerged already. A fight had ensued over one of the intact lifeboats, and fresh blood swirled in the deepening water.

Far away from the others, the companions were at the broken bow of the ship guarding a small skiff piled with their backpacks. At the tiller, Ryan stood holding a lantern salvaged from the quarterdeck. Mildred did the same at the bow, covering the skiff in a nimbus of light. Over the side of the skiff, the splintered planks of the *Connie* were barely visible below the inch of water covering the main deck. On their other side was the stygian sea, stretching to the stars on the horizon, and countless miles deep. With every tiny wave, the bottom of their boat scraped against the planks and became a little more buoyant.

"Where the hell is he?" J.B. demanded, squinting into the growing darkness.

"Shoulda gone with," Jak stated, frowning.

"He's taking way too long," Ryan said, placing aside his Steyr and drawing his hand cannon. "Must be trouble. Give me a lantern, I'll go find him."

"No, wait. There he is!" Krysty cried in obvious relief, pointing into the murky gloom.

At first only a vague shape, Dean suddenly came into view, sloshing through the ankle-deep water covering the deck. A canvas pack over his shoulder, the youth paused, then carefully skirted the invisible hole in the unseen deck.

"Found it," Dean said, tossing his backpack of ammo into the lifeboat. "Give me another minute and I'll grab some more food from the galley."

"No time. Get in," his father said, grabbing the boy by the collar and bodily hauling him into the lifeboat. "Got to make some distance or we'll get caught in the undertow when the *Connie* goes under."

"I could do it," Dean said rebelliously, taking a seat at the stern and straightening his clothes.

Tolerantly Ryan looked at his son. Stubborn as a
Shen mule. Pure Cawdor. "Want to steer?" he asked.

"Sure," the boy replied eagerly.

The Deathlands warrior released the wooden tiller
that controlled the hinged rudder. "Head due south.
I'm standing guard."

Snuggling into position, Dean tucked the tiller under his armpit, holding on with both hands.

"Let's move," Ryan said, working the bolt on the
Steyr. The ship was sinking fast, and there were more
things in the sea to watch for than just desperate men.

Sitting side by side, J.B. and Doc took the first set
of oars. Krysty and Jak took the next set. Mildred
stayed in the bow with a lantern held low to watch
the surface for submerged obstructions, a blaster at
the ready. Just in case.

Awkwardly at first, then with greater ease, the companions started rowing, the oars hitting the planks and
gunwale as the bottom of the skiff scraped noisily
across the deck. Then the lifeboat cleared the bow,
sinking a good foot into the water. The oars dipped
in clean now, without hindrance, and they started
moving freely, rapidly building speed.

Barely visible in the moonlight, two more boats
pulled away from the sinking giant. Jones stood in
one, oddly silent for a change, the short man just staring at the listing vessel. Illuminated by a lantern, Abagail was in the other, along with her team of girls and
a few wounded men.

The creaking of the lowering mast mixed with the
splashing of the oars, the loose canvas sails fluttering

with sharp snaps in the wind. The skiffs were a dozen yards away when a handful of sailors called for the others to wait as they waded through the knee-deep waters on the vessel. Clumsily going into the sea, they started swimming for the moving skiffs. Nobody slowed or waited for them to catch up.

"Damn fools hid until all the work was done," J.B. growled in annoyance, matching his strokes to those of Doc alongside him. "Lazy bastards."

"So die," Jak stated unconcerned. "Plenty more fools."

"Evolution in action," Doc muttered, rowing steadily.

"How many are there?" Krysty asked, hauling the oars up from the water, then down to push. The wound in her shoulder started to throb, and she forced the pain from her mind.

"Don't know, don't care," Ryan said, the long-blaster held ready. "This one is ours."

"I won't turn away people long as there is room," Mildred stated firmly. "We can easily hold two more, maybe three."

"Those who reach us first get a berth," Ryan replied, "and will do all the rowing. But once we're full, nobody else. Not going to risk our lives."

Reluctantly the physician acquiesced to the cold equation. There was no Coast Guard to rescue swimmers, no helicopters to drop supplies and rubber rafts, no Red Cross with coffee and doughnuts and CPR. The companions were alone, and survival always seemed to be a matter of ruthless logic. One died or ten died; there really was no choice to be made.

"And if they try anyway?" Krysty asked.

Ryan leveled his blaster at the approaching swimmers. "Our lives or theirs," he stated. "But I don't think it's going to be a problem."

"What do you mean, sir?" Doc asked perplexed.

"Sharks," Dean answered grimly.

Sharp fins cut the surface of the water, converging from every direction. There had to have been hundreds. A man screamed and fell in pieces, blood swirling around his struggling form. Another went under without a cry. A third reached a skiff and almost made it aboard when he was yanked back down out of sight.

Jones fired a flintlock at the monsters of the deep. A shark was hit by the .75 miniball at point-blank range with no noticeable effect.

Suddenly a tattooed hand grabbed the rim of the companions' lifeboat, and Draco tried to haul himself from the drink.

"Please," he croaked. "Help…me…"

Recognizing the face seen through his sniper scope, Ryan rammed the stock of the longblaster into the pirate's face, breaking teeth. The sailor lost his grip and slipped back into the sea, floundering helplessly as the skiff pulled away. The water washed the blood away from his mouth, and moments later sharks were circling the man. Screaming meaningless words, Draco drew a curved knife and stabbed at the dark shapes, then he jerked as something grabbed him from below. Another fin brushed by, and squealing in madness, Draco was hauled abruptly out of sight into the depths.

Grimacing, Jones tucked his blaster away. The pirate couldn't have died in a better way, or his own crew in worse. The sea was a hot slit that loved you and chilled at the same time. Aye, the biggest bitch in the world, but she was still the only female he'd ever call wife.

"Cap'n, there she goes!" a sailor cried out.

Pausing in their rowing, the companions took a moment to look at the distant ship. A wave broke over the gunwale of the *Constellation,* going fully across her deck. There was a great belch of trapped air escaping from the hold, then the groaning vessel sank beneath the swirling waters. Only the crow's nest atop the mast stayed on the surface for an inordinate length of time, as if the vessel had somehow hit bottom, then it slid out of sight and was gone.

A brief whirlpool formed around the area, hauling wreckage, bodies and sharks below, only to return them again in a few minutes in a rush of water. The churning waves crashed against each other, the force radiating outward, and soon the surface was smooth and calm, as if nothing had ever occurred at that location.

The sharks still circled the lifeboats, but Jones stood and saluted, while most of the sailors slumped over in heart-stricken grief. At the tiller, Abagail stayed safely seated, as did the girls, but even the wounded sailors wiped away tears.

"Why sad?" Jak asked, confused. "They dull-brains? Jus' a wag."

"Merely a vehicle? Oh no. The *Constellation* fought in the Revolutionary War," Doc said softly, "and ran the Rebel blockades in the Civil War."

"Carried troops in World War I," Mildred added, feeling strangely moved by the loss. "And was a radar ship that spotted Nazi bombers in World War II. Moved medical supplies to Korea, too. That ship fought in every major American war."

Doc nodded. "A piece of our history died this day."

"But not us," Ryan said bluntly. He agreed with Jak. It was just a thing, like a boot, or a knife, not blood kin. Sailors were as crazy as the damn scholars.

"They lived and died on that ship. How would you feel if your childhood home of Front Royal was destroyed?" Doc asked simply.

Without answering, Ryan shouldered his blaster and cupped hands to his face. "Hey, Jones! How far to Cold Harbor?"

The other lifeboats smoothly moved closer, only occasionally nudged by a passing shark testing the strength of a craft. The crew backslipped their oars, halting the craft just out of grabbing distance.

"Three days by oars," Jones said, shifting his weight to the rocking of the skiff. "Got any food on board?"

"Enough for a day or two," Ryan said, nudging his backpack with a boot. He knew there were a dozen MREs, some smoked condor and a single self-heat can of soup. But shared with all of the others it wouldn't make one meal. This trip could get nasty real fast.

"Same here," Jones lied. He had made damn sure there was a full sack of dried fish in the skiff before they left, but wasn't about to share any with the outlanders unless absolutely necessary. His crew came first.

"We only have water," Abagail said, resting a hand protectively on a small keg. "Anybody got a net, or a hook and line?"

Dean started to reach for his bowie knife, then stopped. The handle was hollow, and the pommel could be screwed off to hide things inside. But the fishing hooks and predark nylon line had been lost in a whirlpool in the Carolinas. Now it only held a piece of jerky and two live rounds for emergencies.

"Nothing here," Krysty answered, checking under the seats.

"Damn."

"Any place closer where we can hunt for food?" Doc asked hopefully. "Or barter for it. A ville or an island, perhaps?"

"Not that I know of," the captain answered thoughtfully, rubbing the back of his neck. "Cold Harbor is the closest ville. Lots of atolls, most of them only sand and grass."

Then he hesitantly added, "But we can get there a lot faster if we can reach the Jaluit River."

Ryan understood the reference. There were mountains bigger than anything on dry land under the ocean, and the currents followed the ranges making rivers in the sea. A smart ship could catch one going in the right direction and save a shitload of time and effort. Sounded like just what they wanted.

"B-but, skipper," a sailor said, weakly raising his heavily bandaged head, "that river goes by Forbidden Island."

"We got a choice, swab?" The man made no response. "Thought as much. Forbidden Island, it is."

"No way!" Daniels screamed, brandishing a fist. "We got smashed by the storm, captured by slavers, the captain dies, the *Connie* sinks and now this? The Jaluit River? You've gone mad, and I'll not let ya chill us all!"

"Siddown," Jones said, his voice low and dangerous, rising to his feet. "I'm still your captain."

"Never!" Daniels spit. Hauling a blaster from his belt, he aimed the colossal weapon at the short man.

Quickly Jones drew his own hand cannon, but Abagail stood and made a throwing gesture. Daniels gasped as the knife hit his leg. Cursing, he turned the flintlock toward her, and a knife slammed into his lower back, exactly at the kidneys. Crying out in pain, he pulled out the knife and the red trickle became a crimson gusher. Sagging weakly, Daniels tried to aim for Jones again, dying by the heartbeat. A sailor in the skiff grabbed his blaster by the hammer, preventing it from discharging, and another yanked out the knife in his leg. Daniels recoiled and fell over the side to hit with a splash. He clawed at the lifeboat and was pushed away with an oar. Gagging on the saltwater, the dying man tried to stay afloat when the sharks arrived and violently finished the job.

"Anybody else?" Jones asked, pulling back the second hammer of his double-barreled blaster.

"We die either way," a sailor said listlessly, the rest muttering unhappy agreement. "Guess it don't much matter how."

Taking his oars, Jak bumped Krysty and together they did a few strokes to keep the boats aligned for conversation. The other rowers did the same.

"What's wrong with the island?" Ryan asked, relaxing his firing stance. Aside from liking Jones, the pint-sized sailor was their best bet to keep sucking air. He wanted the man alive.

"Don't know for sure," the captain replied, easing down the hammers of his piece and tucking it away. "Some folks say its bad air from the volcanoes. It's got two, and you can see them smoking for a hundred miles away." He glanced to the south, but there was nothing there yet. Just a wine-dark sea and endless stars on the horizon merging into the fiery clouds.

"Is death quick, sir, or do you cough a lot?" Doc asked, rubbing his unshaved chin. "We can easily make masks from our clothing and wet them in the ocean. That should last long enough for us to get by most deadly of noxious gases."

"Been tried," the short man replied hotly. "This air makes your hair fall out, then ya gums bleed, soon ya go faint then vomit out guts and die."

"Rad poisoning," Mildred identified, flexing her

hands. Rowing was a lot harder than she remembered. The gamma radiation had to be off the scale.

J.B. touched the rad counter on his lapel. "We have a device that can warn us if we get too close."

"Really?" a bandaged girl asked, noticeably perking up at the statement.

"Hey, toss it over and let me see," a sailor asked casually.

Faint thunder rolled from the cloudy sky as Ryan glared at the man, and the sailor shamefully looked away. Damn idiot. He had to be the asshole who made it aboard after the skiff left the sinking ship. He made a mental note to keep a watch on the man.

"You show us the way," Ryan stated, "and we'll take the point position, guide everybody past the hot spots."

"And if the currents carry us too close?" Abagail asked, hugging the till. "What do we do then, eh?"

"We die," he answered bluntly.

Thunder sounded again, and to the north the stars disappeared behind a wall of heavy rain.

"Okay, you got another deal, outlander," Jones said, then reached into his pocket to withdraw a small piece of wicker, the dried reeds woven into a very complex pattern. Holding it up to the southern sky, he maneuvered it around until aligning several stars through holes in the material.

"Head that way!" he said, pointing.

Listening for the approaching storm, Ryan added, "And we better hurry."

Chapter Twelve

The sun was a blazing ball of fire above the sea, the storm clouds only thin slashes across the azure sky, the golden rays streaming through to sparkle off the ocean waves.

Standing near the wheel, Captain Bachman mopped the sweat from his face and straightened his wicker hat. The shade it created helped some, but not much. The air felt as hot as a forge, and it was hours until noon. But it was always this way after a storm. As if the world was born anew.

The pirate ship *Gibraltar* was quiet, the slaves working down in the hold, the decks scrubbed, the rigging tight. They had already hauled in a load of fish from the drag nets, and some of the crew were sitting on barrels gutting the fish and separating the meat into one bucket, the inedible scales into another and the guts into a third for the slaves. They'd be delighted over fresh food. Bachman knew his men considered him a little soft on the slaves, but even a horse worked better with food in its belly. Same with people. That was just a fact of life. Whips couldn't make the dead walk.

"Ahoy the deck! Man overboard!" the lookout in

the crow's nest hollered to the deck. "Off the port bow!"

The crew dropped the gutted fish and rushed to the gunwales for a look. A bosun rose from his wicker chair and cocked back both of the hammers on his duck-foot blaster. Bachman approved. Good man. Trust nothing, and stay alive. That was the motto carved into the bow of the *Gibraltar*.

Walking to the edge of the quarterdeck, the captain lifted a predark eyeglass lens from his vest pocket tied to a piece of string. It still frightened him a little that it didn't seem to work for anybody else. Only him. A gaudy slut had once suggested that human eyeballs might be different. It sounded reasonable until he caught her trying to lift his blaster when they were fucking. Drove a knife into her ear, and finished the job anyway.

Closing an eye, he held the lens at different distances from his face until he could see wreckage floating on the water, what looked like a piece of a ship's deck. A man was sprawled facedown on the sodden wood, the toe of one boot dipping into the waves.

"Red Blade!" the captain shouted, tucking the lens away. "Send a skiff to rescue the bastard."

A man at the railing guffawed. "Davey brought us a nice new slave!"

"Mebbe," Bachman said warily. "Let's talk to him first before dress his hands in shackle."

Pulleys squealed as the skiff was lowered, and Bachman had a mental note to flog the crew for not greasing the metal. In a battle, that could cost the ship.

Standing at the bow, Red Blade shouted orders as the skiff was rowed over to the flotsam and hauled the unconscious man aboard. The bosun watched from the bow of the *Gibraltar,* his blaster tracking everything. Occasionally he would look over the other side of the ship, just in case this was a ruse to divert their attention.

Minutes later, the lifeboat was hauled back into position, and the curious crew laid the wounded man on the deck. His face was a battlefield of acne scars, tattoos covered most of his skin and there was a scabby wound on his arm. He was carrying several weapons, which Red Blade took and tucked into a wide leather belt.

"He got da same," a sailor said, tugging on the belt. "Must be one of us."

"Could be," Red Blade agreed in a growl, a thick white scar crossing his neck from ear to ear.

Bachman walked over and studied the man for a minute.

"Don't know him," he said. "But then, I don't know all of us. More every day with the lord bastard making ville fight ville. Smoky, give him some water and wine. Let's see if there's any spunk still in this pile of fish bait."

"Aye, Cap'n," a pale sailor said, and swung around a gourd suspended on a leather strap. He pulled out a cork and carefully dribbled some of the mixture into the man's slack mouth.

At first nothing happened, then the unconscious sailor breathed in some of the fluid and violently awakened, hacking and coughing for breath. Smoky continued to pour, and the man swallowed some simply to clear his throat. Almost immediately, he sat up fully alert, then bent over and vomited on the deck.

Crossing his arms, Bachman frowned at that. Idiot had to have been sipping saltwater. His guts would be all twisted up inside.

"Got a name, matey?" the captain asked gruffly.

"Giles, lieutenant of the…" He wheezed and gasped. "Got to find them…"

"We'll find your ship. If you're a brother," Red Blade rumbled.

"Blade, blood and bones," Giles croaked, and took the gourd away from the pale man to drink greedily, excess flowing over both of his cheeks. Lowering the container, he poured some more into his palm and wiped his face.

"Powder and blades," he finished, placing a fist to his heart.

"Welcome aboard," Bachman said, and waved off the bosun. As the guard eased down the hammers of his longblaster, the crew relaxed, and Red Blade offered the fellow pirate a hand, easily hauling him erect.

"Damn near went to Davey there," Red Blade said, offering back the weapons.

Giles brushed them aside and drank some more. "They're yours. I won't stand beholden to no man."

Red Blade merely grunted and tucked the blaster into his boot, then forcibly put the knife into Giles's belt.

"No man walks naked on the *Gibraltar,*" he said roughly. "Don't fuck with me, or I'll toss ya back."

"Fair steven," Giles said, turning the handle about so it would be easier to grab. "Owe ya."

"No," Bachman said, "you owe me. Where's your ship?"

"Sunk," Giles said, almost sputtering, hate distorting his ugly face into something worse. He staggered, then stood straight. "Bunch of outlanders got the *Delta Blue.* Fuckers had rapidfires, grens, plas. You name it!"

Although intrigued, Bachman managed to control his reaction. He had heard such tales before. Outlanders with nuke batteries, MRE packs, whiskey, nukes, airplanes, all sorts of crap. He was too old to believe in lost tech and a world beyond the last island.

"Bullshit," Red Blade said bluntly.

"On my oath," Giles shot back hostilely, staggering again. "Brass shells were everywhere from that little blaster. Rad me, I'd give me left nut to have them in my sights again. Draco was the best captain ever!"

"Until now," Bachman corrected sternly, a hand going for the whip on his belt.

Not a fool, Giles nodded vigorously. "Aye, skipper. But we got to make them pay," he said, staggering again. Then he started coughing, and the pirate spit bile on the deck.

"Know where they harbor?" a sailor asked.

"Cold," Giles slurred, dropping the gourd. As it rolled away, he went slowly went to the deck and lay slumped into a heap. A few moments later, he started to snore.

Bachman put a finger on the man's throat. There was a pulse, weak, but steady.

"Exhaustion and exposure," the captain declared. "Smoky, haul our brother to my cabin. Wash him off, get some fresh clothes and a blaster, but no ammo."

"Aye, skipper." He grinned. "Comfortable, but helpless."

Red Blade turned to another pirate. "Cookie, get him food. All he wants, a woman, too, if he says he can handle one when he wakes."

"Done." He saluted and started for the closest hatchway.

"Everybody to your posts!" Bachman shouted. "Man the rigging and watch for any other survivors! No work for a day to the swab that finds another!"

Whooping in delight, the pirates swarmed into the ropes above, eagerly scanning the surface for any more wreckage or people. When the officers were alone, they spoke low and quickly.

"What do ya think?" Red Blade asked eagerly. "Sounds legit to me. Outlanders with rapidfires!"

"It isn't impossible," Bachman said hesitantly, pulling out his lens and polishing it on a sleeve. "Sure as shit didn't sound like a drunkard's boast. And if they knew a way in, by Davey's bones they might just know the way out."

"Touch of a knife up their arse will make them talk," Red Blade said, cracking a toothy grin. "Makes anybody talk."

"For a while," the captain agreed, still polishing the clean lens. "And we know where they can be found. Cold must mean Cold Harbor ville."

"Baron Langford." The pirate chief scowled hatefully, touching his scar. "His ma gave me this. Be happy to do the son the same. But not gonna use a dull blade and only get half the job done."

Bachman tucked the lens away. "You've been there? How good are their defensives?"

"Too good. Island got cliffs on every side. Only way to reach land is the main harbor. Ville has stone walls and lots of cannon."

"And their gunners are good shots, so I hear from others who have tried to raid the island," the captain mused. "Tried and failed."

"Aye, sir. Must be a dozen ships lying at the bottom of that harbor," Red Blade agreed. "Almost as many as Maturo Island itself! One of them is me old ship, the *Manatee*."

"A good vessel, and a smart captain," Bachman said, removing his hat and mopping the sweat off his face with the damp handkerchief. It was lace, and he swore he could still smell lilac flowers, a token from the chilled slut who had made a child into a man and taught him the truth of the world. Trust nobody.

His tanned skin brown as dirt, Red Blade stood directly in the streaming sunlight completely unaffected, as if he were carved from cool stone.

"We can't risk a direct assault," Bachman said, tucking the cloth up a sleeve, "unless we get another ship to ride in first and draw their fire. Some newbie who doesn't know any better and only wants to split the booty."

"Aye." Red Blade grinned. "The *Amsterdam*, maybe, or the *Cortez*."

"No, not those," Bachman muttered. "But at least one more ship. Maybe a lot more."

ONE HUNDRED MILES AWAY, three lifeboats floated along under the blistering sun with oars out of the water, no movement, no sounds. Hungry seagulls circled the drifting boats, watching the motionless human forms lying inside the wooden shells. Nuzzling close to the skiffs, a shark swam alongside, patiently waiting for more food.

Slumped over at the tiller, Doc held the hot wooden handle, a damp handkerchief draped over his head as protection. Scooping his hand into ocean for just a moment, he dribbled some more water on the cloth and waited for his shift to end. The rest of the companions lay on the bottom of the boat sheltered by the shadows of the jackets. The other two lifeboats were pretty much the same, one man at the tiller, while the rest sought shade from the blistering sun. Rowing was done only at night.

Only yesterday, they had all grabbed an oar as the oceanic river carried them directly toward Forbidden Island. They managed to break out of the current just in time, and then Ryan and J.B.'s rad counters loudly indicated why the landmass was considered taboo. Twenty miles away, the Geigers started clicking, and quickly rose to an almost steady burr. Without the advance warning, they would have sailed into a harbor ringed with green glass, the vaporized shadows of battleships cast on the half-melted rock of a tall mountain range. Twin volcanoes towered above everything, wisps of steam rising from the truncated peaks, the southern face lined with the flowing red river of molten lava working its way into the sea. There was a strong stink of sulfur. The chemical was often referred to as brimstone in his time, but apparently now it was called flash.

The ruins of a predark city rose behind the glowing harbor. The wealth of the ancient world was just waiting to be taken, protected by the deadly, invisible field of hard radiation. Figures could be seen moving among the ruins, and he wished the muties well to their cornucopia of technology.

Dipping a hand into the water again, Doc jerked as he felt a brief contact with something rough, and knew he had just brushed against a shark. Gasping for breath, he waited for his heart to slow to normal again. The creature was still tracking them after two days! Its dorsal fin and body had several bullet holes from their blasters, but the creature had suffered no deleterious effects from the sudden infusion of subsonic lead. Mildred said the creatures had been on the endangered species list in her time. The scholar had absolutely no idea how the adamantine killers could be in danger from anybody.

Her bearskin coat made into a tent with his swordstick, Krysty muttered something and rolled over just as Doc caught a whiff of living plants in the wind.

Shading his face, he looked about and saw an island on the horizon coming ever closer. A huge waterfall was visible even from this distance, falling from the slopes of cool misty mountains that rose majestically over the jungle landscape. Formidable cliffs rose straight from the ocean, but to the north side there seemed to be a beach. Then the sharp greasy aroma of frying fish arrived.

He tried to speak, but could only croak. Grabbing a canteen, he unscrewed the top and drank deeply of the tepid water for the first time in days.

"Land ho!" Doc shouted. "Land!"

Everybody shook themselves awake and struggled out from their impromptu shelters to blink at the blinding daylight.

"Trouble?" Ryan demanded, holding back a yawn, but with a blaster at the ready.

"On your left," Doc said, gesturing, keeping a hold of the tiller. "Behold an island as green as Walden Pond!"

"Smell fish," Jak said, rubbing his tousled hair.

Holstering his piece, Ryan checked his lapel. The rad counter was silent. "Clean," he announced.

"Same here," J.B. agreed, doffing his fedora. "Dry land, at last!"

"Is that it?" Krysty asked, her red hair flexing in anticipation. "Is that Cold Harbor?"

"Yes," Abagail answered, exhaling in relief. "We're home."

In the second lifeboat, Jones smiled widely, causing his dry lips to crack. "Beautiful!" he croaked, then shouted. "Ahoy, Cold Harbor!" His words disappeared over the surface, and there was no response from the distant ville.

"Too far," he grunted, then spit on his hands and flexed the palms. "Okay, slip to port! We gotta break out of the river or head straight for Chang Island and Butcher Ratak!"

"Heave to, ya swabs!" a sailor ordered, taking an oar. "Put your backs into it, unless ya wanna visit the cannie baron!"

Taking a seat with the other companions, Ryan and Mildred held their oars still, as Doc leaned hard into the tiller and the rest stroked deep and fast. The skiff sluggishly fought free from the underwater river once more and slowed as it reached calm sea.

Doggedly the shark left the warm currents of the river and followed after the boats, its fin cutting the water as it circled eagerly, searching for more of the soft red food to fall into its massive jaws.

An hour passed of steady rowing, the sun draining their strength and blistering exposed skin. A westerly breeze made the waves crest toward the skiffs so that it seemed as if the boats were traveling backward. But the green island came ever closer, and soon Ryan could see the defensive wall around the ville. Ten or more feet high, made of red brick, with several holes in the side. Probably for cannons. A lot of them.

The smells of food and green plants soon masked the tang of the salty sea, and now they could see people moving on the shore and docks, sec men running along the top of the wall. There were several dugout canoes and a battered trawler at the dock, but Ryan was pleased to observe that there was nothing like the *Constellation* or the *Delta Blue*.

The choppy water became suddenly smooth as they neared the island, and Ryan noted they were passing over an undersea reef of bright pink coral, with natural breakers. The boats shot through without any trouble, but the persistent shark skirted away from the deadly sharp coral, swimming ruthlessly back and forth on the other side. Waiting, ever waiting.

"Baron Langford is gonna shit when he hears about the *Constellation*," a sailor said, the muscles in his bare back coiling as he stroked the oars.

"Screw him," Jones replied. "If he hadn't been in such a rush for us to come back, we would have waited out the storm that damaged the *Connie*."

"Gonna tell him that?"

"Hell, no!"

In the companions' skiff, the rowing became slow and the boat eased behind the others rushing for the shore.

"Don't like this," J.B. said, pausing in the work.

Ryan grunted. "The dock is clear," he agreed. "Almost as if they were preparing for a fight."

Mildred glanced ahead at Jones, beaming with delight and waving at the ville. "Something's wrong," she agreed, and slipped an arm through the strap of her med kit to keep it close.

Suddenly there was a puff of gray smoke from the brick wall, and a moment later a geyser shot into the air near the front lifeboat. Then the boom of a cannon rolled over the surface of the harbor.

"Ambush!" Jak cursed, drawing his Colt Python.

"Wait," Ryan commanded, slipping the oars out of the water. "Mebbe it's just a warning shot. They're traveling with outlanders."

"Yeah, us." The teen frowned, but slid the blaster away. Made sense.

Furious, Jones stood and shook a fist. "What in hell are you doing?" he bellowed. "I'm Jones of the *Constellation*!"

A crackle of longblasters sounded from the wall.

"Wh-why are they shooting?" a girl demanded, sounding more angry than frightened. "Don't they know it's us?"

"The sec men know," Krysty said softly, stopping rowing completely. Briefly she checked her weapon. Loaded and oiled. The salt air was tough on steel, and J.B. made sure everybody used extra lub on their weapons.

Now a line of blasters from the ville shot cannonballs, impacting into the water on every side of the three skiffs.

"Getting our range," Ryan warned, grabbing his backpack. He glanced at the breakers, a good ten minutes of rowing distance and well within the range of those huge cannons. Fireblast!

"Captain?" Abagail asked anxiously.

"Fuck this," Jones said reluctantly, then sat down and started pushing the oars to slow the progress of the skiff. "Head back to the sea!"

Quickly, people reversed their seating and started stroking for their lives when the lead lifeboat exploded into pieces, wood and bodies flying everywhere. On the shore came a faint cheering.

"Jones!" Abagail screamed, covering her face.

More smoke puffed from the ville, and a cannonball hit only feet away from the bow of the companions' boat, the water spout going ten feet high, completely hiding them.

"Everybody overboard!" Ryan shouted, dropping his backpack and diving straight over the side.

He hit the water in a clean dive and cool silence engulfed the man as he kicked for the depths. The water was clear and barely stung his eye. He guessed that was from the freshwater of the big fall mixing with the ocean, diluting the salt. The sunlight streamed down to the bottom, and he could actually see the sandy floor of the harbor some thirty or so feet away. There were a lot of wrecked ships scattered about, schools of brightly colored fish darting about in the nautical graveyard. Ryan leveled off at about ten feet above the derelict ships, and checked for the others.

His friends were close behind, Mildred swimming awkwardly hauling her med kit, Krysty swimming in spurts, her waterlogged coat lagging behind like a boneless corpse. Doc was fumbling in the water with both hands at something, then watched as his swordstick disappeared into the amassed wreck below.

Feeling his heart beat in his chest, Ryan pointed a finger, then jerked a thumb. Dean and Jak swam by as the women dropped their excess weight and also headed directly for shore. Nobody needed to be told the only safe location from the cannons was at the base of the ville wall where the black-powder blasters couldn't aim. Once on shore, the matter would be more in favor of the companions.

Hissing a trail of bubbles, a cannonball shot through the group, and they faintly heard a muffled crackling of wood. Dean glanced back to see the wood and dark objects descend from the surface, blood spreading out from the limbs and torsos of the dead. The loss of the girls hit him harder than the death of Jones for some reason, but then the strain in his lungs urged him onward and he continued kicking to reach land.

Then he caught a flash of gold amid the broken spars and ghostly rigging. Drawing a knife, the boy relaxed when he saw the gleaming bones of a skeleton half covered with barnacles grinning blindly from the tilted crow's nest of a sunken vessel. A gold tooth reflecting the sunlight from above. Dean marked the location in his mind and rejoined the others, concentrating on staying calm and conserving his supply of air. Surface now, and the ville sec men might see them in the clear water and be waiting for them on shore with blasterfire.

An eerie peace enveloped the laboring group, the only sounds coming from the movements of their arms and legs. Each was alone in the world of his or her private thoughts as schools of tiny fish darted about without logic. The fields of broken ships

abruptly stopped once the companions reached the
shallows. With burning lungs, they immediately angled for the shadows underneath the wooden dock.
From there they could sneak onto the shore. But as
the land rose, visibility dangerously increased to the
point that they feared being spotted by armed sec men
who had just aced their own incoming people. Waving gently in the currents, lacy fronds of seaweed
reached for them from the seabed, the long tendrils
of the plants the exact same color of the cigs the
sailors smoked, but the companions steered well clear
of the entangling plants.

Sloping gently to shore, the shoals were covered
with wide fields of oysters, their shells splayed open
wide to catch the droppings of passing fish. Only a
small section of the oysters were protectively closed
against an invading starfish. Using its massively thick
five arms, the bright yellow starfish was slowly forcing the dusky shells apart despite the desperate strug-
gles of the mollusk inside. Once the shell opened, the
oyster would be helpless and the starfish would feed.
It was a contest of raw brute strength that the starfish
almost always won.

Soon the ancient concrete pillars supporting the
dock came into view, more barnacles peppering the
cracked columns, their tiny beards waving invitingly
back and forth. Wasting vital moments going around
a thick clump of seaweed, Ryan swam into the shadows and knifed eagerly upward. Upon reaching the
surface, he covered his mouth, and took only tiny sips
of air through his nose so he wouldn't gasp loudly

and announce their presence. The others rose in the strips of darkness and followed his example.

Minutes passed before they dared to breathe normally. While the companions checked their weapons, Mildred hopefully studied the harbor, but couldn't spot any of the others in the skiffs. They appeared to be the only ones who made it to shore alive.

Krysty and Jak drew their weapons, water trickling from the cylinders of the revolvers. The tough blasters would even fire underwater, but it wasn't recommended for long life. Ryan, Dean and Mildred eased their blasters out of the water and patiently waited for them to dry. Unfortunately, Doc's black-powder handcannon had been rendered useless the moment he entered the water. That would have to be laboriously cleaned and dried before reloading was possible.

Blinking water from his bare eyes, J.B. eased back the bolt on the Uzi. Nothing stopped the resilient Israeli machine gun, but the thirty rounds in the clip was it for ammo. The rest was in his munitions bags at the bottom of the harbor. Along with a lot of other vital supplies.

Standing in the chest-deep water, the companions waited a good hour before the gates to the ville opened and footsteps could be heard crunching in the loose sand.

"Any sign of them?" a gruff voice asked.

There was a snort. "Course not. Jimmy's the best gunner in a hundred islands."

"Still got to check."

"Aye, that we do."

Now the footsteps approached and stomped over-head, causing a patter of dirt to fall from the weath-ered planks. With the loss of his sword, Doc drew a knife and Ryan shook his head. The scholar nodded and reversed the blade in his grip so that it was pom-mel first. No chilling; he wanted prisoners first.

"Frank, Arnold," a voice above said, "go walk the beach to the point to see if anybody got out and tried for the jungle."

"Their bad luck if they did," a man stated.

"Aye. Billy, check under the dock."

There was the sound of clothing rustling, and a yellow stream arched off the dock into the water. The companions forced themselves not to move.

"Just warming it up first," a man replied, laughing.

"Stop fucking around. The baron might be watch-ing us."

"Yeah, yeah, well, fuck his highness and the bitch who bore him."

"Wanna say that to his face?" the first voice asked, chuckling.

"Hell no!" the second answered.

Ryan realized that was nearly the exact conversa-tion Jones and a sailor had held in the skiff. Had to be a local joke. Obviously the baron wasn't well loved, or even liked for that matter. Few were, unlike his nephew Nathan Cawdor. Not liked and not feared, if they told jokes behind his back. This info might just work in their favor.

Trying not to splash, Ryan moved toward the di-

rection of the second voice and waited until a face
appeared from above. Instantly he grabbed the man's
throat in an iron grip and hauled the sec man into the
shadows. The prisoner tried for his blaster, but Doc
snatched it away and splashed about in the water as
if trying to swim.

"Oh, for fuck's sake," the first voice complained.
"The moron fell in again. Maggot, Bruiser, haul the
stupe out of there before he drowns."

"Why us?" a young voice demanded.

"Nobody here but us, and I ain't gonna do it. Go."

Two men jumped into the chest-deep water and the
companions charged, swarming over the sec men and
taking them captive in a heartbeat.

"Shitfire!" a bearded man standing on the dock
cried out as the companions came into view with
knives to the throats of his men.

"Hold by order of the baron!" he shouted, backing
away from the outlanders. But then a large hand
reached up over the side of the dock and grabbed hold
of his right boot. Unexpectedly the sec man found
himself tumbling into the sea. He hit hard, water going up his nose, choking the guard for a moment, then
he was roughly hauled from the harbor onto the beach
by a one-eyed man who looked grimmer than death.

"Y-you're the people from the skiff!" the sec man
sputtered, blowing water and bubbling snot out his
nose. "How the hell can you still be alive?"

"Mebbe later," Ryan said, sliding his blaster under
the man's chin while he took his weapons. The local
baron really had the sec men scared, or was it some-

thing else? When the man was unarmed, Ryan pushed the SIG-Sauer into his chin until the sec man was looking into the sky. "Why did you shoot at us? Talk quick."

"Why? Doing you a favor, idiot," the man muttered through a clenched mouth. "You're already aced. Guess I am, too, now that I've touched ya. Use the blaster on us both and end it quick and clean. Don't wanna die puking blood for days."

Ryan almost released the man in the shock of understanding. "Think we're hot, eh?" he growled.

"Of course ya are! We seen ya using the river. Must a gone right past Forbidden Island." He was trying to wiggle away from touching Ryan. "Got no idea why you're still walking. Should be aced long ago. Guess I'm a dirt-eater myself now."

Lowering the SIG-Sauer, Ryan lifted the sec man off the ground. "Do we seem weak?" he breathed into the man's face. "Hair falling out, gums bleeding, puking our guts out? Triple-stupe bastard. We never got close to the reeking pesthole!"

The sec man stared at Ryan as if expecting him to topple over, the flesh falling from his bones. But as it became clear this wasn't going to happen, the man started to quake in fear.

"It's true," the man whispered. "You're not hot. Gods above, the baron will use the cage on me for this fuckup. Let me go! I'll risk the jungle. Please! Have mercy!"

"Not my problem," Ryan stated, shoving the sec

man toward the gate. "I got a deal for the baron and you're part of the price. Lead the way."

"To the baron?"

Ryan shook the man hard. "Start walking."

Suddenly there was a commotion on the wall, and a metal gong began to sound. The sec man on the beach started running back at top speed.

"More coming," Jak announced, clicking back the hammer on his damp pistol.

Instantly J.B. worked the bolt on his Uzi and swung the weapon back and forth. "Where?" he demanded anxiously. "Which direction, dammit!"

Shocked at the outburst, Krysty stared at the man until she noticed how hard J.B. was squinting. Soaking wet, the Armorer was dressed as always, combat boots, Army fatigues, fingerless gloves, leather bomber jacket and tilted fedora. But his wire-rimmed glasses were gone. Without those, the gunner was nearly blind.

"To the right," Mildred said softly, moving behind the man.

Turning fast, J.B. triggered a burst into the air in that general direction, and the sec men stopped in their tracks. The stutter of the rapidfire echoed across the harbor like a million ghostly blasters.

"Cease firing!" a new voice commanded as the gates of the ville swung open wide.

The companions formed a firing line as a group of armed men walked from the gateway. Most held flint-lock muskets, a few hastily loading crossbows, but one man was a bald giant, taller than even Ryan. All muscle, the goliath was wider than two men, and stood bare chested, bandoliers of brass ammo crisscrossing his Herculean torso. Cryptic tattoos in swirling patterns covered both arms, and matching knives with carved bone handles were sheathed at the belt buckle. The baron carried a huge revolver in each hand, a steel Magnum and an Old West revolver, the black-powder blaster very similar to the monstrous LeMat carried by Doc.

"So they're not hot," the baron stated as a greeting. "Corporal Williams, you're a fool."

"The outlanders lie, my liege," the prisoner countered.

The aim of his hand cannons never wavering for a moment, Baron Langford glanced at a shiny device strapped on his wrist.

"No, it's the truth," he announced. "I can tell these things. Corporal, you wasted pounds of black powder for no reason, and chilled a dozen of my men. Guards, put him in the cage. The little one."

"No!" the corporal screamed, and struggled to break away from Ryan.

Curious to see what would happen, the Deathlands warrior released the man. The corporal staggered away and then pulled a small concealed knife from his boot, plunging it into his belly. Before he could do so again, the guards had him in their grip.

"Leave the knife there, it'll make his time more...memorable," Langford directed as the guards carefully carried the bleeding prisoner into the ville. The bleeding man continued to beg for death until he

was out of sight. Now the baron turned his attention
to the companions.

"Unusual blasters," he said.

Ryan didn't reply.

"No smoke when the rapidfire fired."

"Wanna see it again?" J.B. offered.

"Not right now." Langford weighed the answers.
"I'm Langford, baron of this ville. Who are you?"

"Nobody important," Ryan replied.

A crowd of people had gathered at the gate in the
brick wall, slaves holding brooms, pregnant women,
children, a blacksmith in a leather apron, his face
burned from the forge, probably most of the ville.
None were venturing out of the short tunnel, but
watched from within the barrier.

"I saw the skiffs. Is the *Constellation* damaged
somewhere on a beach?" Langford asked pointedly.

"Sunk by pirates," Ryan answered, seeing no reason to lie. "Jones and the others chilled in the harbor
were all that remained of the crew."

Blast. Years of salvage and repairs gone. Men
could be easily replaced, but not the ship. He had
dozens of dugout canoes, a couple of trawlers and the
racing yacht, but nothing like the oceangoing *Constellation*.

A scream wassailed from within the ville, the on-
lookers cringing at the sound. The sec men chuckled
and nudged each other with their elbows.

"Williams has been introduced to the cage," Langford said, smirking.

"Don't care," Ryan said bluntly. "We're here to trade with you, not him."

The baron pretended to think for a minute. "I'll swap you a dozen slaves for that rapidfire."

Ryan shook his head. "No deal."

"Two dozen."

"Don't want slaves," Ryan countered. "Need a ship."

"Okay, a trawler for the blasters." Then he added, "And ammo."

"Weapons aren't part of any deal," Ryan stated curtly. "We're here to offer information."

The baron snorted a laugh. "For a ship? What kind of info could possibly be worth that?"

While the two men talked business, the sec men started to spread out across the beach. The companions shifted their positions to match them, and the sec men retreated to the gate. But more appeared on top of the wall carrying longblasters.

"Out here?" Ryan asked, glancing at the crowd of people watching them from the tunnel. The wall had to be ten feet wide, but then it was built to stop cannonballs.

Langford shrugged. "Inside, outside, makes no difference. This is my island."

Fair enough. Ryan stepped closer and spoke softly. "We know the formula."

The baron wasn't impressed. Many times over the years, he had heard men tell him that, usually while they were being stuffed into a cage, trying to bargain for a fast death.

"The lord baron deals harshly with folks about such matters," Langford whispered back, confident the breeze along the shire would hide their words. "Very harshly."

"Doesn't matter. We can also tell you how to make it better than him," Ryan added. "The powder he sells isn't as strong as the stuff he uses. Right?"

That was correct, but Langford wasn't ready to concede anything yet to the cocky outlander. "Mebbe," he hedged. "But that's common enough knowledge. Gotta tell me more."

Debating the options, Ryan chose the truth. "Three ingredients," he said. "But they have to be mixed in just the right amounts, or it's as useless as dirt."

Now the baron felt a surge of excitement. Rumors among the slaves told about three chems. But this was the first confirmation of the fact. Maybe he was being offered the real thing.

"Perhaps we should continue this in private," Langford offered slyly, trying to ooze charm. "Over dinner in my palace."

Another scream sounded from within the ville, but Ryan already knew that getting out of the ville was going to be a lot tougher than going in. Dinner would be drugged wine, poisoned food and then a long lifetime in a small room with many knives until the companions had told the baron everything they knew.

"Out here is fine," he countered, grateful for all those years he traveled with the Trader learning to cut a deal. The baron was no fool. "Or we could talk on one of the trawlers."

Away from the longblasters, where only the cannon could strike? Langford thought. Fuck that. "Tell me an ingredient first," he offered in reply. "Then we talk on the ship."

On the ground, a blue crab scuttled by, unconcerned with the world of the humans.

"Sulfur," Ryan said. "You call it flash. The yellow powder that smells like bad eggs and comes from a steam vent near your volcano."

Trying not to show it, Langford was stunned beyond words. The outlander knew everything! So the lord baron had lied, it was part of black powder and not something for his disease. The healers used flash to treat minor wounds. They healed faster that way, so it seemed only natural to assume the lord baron was doing the same for his strange illness. Another lie. Had the fat bastard ever said anything that was true? Probably not.

"Good enough," Langford grunted, tucking away his blasters. "What's your price for the rest?"

"The trawler and a load of shine," Ryan said doing the same.

The baron waited for the rest of the demands, but no more seemed to be coming. "That's it?"

"All we need."

His suspicions confirmed, the baron began to get truly angry. It was much too cheap. This was a trick. Or some sort of loyalty test from Kinnison to see if he would deal with whitecoats. Well, it wouldn't work!

"Well, I don't deal with traitors!" the baron

shouted, backing away from the man so the snipers would have a clear target. "Chill these bastards!"

The crowd of people turned and ran, while the sec men cut loose with their flintlock miniballs humming past the companions. The range too great for the crude smoothbores.

Trapped on the open beach, the companions dived to the ground, and J.B. cut loose with a full stuttering stream at the group of sec men. Mildred fired the shotgun while Ryan shot the baron twice in the chest, then aimed for the guards at the gate, the 9 mm blaster chugging hot lead death into their midst. Ryan had no idea how the talk had gone sour so fast.

Meanwhile, Jak raked the beach with his Colt Python, taking out the nearby guards, Dean hit a sniper on top of the wall and Doc slammed the pommel of his knife into the temple of the other sec man they had been holding as a prisoner. As the groaning man fell, the scholar grabbed his flintlock. The discharge was louder than his LeMat, but the .75 miniball slammed into the man with the crossbow, spinning him, and the arrow hit the wooden gate, going in a good foot. The rest of the sec men retreated along the tunnel firing at every step, the billowing smoke soon hiding them from sight.

"Head for the trawler!" Ryan shouted, rising and shooting as he sprinted. That would give them cover from snipers until reaching the jungle.

Firing at more sec men appearing on top of the wall, Krysty raced after the man but tripped in the sand and came down hard. Trying to move, she found a gnarled hand clamped on her ankle, then her wrist, and Baron Langford stood, pulling her close. Point-blank, she fired the S&W at the man, but he only grunted as the .38 bullets slapped into his chest. Then the baron wrapped tree-trunk-size arms around Krysty, pinning both arms at her sides. The pressure was incredible, and her blaster soon dropped from numb hands.

Drawing his revolver, Langford started backing to-ward the gate, holding the trapped woman as a human shield. Ryan and Mildred both took aim, but held off firing, afraid to hit their friend. Barely able to breathe, Krysty clawed for her belt knife but was unable to find it with her clumsy hands. His arms were so tight that all of the sensation was fading from her body. In desperation, she drove a knee into his crotch. Firing his weapon, Langford only squeezed harder, making her ribs creak.

Risking a shot, Ryan got the baron in the shoulder, and he fired back with the booming revolver. Lang-ford's arm jerked as blood spurted from his shoulder and the heavy combat round plowed into the sand between Ryan's boots.

Fireblast! The son of a bitch had to have a dozen slugs in him, and was still moving. He had to be some sort of mutie, norm on the outside, but who knew what lay under the human-looking skin?

Now the baron and his captive were directly be-tween the companions and the sec men, neither side able to fire for fear of hitting one of their own. Only Langford was free to shoot, and he emptied the re-

volver at the companions, then tossed the blaster
away and drew the black-powder Colt .44 to start firing again. But the companions were back in the water,
the angle of the beach making it hard to get a bead
on them.

Reaching the mouth of the tunnel, Langford paused
and grinned in triumph. "Drop your blasters, or the
bitch dies!" he bellowed, brandishing the Old West
hand cannon, trails of smoke snaking from its pitted
muzzle.

A wild rage boiling inside, Ryan started to charge,
then forcibly held himself back, knowing that if they
attacked or surrendered, they would get chilled. Desperately he tried to conceive of a third option, but
every plan ended with Krysty dead. They were going
to have to leave her behind. It was a choice between
her or all of them. The Deathlands warrior felt madness tug on his sanity as he realized there was no way
around the awful decision. Shooting at the wall
around the gate, he tried to keep the baron off balance
and buy some time.

"Gotta go," Jak said urgently, wading closer.
"Come back later."

"Not yet," Ryan growled, splashing through the
surf.

J.B. started to charge, and Mildred held him back.
"Don't want to lose you, too," the physician stated
bluntly.

Furious, the Armorer did as she asked, cursing his
inability to help.

SWIRLING COLORS FILLED Krysty's vision, and only the thundering blood in her ears could be heard. Death was near, and Krysty knew she had only one chance. Calling on Gaia to aid her, mentally saying the prayers that would summon inhuman strength, the woman experienced a rush of electric power that banished the pain and returned the feelings to her arms. Now Krysty tried again to break free from the baron's grasp, and his arms parted easily, his face reflecting his utter astonishment.

As she got loose, Langford aimed his blaster and Krysty knocked it aside, the miniball tugging at her khaki jumpsuit as it tore a new hole in the cloth.

His left wrist throbbing, Langford dropped the exhausted weapon and threw a punch. Krysty swayed out of the way, feeling it brush her chin, then leaned in and hit him twice with blows that would have aced a norm. Snarling, the baron buried a fist into her stomach, but the blow, although devastating, seemed to have no effect on her.

Backing away, she kicked dirt in his eyes, but the giant laughed and grabbed for her throat. Krysty feinted to the right, and incalculable agony shattered the universe. Langford had yanked loose a handful of her animated hair.

In spite of the pain, Krysty swung out her legs for a trip, and the baron cursed as he landed sprawling, red filaments still clenched in his fist. The sight fueled her anger, and Krysty rolled on top of the man to slap cupped hands onto his ears.

Howling, the giant rose to his knees, throwing her

off. Rolling to her knees, Krysty saw trickles of blood flowing down his neck and knew she had successfully burst his eardrums.

Spinning on a heel, Langford kicked at her, lightning fast. The boot scraped her side, and Krysty swayed out of the way just in time to avoid the expected second kick from his other boot.

Her hand brushed one of the dropped blasters on the ground, and she threw it at his face. He ducked and then lunged, arms splayed wide for a deadly bear hug again. Krysty dropped and rolled, the baron plowing into the wall of the tunnel, shaking the huge structure.

As he turned, Krysty stepped in close and rammed the heel of her hand into his nose, intending to drive the fragments into his brain. She heard the bones snap and felt them move. Instantly the baron's face went slack, and he fell to his knees drooling. Fumbling for her belt knife again, this time she found it and slashed him twice across the throat, then stabbed the blade into an armpit to sever the major artery hidden there.

Langford limply fell forward onto the ground. He shuddered all over just once, then went completely still.

Minutes later, as Krysty weakly stood in the tunnel, a faint sound permeated her consciousness. Dozens, maybe hundreds of people were chanting, their voices swelling in power in volume until the very ground seemed to shake with the endless repetition—their hailing her as the new baron.

Chapter Thirteen

"There!" a sec man shouted, pointing at the distant horizon. "Black dust, it's the biggest I've ever seen!"

"Silence, fool," Brandon hissed, leaning over the railing that surrounded a .50-caliber machine gun attached to a gimbal stanchion. The officer held a pair of binocs to his face, and manually dialed the focus. The batteries were long dead, and many of the functions of the complex device were unknown, but the prism-based optics worked just fine.

"Shitfire, it's a monster!" Brandon cursed, then lowered his tone to a hush. "Pilot, kill the engines. I want dead silence."

Keeping one hand on the wheel, the pilot of PT 264 threw a switch, disengaging the propellers from the thumping steam engine.

"Engine room to bridge," a voice shouted up the speaking tube. "What's going on up there?"

"Shut up. There's a sea mutie on the horizon," the pilot said clearly into the tube, his lips less than an inch away. "No sounds, no walking, nothing until the lieutenant says so."

"Aye, aye, sir," the engineer whispered up the tube, his voice barely audible.

"And if you hear Firebirds launch," he added sourly, "then kiss your ass goodbye."

Going to the stern, a bosun waved a bright orange flag at the other nine boats as a warning. But most of them had already gone silent, and soon the entire armada was coasting along by sheer inertia through the Pacific Ocean, props still, engines banked and quiet.

To the naked eye, there was only some rough water ahead. Maybe an underwater volcano bubbling up steam or a school of sharks in a feed frenzy. But under the glass, Brandon saw it all. A humpback whale was fighting for its life. Bleeding from a hundred wounds, the creature frantically rolled over and over, trying to get loose from the writhing tentacles ripping off chunks of its flesh. An eye was removed, the blowhole ripped wide. The whale slammed down a tail that could have crushed the PT boat flat, rolled over once more, but to no avail. More of the tentacles stabbed into its huge body and began to pulse as they pumped out the life fluids. Pitifully moaning a warning to others of its kind, the humpback still tried to swim away, but was dragged backward under the choppy waters. Then a red geyser shot into the air, going up a hundred feet as the horrible feeding began.

"Nuke me," the pilot breathed, and grabbed his blaster for no sane reason. The weapon would be totally useless against one of the ocean leviathans. Its only possible function was to blow out his brains and save the man from being swallowed whole, boat and all, in a single gulp, by the underwater mutie.

Padding along in bare feet, Thor approached the

machine-gun nest. The lieutenant was leaning over the railing, watching the death match closely through the binocs.

"Never seen one before," the sergeant said, cracking his knuckles, then abruptly stopping and staring at his hands as if they belonged to somebody else. The sea muties were attracted to sound, the more the better. As a child he heard stories of the muties attacking an island ville celebrating their baron's birthday, the finishing of wall, whatever, and dragging most of the people and the buildings into the sea. He had never believed the tales until this moment.

"What's wrong—scared?" Brandon asked, a touch of amusement in his words.

"Yes," the sergeant answered truthfully.

Standing erect, Brandon lowered the binocs and tucked them into a cushioned bag at his side. "Me, too," he admitted. "If that thing attacks, we don't have a chance in hell of reaching land in time. Even if I sacrifice the other boats, it'll still swallow us all, then go looking for more."

"So we wait."

"Aye, wait in silence, until it leaves."

Thor started to crack his knuckles again, then stuffed both hands into his pockets. "Shouldn't be too long," he ventured, watching the mutie tear the whale apart. "Mebbe only a couple of hours. It's about done."

"We stay right here for however long it takes," Brandon whispered. "Cold Harbor isn't going anywhere."

"Aye, sir," Thor agreed. "What's another couple of days?"

SLUGGISHLY Krysty awakened to find herself naked under the covers of a large bed. The mattress was softer than anything she had ever been on, the quilt warm and heavy. The woman almost went back to sleep it was so comfortable, then the images of the fight on the beach flooded back into her conscious mind, and Krysty abruptly sat upright, reaching for her blaster.

But she was alone. The room was big, brick walls, bare concrete floor with thick rugs of different designs. All of the furniture was oversize, the two wooden chairs before the fireplace old leather shiny with polish. There were no windows; the light came from bright white lanterns. The door was lined with bolts, all of them on her side.

Obviously this was no prison, and aside from her lack of clothing there were no indications she had been violated. Lots of bruises, but only where she remembered Langford pummeling her with his massive fists. Then she noted the wounds had been tended, cuts stitched closed. Krysty recognized Mildred's style of a battlefield dressing in the bandage on her shoulder. There came a fuzzy memory of the tunnel fight and a confused impression of being carried through the ville by Ryan and J.B. with people cheering. Had she aced Langford, and was the baron now? Or was he still alive and softening her to be his bed partner?

Rising from the soft cushions, Krysty shivered more at the thought than the cold floor, then remembered slashing his throat. No, Langford was dead— no doubt of that.

Goose bumps running along her skin, Krysty stepped off the floor and onto a rug. Ah, better. Across the bedroom was a fireplace with a cheery blaze, a couple of chairs set tandem and a large table covered with what looked like her clothing. As Krysty padded over, a young girl rose from one of the chairs holding a blaster, then gasped and fell to her knees bowing.

"Morning," Krysty said.

The girl raised her face and touched her throat, shaking her head no.

Ah, a mute, as Mildred called them. Most were deaf and dumb, but obviously this one could hear, just not speak. A perfect bed warmer for any baron.

Walking past the kneeling girl, Krysty examined the articles on the table, running fingertips along the patches. There were new buttons, and her boots shone.

"Your work?" she asked.

A head nod, shoulders braced for a strike.

"Excellent work," Krysty said, looking at the inside seams. "Well done...ah, what do I call you, girl?"

Rising timidly, she touched the toe of the cowboy boot.

"Steel?" Krysty asked.

A head shake.

"Silver," she stated, and the girl nodded. "Well done, Silver. Should be the head seamstress for a big ville with talent like this. Predark clothes aren't this well made."

Silver blinked rapidly.

"Baron not much with compliments," Krysty stated. "Even when they were due, eh?"

A shy smile and a vigorous head shake.

"Well, that changes today. New baron, new rules," Krysty announced, stepping into her khaki jumpsuit.

Quickly getting dressed, she was amazed that somebody had even curried her bearskin coat. The thing never looked so good. Lying nearby were her weapons, cleaned and oiled. Along with the baron's matching set of knives and two blasters.

"Where are the others?" Krysty asked, strapping on a gun belt. She checked the load in her blaster and tucked it into her belt. Only a few rounds were left. The baron's weapons she left where they were. Too many was the same as not enough.

Silver bowed again and gestured toward the door.

"Take me to them," she said, giving her first command as a baron.

Silver scurried to unlock the bedroom door. On the other side was a long hallway without furniture or windows. Krysty recognized it as a killzone. Invaders would have no place to ambush the baron, or hide when he shot back.

Proceeding to the far end, Silver gave a coded knock on a heavy door banded with iron. On creaking hinges, the massive portal was pushed aside by frowning sec men, longblasters in their hands, but then both of the guards beamed smiles and saluted.

"Good day, Baron," they chorused.

Not used to such servitude, Krysty merely nodded in passing and started down the wide brick stairs and into a tremendous room with cinder-block walls. It was obviously the throne room. At one end was a dais and a massive chair covered with intricate carvings of mushroom clouds and other symbols of war. Swords and axes decorated the walls. Four chandeliers were suspended from the ceiling, but only one was lit, casting most of the room into shadows, including the chopping block, the neck rest stained dark with old blood.

Crossing the room, her boot heels clicking on the floor, Krysty paused by the dais and noticed the bullet holes, then went to the chair and easily found a knife and a blaster tucked away in hidden folds. Even here, Langford had expected betrayal.

Silver patiently waited for Krysty to decide to continue.

Going to the windows, Krysty threw back the shutters and saw it was night outside. "How long did I sleep?" she asked.

The girl went to a lantern and, touching it, raised just her forefinger.

One lantern burn. About eight hours. It was the same day.

"Good," Krysty said, then her stomach rumbled. "But you better show me that dining hall fast before I start eating the throne."

The girl was startled, then almost allowed a smile to cross her pretty young face as she darted across the room.

Past an iron portcullis, another set of double doors opened into a courtyard of flowering bushes and stone benches. A gravel path circled a marble fountain with a predark bronze statue, and orchids dotted the basin with tiny fish darting about in the clear water. Smoky torches lit the courtyard, and a dozen sec men stood smoking green cigs, talking softly. But at the sight of the two females, they snapped to attention and briskly saluted. Silver stayed in the background, head bowed, hands folded.

"Ready for inspection, my lord," a sergeant stated, holding a salute until it was returned.

"Is the ville secure?" Krysty asked.

"Yes, sir!"

"Then continue as you are for the time being." Krysty turned to go, and the man cleared his throat.

"What?" she snapped irritably. Hunger was growing inside her belly like a fire. It had been days since her last full meal, on top of which summoning the power of Gaia always left her weak and hungry. Her stomach loudly gurgled again, and the sec man flicked his attention to her midriff then back.

"You shouldn't walk alone, my lord," the sec man said. "Which of us do you want as an escort?"

Damn, she was the baron now and had to tolerate such things. Krysty briefly looked over the guards, none of them very impressive.

"I need no escorts inside my own castle," she retorted, touching her blaster and briskly walking away.

The sec men frowned at each other, their confused and angry voices mixing with the splash of the fountain in the private garden.

A side path led to another door of iron and wood. Silver pushed it open with some difficulty, and Krysty entered a long room with a vaulted ceiling. Instantly she was assaulted by the rich smells of roasting beef and fresh bread. Then a wave of weakness washed over Krysty, and she nearly stumbled. The need for food was a knife in her guts by now.

Over by a roaring fireplace, the companions were seated at a massive table looking over maps and cleaning their weapons. The other end was covered with dirty dishes.

Ryan snapped his head up at her approach and smiled widely, the first such expression she had seen in months. It faded quickly, but she went directly to the man and kissed him soundly.

"I'm glad to see you, too, lover," Krysty said, stroking his smoothly shaved cheek. "Now get the fuck out of my chair, I'm the baron."

"My lord," he said, chuckling, and shifted his chair to the side to make room for another.

"Silver, have you eaten yet?" Krysty asked, then she glanced about. The girl was gone, moving as silently as morning mist. Maybe there was more mutie in that mute than she expected.

Judiciously Mildred watched as the woman stiffly took a chair from a line of them along the wall. She had tended Krysty as best she could under the circumstances. The redhead had several sprains, and quite a few bone bruises, painful but not life-threatening. Good news, as without her med kit there was little Mildred actually could do. And the local healer knew nothing of basic hygiene, much less surgery or chemistry. She used a lot of wild herbs, and seemed to have a pathological fear of science. Understandable, considering what science had done to the entire world a hundred years ago.

Krysty sat down heavily at the table, and serving girls appeared from a steamy kitchen to lay down bowls and plates of food. There was a whole loaf of brown bread still radiating warmth from the oven. Plus a tiny dish of honey with a piece of comb. A heaping bowl of steamed kelp, with some sort of chopped nuts on top, a tray of boiled crab, baked fish, a bowl of fresh oysters still in their shell with a curved knife on top for easy opening. There was no glassware, but the wooden mugs were carved with scenes of sailing ships and naked women.

Taking a sailing ship, Krysty poured it full of water and greedily drank.

"How are you feeling?" Mildred asked, going to the woman and lightly probing her here and there.

"Better than Langford," Krysty replied, ignoring the ministrations while she hacked off a piece of the bread and stuffed it whole into her mouth. After a short prayer to Gaia, she swallowed and ripped off a crab leg to crack the shell apart and start picking out the sweet white meat.

"I told them to bring enough for five," Ryan said, pouring her some coconut milk. There was no wine or beer. But he would tell her about that later.

"Smart move," Krysty mumbled, tossing the hollow leg onto an empty platter and starting on another. Crab was a favorite of hers, and they didn't find much of it in the deserts of North America. Doc said it was kin to spiders, but she had eaten those and the two tasted nothing alike.

"Aside from your hunger, you're fine," Mildred announced, returning to her chair. "Just some bruises, abrasions and a minor flesh wound. Although those ribs need to be watched. You start having any trouble breathing, let me know."

Nodding her agreement, Krysty put aside a wooden mug of water and began shoveling the kelp into her mouth. It was surprisingly good.

"How do we stand?" she mumbled, sucking a loose strand off her chin.

"The people worship you and tolerate us," J.B. said, blowing a smoke ring at the ceiling. The seaweed cigar was very similar to tobacco in taste, if not appearance. Four more were tucked into the pocket of his clean shirt.

"Langford major buttwipe," Jak added, cleaning his nails with a knife point.

"From what we can discern, dear lady," Doc rumbled, brushing crumbs off his shirt, "he ruled by sheer intimidation."

"No rewards for loyalty?"

"None," Ryan stated, leaning back in his chair.

"Which explains the party over you chilling the man."

Even over the fireplace, they could hear faint sounds of celebration from the ville. Laughing, singing, even the occasional gunshot.

"To be blunt," Doc added, "unloved would be a polite way of assaying his general social demeanor."

"Got that right," J.B. agreed, stubbing out the butt of the cig on a dirty dish.

Seeing the Armorer without his glasses brought her attention to the pressing matter of ammo. "We have to get those backpacks," she said urgently. "I'm down to five rounds."

"Same here," Mildred agreed.

"Less," Dean admitted, and placed a flintlock on the table. "That's why I have one of these now."

Jak made no comment. Langford had owned a .357 Magnum pistol, and the teenager had taken all of the spare ammo off the dead man. It fit his own blaster just fine. Doc had done the same with the baron's Navy Colt .44, reaping a harvest of primer caps and lead for his Civil War hand cannon.

"Five for the Steyr, one clip for the SIG-Sauer," Ryan said, taking a sliver of wood off a small dish and began picking his teeth. "But even with torches it's too dark. We'll send divers to reclaim our backpacks at first light."

"Under tight guard," she added.

"Bet your ass."

Krysty drew her belt knife to smear honey on another piece of bread. Then she paused, recalling where it had last been, and dipped a finger into the gooey sweet to do the job.

"Also, your sec men aren't too happy to get replaced by us," Ryan said, watching them through the windows as they stood around the fountain outside. A man hatefully glanced their way, caught Ryan's eye and hastily looked away.

"Tough," Krysty said, looking in to the courtyard. The sec men stood straighter and stopped talking. "Probably only afraid you'll take away their privileges in the gaudy house."

"Langford was a human, by the way," Mildred said. "Just really strong and heavily muscled. Not a thing out of the ordinary. I cut him open to check."

"And to make sure he was dead," Ryan added grimly. "But it's a good thing we're not planning on staying here. The ville is a pesthole. Seen cleaner ruins after a shitter exploded."

"Disgusting," Dean added, holding his nose.

"The latrines are far enough away from the wells," Mildred announced. "But not by anybody's plan. Pure chance."

"Lots of slaves, but they're all captured pirates. For some reason, Langford didn't use slave labor."

"Even Hitler liked dogs," Mildred said.

"Damn. I was almost hoping this was the good land we've been searching for." Krysty sighed, pushing away the half-filled plate. "Guess not."

"Aside from the crap in the streets," J.B. said, "the ville is okay. Walls are sturdy, the gate solid. But as a precaution, I've had two of the wall cannons elevated to point down at the beach before the gate. Jak had the idea of loading them with pieces of coral and broken clamshells.''

"Short-range only," Ryan said. "But it'll blow any boarding party onto the last train west, that's for sure."

"Piecemeal," the albino added. "Nobody try twice."

"Expect trouble?" Krysty asked, wiping off her mouth of a cloth napkin. She was the only person at the table with such a luxury.

"Only known way to avoid it," Ryan answered succinctly. "Unfortunately the ville is low on black powder again."

"Low?"

"Damn near out."

"Shit!"

"Now Doc and I checked around," J.B. said, tapping some ashes onto the floor, "and there's everything we need to make more. Give me some ceramic or plastic bowls, and I'll have folks filling barrels with gunpowder in less than a day."

"Like we use?" Dean asked, sounding surprised. He had never seen bullets reloaded except from vacuum-packed tins of silvery powder from a redoubt.

"Our blasters don't use gunpowder," Ryan explained. "I know we call it gunpowder, but it isn't. Stuff is called cordite, a mix of powdered nitroglycerin and guncotton. That's why it's smokeless, and doesn't cause shells to jam."

"Gunpowder is the same thing as black powder,"

J.B. finished. "Just processed differently. And got ten times the power."

"Going to need plastic window screens," Doc said, patting the LeMat at his hip.

J.B. smiled. "Yeah. You would know that."

"If what we heard about the lord baron is true," Krysty said, pushing away her dirty plates, "he'll go ballistic when he learns we've got the secret."

"No choice. When folks hear there's a new baron, somebody is going to try and attack before you're dug in deep. We'll have to move fast, and leave soon as we can," Ryan agreed. "Then the locals can settle who's in charge among themselves. Not our business."

"True enough."

"Hopefully there is something useful in the vault."

"You mean the armory," Krysty corrected.

"Nope. That was full of powder and shot for the sec men, a bunch of crossbows, axes, spare parts from broken weapons, that sort of stuff." He glanced sideways. "But your faithful guards wouldn't let us in without bloodshed, or you."

"Because I'm the baron," Krysty said with a sour expression. Loyalty was one thing; stupidity was another. "Okay, let's see what Langford was hiding from everybody."

"Could be a pile of predark porn," Mildred suggested.

"Or a nuke. Only one way to find out."

Rising from the dining table, the companions headed for the door. Outside, the squad of armed sec men in the courtyard moved quickly out another door, weapons at the ready.

IN THE NOISY gaudy house, the madam was crouched over a basin of warm water, washing herself in preparation for the next sec man who lay naked on the sweaty bed, when she heard a snatch of conversation from departing customers.

"...he said it's gray?"

"Yeah, and supposed to be a lot better than our black powder."

"Gray powder. Ain't no law against making that, is there?"

"Nope!"

Brushing past the nude man, the madam rushed to the doorway, but there was a crowd of sec men waiting in line, and it was impossible to tell who had been talking. Nuking hell!

Going to the railing, she leaned over, receiving a horde of catcalls from the men below over the glorious cleavage on display. She flashed some to make them happy, then closed her robe, cinching the belt tight.

"Sue-Ann!" the madam shouted over the moaning and panting coming from everywhere in the predark library.

"Yeah?" a voice called from behind a marble column. A topless woman stepped into view, her hand still busy.

"I'm going to the dock for a minute," the madam said. "You're in charge till I come back."

Her straggly hair in wild disarray, the slut slowed in her work while staring thoughtfully at the excited older woman.

"Half," she mouthed silently.

Expecting that, the madam nodded agreement and rushed down the stairs and into the muddy streets, heading straight for the front gate of the ville.

Chapter Fourteen

Stepping outside the post office, Krysty looked over Cold Harbor ville while the guards on either side of the door dropped their cigs and snapped to attention.

"Evening, Baron!" one shouted, while the other man clumsily ground his cig under a boot.

The woman walked past the sec men, wrinkling her nose at the thick smells in the night air. The ville was ablaze with crackling torches and fish-oil lanterns. In the flickering yellow light, chickens ran wild along the dirt streets, and a group of mangy dogs tormented a squealing pig wallowing in a mud hole. Swarms of flies buzzed thick around a public latrine, and the houses were ramshackle predark buildings badly fixed with banana leaves and bamboo. Most had no glass in the windows, and only a few possessed doors of any kind.

In the street, a hooting crowd was gathered around two sec men having a slow-motion fistfight, while naked children ran about screaming and a woman openly relieved herself in the weeds along a blacksmith shop. On the corner was the local gaudy house filled with a riot of partially clad people having sex in every possible combination, then a sec man stuck his head out a window and retched into the street, almost drenching some folks hurrying by. Only the dimly seen silhouettes of the guards walking along the top of the brick wall had a semblance of order.

"Mother Gaia," the woman muttered. "It's a drunken pesthole."

"That's 'cause it's not their ville," Ryan said, brushing away some buzzing flies. "The kitchen staff told me that the original builders of the place got aced by a plague. These folks found it empty and moved in."

"That explains a lot," J.B. said, trying not to breathe. "You build something, you take care of it."

Her hair flaring in anger, Krysty turned to the closest sec man. "Where is the vault?"

"Behind the palace," he replied, the words slightly slurred, showing that he had been celebrating while on duty, a capital offense under most barons. "Here, I'll show ya."

"Stay," Ryan ordered loudly to get through his fogged mind. "I know the way."

He shrugged. "Sure…"

Stepping over the defensive sandbags, the companions started along the main street, dodging revelers and pools of ripe offal.

"Whole ville must be drunk in celebration," Krysty said, watching her step. "Great time for us to be attacked."

"I know," Ryan said grimly. "And it's not booze. They don't know how to make it."

"Not know how shine?" Jak demanded, then gave a bitter laugh. "Stupes."

"There we agree, my taciturn friend," Doc rumbled in his deep voice.

"Dark night," J.B. cursed, squinting at the ground so he wouldn't trip. "We'll have to start from scratch to make the juice we need. Be trapped here for weeks."

"So what is it they're drunk on?" Krysty asked. "Jolt?"

"No, some local herb called ralk," Mildred explained dourly. "They chew it or make tea. Gets them high enough, but it's not wolfweed or marijuana. Nothing I've run across before. Some local mutation. Harmless enough."

A sudden movement made her pull a blaster, and then a man staggered from the shadows with his pants around his ankles and holding a panting woman to his chest, her dress unbuttoned to the point where her sagging breasts bounced freely. Arms wrapped around his neck, legs around his waist, she gave little jumps as he steadily hiccuped and fed her sips of some fluid from a striped gourd.

"If taken in small doses," the physician finished, replacing her blaster. An entire ville of people hooked on drugs. She shook her head in disbelief.

Following the sandbag wall, the companions reached a quiet area behind the palace. Nobody was singing or dancing there, and it was obvious why. The area was ringed by a series of short poles with human skulls balanced on top. A row of crosses with skeletons tied to the crossbars gave mute testimony of public executions. There was a series of sharp metal poles, bones scattered below, a skeleton impaled halfway down on the thick shaft, the pole entering between his legs and exiting out his gaping mouth. Nearby was a shallow pit with the ground blackened from flames, a fresh new stake standing in the middle, waiting for the next victim. A complex collection of rusty iron pipes formed a sort of dome, and hung inside the kindergarten jungle gym was a series of tiny iron cages, more dead jammed inside, some still possessing faces, one prisoner's arm extended through the bars clawing for freedom. Fat seagulls roosted on the cages and pecked for tidbits of rotting meat from the decaying corpses.

Nobody spoke as they passed the killing field. It wasn't the first seen, nor would it be the last.

"There's the armory," Ryan said, pointing.

Set in a pool of light between the brick palace and execution ground was a squat brick building, lit by lanterns and guarded by more sec men. These seemed wide awake and studied the people coming toward them intently.

Heading directly for the armory, the companions passed through the execution ground, when a faint cry caught their attention.

"One is still alive," Krysty said softly.

Fumbling in her pocket for the flashlight, Mildred pumped the charging handle several times, then hit the button. Sweeping the area, she saw movement in the cages, and now could see the birds stabbing the man inside a cage with their sharp beaks.

"Chill me..." a hoarse voice pleaded from within the iron bars.

Ryan started for his blaster, then remembered how little ammo he had and pulled his panga instead. Mildred held the light steady as Ryan went to the cage and chased the birds away.

The seagulls cawled their annoyance and took wing while Ryan tried to reach the throat of the man inside, but the spaces between the bars were too small for his big hands. Checking the hinged door, Ryan saw it was closed with a heavy padlock. The prisoner whimpered again plaintively, as Ryan reluctantly drew the SIG-Sauer and took aim, but then paused.

"You," he growled in recognition.

"Please..." the sec man whined, his face a scabby ruin from the hungry birds, a blood-encrusted knife jutting from his belly, wads of cloth and ropes holding it in place.

Without a word, Ryan holstered his piece, turned and walked back to the others while the prisoner pleaded for death.

"Let him rot," he growled, giving back the flashlight. "Move on."

J.B. tilted back his fedora. "That the guy who aced Jones?"

"Yeah."

The group only got a yard before a thundering roar lit up the execution grounds, and there was a terrible cry from the man inside the cage. As the blast faded into the night, there were no more sounds from the prisoner, except for the drip of blood falling onto the ground.

"Misfire," Dean said, holstering the blaster.

Ryan gave his son a hard stare. "No more," he ordered. "We're low enough on ammo as it is."

"My ammo," Dean answered defiantly, then relented. "But you're right. It was a waste."

Waiting a minute, Ryan decided the boy meant it and started walking again. Dean was becoming a man and didn't blindly follow orders anymore. That was good and bad. But they would need a serious talk about this real bastard soon.

A group of sec men charged around the palace, their weapons at the ready. Ryan recognized them as the guards from the palace. He had thought they were being followed, but in all the chaos on the streets, he hadn't been sure.

"We heard a shot," one panted. "What's the problem?"

"You okay, Baron?" another asked, wheezing for breath.

Easing J.B.'s Uzi off her shoulder, Mildred glanced over the sec men in disapproval. Too much good living. They were in terrible shape. If invaders got past the wall cannon, it would be a slaughter.

"We're executing a prisoner," Ryan said shortly. "Why aren't you at your posts?"

"We are," a man explained awkwardly. "We're her bodyguards."

"Said you didn't want any in the palace," another added. "But we're outside now."

"Got us," Jak said.

"Any problem with that?" J.B. asked, jacking the slide on his pump-action S&W M-4000.

Mildred did the same with the Uzi. Without his glasses, J.B. was more of a threat to the companions with the rapidfire than others.

"Course not," the sergeant said, through gritted teeth. "Baron can choose whoever the fuck he…she wants for bodyguards. She won the fight. Wroth is the baron. She wants you, that's all I needs to know."

"Just ain't heard her say it," another added. The others muttered agreement and didn't relax their stance.

"How dare you speak in that manner?" Krysty said, walking closer and slapping the sergeant. She didn't want to, but there was no other way to make the point. "This is my ville, and you will do as you're told!"

"But, ma'am," he answered, rubbing his stinging cheek, "we were only—"

"Silence! These people are my blood kin," she lied. "Obey them as you would me. Understand? Or do I need new sec men?"

"Of course, my lady," a guard said, hastily lowering his blaster. "Our apologies."

Ryan watched the other sec men. The troops were unhappy with the idea and would bear watching. The son of a baron, he knew what to do next in this situation, but did she?

"My lady," he spoke urgently, "a word, please."

"Later," Krysty said. "You there, name!"

Shifting the blaster to his other hand, the man saluted. "Sergeant Armstein, Baron."

"Take your squad and shut the ville down. No more parties. In one candle of time, I want the streets cleared and everybody sent home. Use the gaudy house as your base to coordinate everything. There's a lot to do tomorrow, and I don't want the entire population too exhausted to work."

They were being placed in charge of the gaudy house? Armstein tried to hide his pleasure at the news, while the other sec men openly grinned and nudged each other.

"It will be done, Baron," the sergeant stated. "Anything else?"

"Get moving," Krysty said brusquely. "We're going to do an inventory of the armory. And remember, you have only one candle. Do not fail me, Sergeant."

The familiar words sent a chill down the man's spine, and he gushed loyalty to the woman as he and the squad started off at a brisk run.

"Go straight to the gaudy house, kick everybody else out, then grab a quick one," Mildred said, easing off the bolt on the Uzi. The spring of the tough little blaster had been repaired many times, and there was no sense putting a strain on the metal for no reason. They were safe enough now.

"Which will keep them busy until tomorrow," Krysty said. "If we're going to be here for a while, got to find some to win their loyalty."

"You have it already," Ryan said. "It's only us they want to chill."

"Was going to use sec men to make black powder," J.B. stated, sliding the shotgun over a shoulder. "But mebbe I'll use the slaves instead. Less chance of any trouble."

"From pirates?" Dean asked.

The Armorer grinned. "Under a death sentence anyway. But if they can escape with the formula, be rich enough to buy a ville."

"Or a new ship," Ryan finished. "Yeah, smart. The slaves won't try anything until they know what to do. Then they'll try to escape. Makes sense."

"Trader always used to say that the only person you can really trust is an enemy with a hand in your mag."

"Got that right."

As the companions finally turned and walked away, the circling seagulls eagerly descended in a flock upon the jungle gym and began to continue their interrupted meal.

In the golden illumination of the lanterns, the armory could be seen as a stout brick building, with rusty nails sticking out of the mortar between the bricks like porcupine quills. The door was formed of wooden planks held together with iron bands, and two guards stood outside, holding bolt-action rifles, not flintlocks. Ryan spotted another man on the roof who was trying to stay out of sight. That guard carried a sawed-off shotgun and a brace of revolvers.

The guards snapped to attention as Krysty came forward. One was a lanky man with a goatee, the other short and seemingly made of solid muscle. Both sported a lot of scars, and had the neutral expressions of coldhearts. Exactly the sort any smart baron would use to protect the blasters. Men like these couldn't be bullied or bribed. They were just waiting for trouble to arrive so they could use their fancy blasters.

"Door," she said bluntly.

"Yes, Baron Wroth," the bearded guard said, fumbling at his belt and rushing to unlock the door. Shouldering his blaster, he pushed open the door with a lot of grunting. The other didn't assist, but stepped back to have a clear field of fire. Finally the first guard moved it aside enough for the companions to enter.

"Here, Baron," he said, reaching into a box on the ground and extracting a lantern. He lit it with a glowing piece of bamboo from the flame of his own lantern and gave it to her. "You'll need this. No windows inside, or lanterns, either."

"Smart. Thank you," Krysty said, accepting the light and going inside.

The others followed, with Ryan going in last. Halfway through the door, he paused and turned at the waist.

"What was that again?" he demanded hotly.

"I said fuck you, outlander," the sec man with the Remington snarled. "Can't stand you hangers-on. She's the baron, and you're just some leech sucking on her ass. Baron gives the word, and you're all in a cage."

"Should chill ya right here," the short man snarled, swinging his big-bore weapon around.

"Go for it," Ryan muttered, dropping into a gunfighter's crouch, his hand inches away from the SIG-Sauer.

"Not with her inside," the sec man growled, lowering his blaster. "I miss you and a ricochet might set the whole place off."

"Later," the goateed man promised, shaking his longblaster.

"Any time," the Deathlands warrior replied and walked backward into the building, never taking his eye off them. Once inside, Ryan rammed the interior bolts home.

"From now on," he said, "we travel in pairs. Nobody goes anywhere alone. The locals are itching to replace us as the baron's bodyguards."

"Definitely using the slaves," J.B. said, craning his neck to see around the dark room.

Lit only by the one lantern, the armory was masked in heavy shadows, but they could still see that the walls were made of a different color brick than those outside, so there was probably two layers of brick, maybe three. It would be extremely difficult for anybody trying to break in. And the floor was composed of slabs of sidewalk concrete. Ryan thumped a boot heel down hard and heard only a muffled thump of solid rock.

"Whoever built the bunker knew what they were doing," he said. "The original builders must have disassembled a city to make this place."

"I'll bet they had plans to do the streets, too, before they died," Krysty added, checking out the ceiling.

More sidewalk slabs, and there was no sound of the sec man walking on the roof.

"Makes sense."

To the left side were racks of longblasters lining the brown brick wall; to the right was a quadruple row of hand flintlocks. Barrels of black powder were stacked on bricks to keep them away from any water in case of heavy rain, and buckets of white sand hung from brass hooks attached to the brick column supporting the ceiling, crude protection against a fire.

In the middle of the room was a ship's cannon, set in a wall of sandbags, a fuse sticking out of the glory hole, the big muzzle pointing straight for the front door.

"In case of attack," J.B. said, reaching up to adjust his glasses, then angrily lowering his hand. "Triple stupe. The concussion would deafen, if not kill, everybody in the room."

"Unless there is another way out of here," Ryan said thoughtfully. Now he moved among the barrels, rapping them with a gun butt and listening for echoes.

Along the back wall was another door, and several long tables. One held a small brazier, bullet molds and a lot of miscellaneous lead, some misshapen lumps streaked with brown.

"They dug the bullets out of the dead to reclaim the lead," Mildred muttered, lifting a lump for inspection. "Grisly, but efficient."

"War is a nightmare," Doc remarked, pocketing a nice bullet mold. "And we are but the dreamers."

The other table was covered with pieces of flint and

cigar boxes. Krysty lifted a lid and found steel chisels nestled on a bed of fragrant leaves. Curious. She lifted a piece to briefly inspect it, then felt the oil on her fingertips. Ah, it was to ward off rust. Not total fools, then.

"All crap," Jak snorted, moving from table to table, glancing briefly at the collection of crude blasters before moving on. There was nothing here of any use that he could see. "Where vault?"

The back door was heavy wood bolted in a zigzag pattern to more wood, but it proved to be unlocked. The next room was a lot smaller, containing small barrels of assorted pieces of blasters for repairs, coils of cannon fuse and more buckets of sand. There was also a third door, but this was made of burnished metal, its seamless expanse unmarred. There was a combination dial and a swing lever. The hinges, if any, weren't readily located.

"Stolen from a bank, I'd wager," Mildred said, amused by the concept of somebody raiding a bank to take the doors and leave the money behind. Dollar bills were useless these days. They didn't burn hot enough to help start a campfire, and were way too rough to use in the latrine.

"Where is the black powder and shot for the wall cannons?" Krysty asked, hands on her hips. "Don't tell me the ville is completely unarmed."

"There are four more places like this spaced along the outer wall," Ryan explained, pounding on the walls. "Shot is too heavy to move fast. You have to keep it close to the cannons."

"What do you think, John?" Mildred asked, rapping the steel door with a knuckle.

"Give it a try," J.B. said hesitantly, and started running his hands over the door. No warm spots. Then he swept it with his compass. The needle never wavered. No mag fields. Even better. The rest of his tools were in his backpack, rusting at the bottom of the harbor. Saltwater would ruin his collection of munitions, and he had no idea what it would do to his prized timing pencils. The C-4 should be okay, but everything else was most likely dissolving while they waited for daylight.

Placing his ear to the cool metal, J.B. held his breath as he slowly turned the dial listening for any clicks. Having seen this before, the companions stayed still and made as little noise as possible. Sometimes the doors opened easily, but that was only because of something on the other side that wanted out.

"Couldn't try this last time," Ryan whispered to Krysty. "Guards wouldn't leave us alone."

"The original ten-second tour," Doc added softly. "Then a most improprietous bum's rush."

Smiling in satisfaction, J.B. leaned away from the bank door and worked the lever. There was a ratcheting sound of moving gears, then the heavy thud of a big lock disengaging.

"Anything you can't open?" Dean asked.

"Not yet," he answered, sliding the shotgun off his shoulder and snicking off the safety. "Wanna take cover in the next room?"

"Here is good. Open it," Ryan said forcibly.

Keeping the scattergun in his grip, J.B. tried pulling the door open, then pushing, but it refused to budge. Chewing a lip, the wiry man attempted to shove it sideways, and the massive portal slid easily on greased tracks out of sight into the wall. Beyond was dark tunnel that angled into the ground. The floor was metal grating, the smooth concrete sides rising to curve overhead.

"Blasted sewer pipe," Doc rumbled.

"Heads straight for the palace," Krysty said, sniffing the air. There was no smell of sewage. "Vault, my ass. It's the baron's secret entrance to the armory."

"Could be," Ryan agreed, inspecting the walls and ceiling with the lantern. In the tight confines of the tunnel, the meager light was magnified to a much brighter level. "Single file, one-yard spread. I'm on point, Jak cover the rear."

As the companions entered the tunnel, Jak rolled over the barrel of spare blaster parts and placed it directly in front of the bank door, hopefully forcing it to stay open. Checking the load on his blaster, the teenager then followed the rest into the predark sewer.

Walking along, their steps rapping on the grating, making stealth impossible. The air was stale and slightly cold. Side openings for feeder pipes had been cemented shut, water trickling through tiny cracks and going down under the flooring. Every ten yards or so, there were stacked bricks bracing the arched ceiling, moss edging the brick as it followed the path of the descending moisture.

"Must be under a stream," Dean suggested.

"Or the fountain," Mildred countered.

A gentle curve in the tunnel exposed stairs going up, and Ryan automatically stopped. The place was perfect for a booby trap. He looked hard at the darkness and there was something different; the moss lining the bricks here was a lighter shade than the rest. Testing it with a finger, he found it was dry and long dead. Easing the panga from its sheath, he gingerly pried away a piece and exposed a narrow slit.

"Trap," he said softly.

Immediately, Mildred clicked her flashlight and the passageway was brightly illuminated by white light. Now they could see a piece of thin yellow twine stretched across the passageway, the color of the string almost identical to the illumination coming from the smelly fish-oil lanterns.

"Used their own lanterns to hide the twine," Ryan said, running his hands along the taut length. "Damn, it's attached to the pin of a gren. Yellow striped, Willy Pete."

White phosphorous? "Leave it be," J.B. suggested, jerking his head back down the tunnel. "In case of company."

"Good idea," Ryan said, standing and sheathing his blade. "Mildred, keep the light on it. Everybody stay sharp going over."

Carefully the companions stepped over the trigger mechanism while Ryan checked ahead for more traps. But that was the only one found. Hopefully the only one there was.

Proceeding up the cinder-block stairs at a crawl, he reached the top and another banded door. Langford hadn't missed a trick. Checking it for traps, Ryan then slid his knife into the jamb and depressed the spring bolt. A push, and the door swung open easily.

Beyond was a large room, bookshelves full of volumes lining the walls, and large steamer trucks arranged in neat rows along the carpeted floor. The glass flue of a lantern hanging from the ceiling reflected the light of their own lantern, throwing distorted shadows everywhere.

"Bastard maze," the Deathlands warrior growled, stepping into the library. The shag carpet crunched with age at every step, making more unwanted noise.

"Books! I'll start the lantern," Mildred said, lifting it off the hook. Cradling the lantern, she raised the flue and lit it with her butane lighter. The stubby wick ignited with a clear blue flame, and bright white light flooded the room.

"That's alcohol!" J.B. gasped, grabbing the lantern away. Quickly he yanked up the flue and turned down the wick until it died.

"Must be a quart," Ryan said. "Excellent. That's about half of what we need for the generator. See if there are any more around."

The companions spread out in a standard search pattern while Mildred hung the fish-oil lantern from the ceiling hook.

"Two more," Dean reported from a corner, lifting them into view. "But both are empty."

"Got another door," J.B. called, studying the latch, but Krysty moved past the man.

"Don't bother," she said, reaching past him and turning the knob. The door swung aside, revealing a large room with brick walls and heavy wooden furniture. A table covered with extra clothing and some blasters stood before a glowing fireplace.

"Baron's bedroom," Krysty said, checking the other side of the door. As expected, it was carved and painted to resemble brick. More of his work, or another gift from the original builders?

"Now we know how he got in and out," she said, easing the door shut.

"Let's see what's in the trunks," Ryan suggested, and the companions started tearing through the huge collection.

Breaking open the lock, Jak lifted the lid to find a nude centerfold of a woman on the inside of the lid, the photo slightly reddish from a layer of varnish. The trunk was packed with gold and silver jewelry.

"Junk," the teenager declared.

"Mebbe," J.B. said, and started tossing away the antiques. Soon they reached the bottom of a drawer. Lifting it out, both men gasped as they uncovered a rack of automatic rifles gleaming with oil. Stacks of clips covering the bottom of the trunk.

"M-16s!" Dean cried in delight, snatching one of the military rapidfires.

"Kept all the good stuff for himself," Ryan noted, lifting another autoblaster from the nest. He worked the bolt and checked the action. The rapidfire was worn, but with no sign of carbolic-acid corrosion from putting it away dirty.

Dropping the magazine, the man thumbed out a cartridge. Using the edge of his panga, he pried loose the lead ball at the front of the brass and cast it aside. Sheathing the blade, he then poured the contents of the cartridge into the palm of his hand.

"Black powder," he cursed in annoyance. "This would jam after only a few rounds. Even if the powder had enough kick to operate the blowback bolt."

"That explains these," Mildred said, lifting a wooden object into view. Deftly she slid the thing onto the arming bolt of the M-16. It fit perfectly.

"They made the autofire into a bolt action," Ryan said, studying the contraption. "Set the selector to single shot and just work the bolt every time you want to fire. Slow as hell, but better than a jam every few rounds."

"This one is full of clothes," Krysty said, frowning at the contents of another trunk as she lifted out some Navy uniforms. But then added, "And boots!"

"My size?" Jak asked hopefully. His right boot had a small hole in it getting bigger all the time, and the leather patch wasn't keeping out the water anymore.

She checked the soles for size and passed a pair to the teenager. "These should fit."

Grinning happily, he yanked off his old boots and tried the new pair. "Just fine," he declared. "Any socks?"

"Nope."

"Damn."

"I'll take some laces," Dean said, glancing at the tangle of repaired knots keeping his boots closed.

Krysty tossed him a pair, and he started eagerly undoing the stiff military string. It was the same stuff as on the booby trap, he noted and mentally filed the trick away for his own use in the future.

"How sad," Doc said, returning a book to the wall shelves. Every volume in the room was destroyed with age, and fat from being waterlogged, the pages expanded to the point the ink was bleached clean and completely unreadable. Even the leather bindings were cracked and crumbling.

"No Caesar, but time burned this library of Alexandria," the scholar said sadly. *"Tempus morta ergo sum est."*

"You have the syntax of a high-school student," Mildred retorted, looking over the collection. She scowled as she began to browse through the titles. Several books were private printings of experimental research, chemistry, gene splicing, DNA alterations and a lot of coded books with Pentagon and top secret markings.

"There was a biowep research lab on this island," she commented. "Or rather, wherever these books came from."

"We saw the spider," Ryan said, lifting a lump of oily canvas from a trunk full of cables, electronics and circuit boards. They looked like the guts of a computer. Why anybody had saved the stuff he had no idea. Closing the lid, he laid the bundle on top and cut away the stiff string. The unwrapped oily canvas exposed a large blue-steel revolver.

"Webley .44," he announced, hefting the blaster and breaking the top-loader in two to check the cylinder. There were four rounds inside and two empty shells.

"Even with black powder, this should work fine," Ryan stated, closing the huge British hand cannon. "Good blaster."

"I'll take it," Krysty said, and tucked the cannon into her belt. The S&W was nearly empty and she needed a backup piece badly. The Webley slipped down a bit, and she had to tighten the belt to keep it in place. Now she knew why the sailors wore such wide belts. They used them as holsters.

Going to the largest trunk, off in its own corner, J.B. tricked the lock with a knife blade and forced open the lid.

"Jackpot," he announced happily. Nestled in plastic foam were rows of military grens. Underneath was another layer, and another, going straight to the bottom of the trunk. "Six layers of twenty grens. Dark night! We could hold off an army with these."

"If still live," Jak warned.

With practiced ease, Ryan opened one and checked inside. "Dead," he cursed, pouring out some white residue. "The plas has dried into dust."

"If the primers are still good, we could stuff these with black powder," J.B. suggested. "Not very powerful, but better than nothing."

"That work?"

"Sure. Did it before."

Going to the last trunk, Ryan discovered it had no lock or keyhole. There *was* no keyhole. It had to be one of the Chinese puzzle boxes. Probing carefully, he ran fingers along the seams and found a loose piece of wood that slide aside. As it moved, he jerked back fast as steel needles stabbed out from the trunk, then back in again almost faster than he could see.

"Son of a bitch," he growled, and stabbing with his knife, tore the lid of the trunk apart, exposing the clockwork mechanism.

"Spring driven," Ryan announced, snapping off the needles with his gun butt. The steel was smeared with a green substance that he knew to be deadly. Whatever was inside, Langford had prized very highly, more than blasters or grens. Those trunks had simply been locked, not armed.

While the companions took cover, Ryan stepped away from the trunk and carefully lifted the lid with the tip of the Steyr. The broken cover flipped up and flopped over the back. Nothing happened.

"What the hell," he muttered, glancing inside. A pad of foam cushion covered the contents, but lying prominently in sight was a tiny dead frog, yellow in color, no bigger than his thumb.

Ryan tossed it aside and started to look under the foam, when Mildred screamed as she saw the frog hit the floor.

"Sweet Jesus!" she cried, rushed forward to grab Ryan by the wrist. Slamming his arm to the floor, she drew a blade and raised her hand high.

"Is your hand numb?" Mildred demanded. "Answer me, man, seconds count. Is your hand numb?"

"No," he stated angrily. "What were you going to do, slice off my hand?"

"To save your life, yes, but it wasn't necessary." The physician sighed and dropped the knife. "It was too old, just like the grens. Much too old. You are a very lucky man."

"You saved him from a dead frog?" J.B. asked.

"Madam, really," Doc rumbled askance.

Warily Dean went over and stared at the tiny corpse. "Chilled from touching a frog?" the boy demanded skeptically. "Don't see no quills or teeth."

"Poison skin?" Jak asked.

She nodded. "It's called the Golden Arrow Frog. Some of the Amazon natives coat their arrows with the oil on its skin to kill enemies. But they couldn't eat the creature afterward the poison was so strong. The frog naturally makes a powerful neurotoxin that kills seconds after contact."

"Liquid nerve gas," Ryan said thoughtfully, rubbing his wrist. "Good guard. Frogs can live a long time without food or fresh air. Hell, if you're right, even a dead one would kill for months."

"Year," Mildred corrected. "When one of the explorers touched the frog, his hand went numb, then his arm, and seconds later he toppled over dead. Only way to save him was prompt amputation."

"And here is what it was protecting," Krysty said, raising a glass bottle into view from the truck. Its silvery label was faded with age, and the writing wasn't in English, but they all knew what it was.

"Vodka," Ryan said.

"Plus some whiskey, rum, gin and a whole bunch of wine," Krysty recited, going through the bottles. "A lot of these are empty, mostly the whiskey and rum. But we got plenty of vodka. Guess Langford didn't like it."

"Awful stuff," Jak agreed. "Got no taste."

"But it's our ticket home," J.B. added. "That will burn in a motor just fine."

Dean scowled. "Mix gasoline and booze as fuel?"

"Not in a regular engine. But a turbine will burn anything. How many bottles?"

"Six."

"More than enough," Ryan said, pleased. "We have the fishing trawlers, and now the fuel we need. Just have to get our backpacks and we're gone."

"Let's move these trunks into the bedroom," Krysty suggested, grabbing a handle and dragging one across the crunchy carpet. "Don't want anybody to find this bolt-hole. We may need it."

"Safer for us, too," J.B. added, taking the other end. "Not going to night-creep us in your room."

"Hopefully," Mildred grunted, taking a hold of the trunk full of blasters. "But I can't wait to leave these islands."

IN THE NEXT ROOM, Silver jerked her head away from the spy hole in the wall as the doorknob began to turn. Darting into the hallway, she closed that heavier door and began to listen again at the keyhole. They were discussing their plans in detail now. Taking a small golden frog from her pocket, she bit off the head and sucked out the guts, feeling the deadly toxins tingling down her throat. Then she ate the rest, licking her hands clean with a forked tongue.

This was perfect. When her people had spread the white cough among the previous norms of the ville, it chilled them fast enough, but then new norms arrived in the big ship *Constellation* with its many cannons, and her tribe dared not attack.

Ah, but now the new baron was going to sneak away from the ville, taking most of the good blasters with her. The moment the outlanders were gone, her people could attack, and finally cleanse their home of these invaders. But by tomorrow night, maybe sooner, the island would be theirs once more. Nothing would stop them this time. Praise be the maker.

Chapter Fifteen

The companions spent the night in the baron's bedroom, sharing the huge bed in shifts, the door blocked with the heaviest trunk, a roaring fire in the fireplace to forestall any unwanted intrusions.

In the morning, they stayed alert at the dining table, while pretty young girls in oddly low-cut clothing served the men and Mildred breakfast, and older women more sensibly dressed for kitchen work served Krysty.

Not born a fool, Ryan could see what was happening and offered Krysty a slice of pineapple from his plate. But when the redhead reached for it, a serving girl darted forward and knocked the plate to the floor.

"Please forgive me, sir," the girl gushed, almost spilling from her clothing as she bent over to clean the mess.

"The comfort of my kin is very important to me," Krysty said sternly to the busty server. "So I will be tasting everything brought to the table before they eat. Is that clearly understood?"

"But I...as you command, Baron," the girl muttered, and promptly raced into the kitchen. The older women came back in a few moments with different food.

"We could smell it had gone sour," the matron explained, trying to hide a scowl as she filled their wooden mugs with coconut milk.

Ryan took her wrinkled arm and held it firmly in his grip. She gasped, and he offered the mug. "Taste it and make sure," he ordered.

The matron nodded eagerly and drank, spilling some down her clothing. "See? Nice and fresh, sir." She managed to smile, tears in her eyes. "Very good. Just harvested."

"Go," Ryan commanded, releasing his grip.

She stumbled back a step, then darted into the kitchen, cradling the arm as if it were broken.

"What is wrong with these people?" Mildred muttered, releasing the grip on her blaster.

"Poison the latrine seat next," Jak growled, sniffing a slice of grilled breadfruit before chancing a bite.

"Act normal, eat fast," Ryan said, cutting up a smoked fish to look for hidden needles. It was clean. "We're leaving on the noon tide. With or without the backpacks."

Squinting at the warrior, J.B. started to speak, then closed his mouth with a snap. Yeah, made sense. What good were glasses if he was riding the last train west?

"That is," Krysty added softly, feeling watched from every direction, "if they let me leave."

WATER SPLASHING around his neck, Dean reached over the gunwale of the dugout canoe and handed his father the ebony stick.

"That's almost everything," Ryan said, opening the stick and checking the blade within. The steel shone as if freshly polished, its day underwater causing no noticeable damage. There was just the med kit and J.B.'s munitions bag remaining.

Ryan had originally planned on using the local oyster divers for this job, but after the incident at breakfast, he wasn't letting anybody near their blasters and grens.

"How are you feeling?" he asked, rocking to the motion of the waves.

"Fine," the boy replied, kicking steadily. "This is easy." Dean was stripped down to his shorts and a pair of woven sandals, around his waist a canvas ammo belt with the pouches full of rocks. Just enough to balance the natural buoyancy of the human body so he only had to expend strength swimming, and not endlessly fight to stay submerged.

"Any sign of the med kit?" Ryan asked, holding out a canteen and pouring some of the warm coconut milk into the boy's mouth.

Swallowing gratefully, Dean waved, sending a spray of water in the direction. "Sure! Ten feet over that way."

"Hang on and rest for a minute," Ryan said, going to the bow of the canoe. Lifting a large rock, he brought it to his chest and heaved toward the location indicated. It hit with a mighty splash and disappeared, the attached rope snaking along the bottom of the canoe then yanking a fishnet full of inflated pig bladders over the side and down into the water. Using the bladders for air, the boy didn't have to waste time swimming to the surface every couple of minutes and could stay down for long periods of time, ten, fifteen minutes at a stretch. It was how they had gotten so much done so quickly.

The rest of the companions were equally busy. Doc and Jak were staying close to Krysty for protection while the sec men loaded the trawler for her official tour of the island. Mildred and J.B. were with the slaves making black powder, because they said it would be done today. Everything had to appear perfectly ordinary. But once the two came back, the companions would all meet at the trawler and get out of there. There was no way the sec men could stop them once they had sufficient firepower. The trunk holding the rapidfires and grens was already on board.

"That lard working?" Ryan asked, glancing at the sec men and civilians watching them from the beach.

"Nice and warm," Dean replied, the water sliding off his greased face. "But the damn fish keep nibbling on me."

"Bite them back." Ryan smiled.

"Watch me!" Dean laughed, and taking a deep breath, the boy plunged into the harbor. The saltwater stung his eyes for only a moment before they became adjusted again.

At a steady pace, Dean swam all the way down to only a few yards above the crumbling wrecks that covered the harbor bottom, then he started sideways, searching for the skeleton in the crow's nest. It was the most easily spotted object underwater, and served as his anchor for finding things.

Shafts of sunlight sparkled through the clear water, making the recce a relatively easy job. It was only inside the sunken ships that the shadows were thick, the broken hulls still protecting their cargo from thieves and raiders. After a few minutes, Dean was forced to exhale and take a careful sip from the inflated pig's bladder tied to his belt. The clip on his nose was uncomfortable, but his father had been right. There was a natural urge to inhale through your nose, which would easily chill him.

Finding the fishing net of additional pig bladders, Dean replaced his used one for a fresh. Then he glanced about for the crow's nest, and headed that way with a short bamboo spear at the ready. He felt vulnerable without a blaster, but tried not to let it bother him too much.

Then something moved into his field of vision and the young Cawdor turned about fast, jabbing with the spear. But it was only his hair, animated by the currents of the sea. He chuckled and a sip of ocean got into his mouth, momentarily blocking his throat. Exhaling hard to clear the air passage, Dean drained a fresh bladder, making it go flat. Exhaling again, he took a smaller breath from another bladder and felt his heart slow down. Death was everywhere in the depths. Even laughter killed. It was a sobering thought.

A school of brightly colored fish swam past him, and Dean froze, waiting for them to pass. They were only little things, but he knew there was usually something big chasing the smaller animals. He was correct. Only yards behind the school came a black lightning bolt wiggling through the sea—an electric eel, its pointed snout packed full on sharp teeth. As he watched, it snagged a fish and swallowed it whole. The rest of the school darted off at fantastic speed, the eel staying close behind catching another, and another.

His lungs were nearly bursting before the hunting party had moved onward, and he drank deeply from the shrinking supply of bladders. Mildred said he could only dive for an hour before risking damage. The boy was already way past that mark, so he hurried to finish the job.

The med kit was lying in plain sight on a bed of pristine white sand, a small red crab poking at it with claws. Dean chased the crustacean away. The packs were much too bulky to drag to the surface with any ease, so he simply tied on the rope, released the bladder and his father would paddle over to the bouncing buoy and haul them into the canoe.

A dark shape moved on the surface, and the med kit ascended. All right, only a single bag to go, the most important one, J.B.'s explosives.

Studying the undersea vista, Dean tried to reconstruct their hasty swim from the sinking skiffs in his mind. Now, if the lifeboat with Jones sank over there, and he had found his own backpack there, then the last bag should be somewhere near the coral breakers. The tide was going out when they arrived, and a lot of the smaller items had been swept out to sea by the strong currents. Thankfully the breakers removed any possibility of a riptide capturing the boy and hauling him miles away before releasing his drowned corpse. Otherwise, he never would have risked this dive without more equipment, as crude as it was.

Charging his lungs again, Dean headed for coral and swam along the irregular side of the submerged wall. Finally he spied the canvas bag hanging from the spar of a sunken ship lying smack in the middle of the pass. The ship was cracked in two, its broken hull draped over both sides of the reef.

Swimming close, Dean grabbed the spar to slow his passage and heard it break apart, then saw the bag plummeting into a hole in the deck, disappearing inside the vessel. Releasing the rotten piece of wood, Dean went lower and lower until locating the bag of munitions. Most of the bottom of the ship was gone, ripped away by the coral. Through the gaping chasm of the hull, the bag had fallen onto a ledge of pink coral, the straps waving in the currents.

Making a decision, Dean exhaled early and filled his lungs to the maximum, emptying a bladder. Then casting away the excess drag of the bamboo spear, he swam using both hands, going straight into the belly of the sunken vessel.

Trying not to touch anything, Dean maneuvered around the dim recess of the craft. The pink coral showed through the hull, rising from the shattered planks in spurs and sharp peaks, but the coarse material reflected the dim light from above, giving him just barely enough illumination to traverse the razor-sharp obstacles.

However, the water had distorted his estimation of the depth, and his lungs were aching by the time be reached the bag and grabbed it off the ledge. Success! Draping it over a shoulder, he realized how heavy it was when he started to sink. Quickly drawing his knife, he sawed at the leather belt of rocks around his waist to lighten the load. Busy at the task, he didn't notice when he drifted to the stairs and collided with the railing.

Small as the contact was, the entire ship groaned loudly and began to break apart. The deck rose as the ceiling fell. Planks splintered, silt clouding the water, and the mast slowly smashed through the hatch like a falling tree. He dodged clumsily, but blackness engulfed him and something painfully glanced off his shoulder, then the bag was jerked away, dragging him along.

Savagely Dean hacked at the darkness, and the munitions bag came free. As the awesome weight of the rotten hull drove the bow into the sand, the wreckage began to pile upward. Frantically swimming for the stairs, Dean dodged a thrust from the shattering railing, went under a rushing bulkhead and darted into the cargo hold.

The destruction slowed slightly as the aft section of the keel stubbornly resisted, and Dean took the opportunity to get his bearings. Floating between decks, he saw there were still tiny pinpoints of light streaming in from above, which meant he was in the shallows of the harbor. But he had to get out fast, and without touching anything. Next time he might not be so fortunate.

Lungs aching, Dean went to take another breath from the pig bladder and found it flopping loosely, ripped apart by some slashing piece of wreckage. Instantly his heart began to pound, and Dean remembered his father telling him a person used more air when he was scared. Stay calm, stretch every breath. Seconds counted now.

Krysty had told him to always follow the air bubbles, but that was bad advice for this situation. Escape meant going sideways. Rolling on his side, the tiny bubbles trickling along his left cheek, the boy now saw the ship correctly in his mind and headed for the starboard gun ports. A direct access to the outside. If they were in the same place as on the *Constellation,* everything was fine. If not… Dean banished from his thoughts what would be the result if he was wrong.

Swimming quickly, he ignored the moans of the ship, the snaps of its ribs and buckling beams, concentrating on watching the light and the bubbles, his only compass to freedom.

A hatch led up, or was it down? He didn't know. Confusion filled his mind, then he saw the rising bubbles and moved toward what looked to be deeper into the ship but had to be the way to the upper deck. So bastard easy to get lost underwater. He couldn't let that happen again. But it was getting hard to think clearly. He desperately needed to breathe, his heart pounding hard, lungs aching for the tiniest sip of air.

Closing both eyes, he let the currents haul him upward, always following the course of the bubbles that trickled from his nose. He willed himself to think of good times, to stay calm. He recalled watching vids in a redoubt and his first taste of popcorn, the memory of his mother and the first time he met his dad. That day they spent fishing on the Hudson and didn't get a bite. No muties, no fighting, a peaceful day, almost boring then, but now it seemed like heaven.

His lungs began to burn, and Dean clamped his mouth shut as he went by a hatch, then hastily paddled back and went through. Yes! Cannons and broken barrels were scattered about, rope snaking through the darkness as if alive, and a row of open hatches forming a vertical line of sunlight.

Kicking away, he felt the sandal hit the hatch and there came the terrible sound of splintering wood once more. As fast as possible, he headed for the middle hatch and saw the hull of the ship descending from his left, the opening going by to be crushed flat on the sand to his right at a frightening speed. Summoning his last ounce of strength, Dean charged and darted through the last opening, the jamb slamming into his legs, a heel catching for a second, then he was out!

Clamping a hand over his mouth, Dean moved away from the disintegrating vessel, then headed for the surface. It was just a matter of time now. Only thirty feet to go. But his movements were feeble, his meager resources of stamina gone in his flight from the craft. Worse, the noon tide seemed to be pushing him sideways, and he was much too weak to fight the current. Dean banished a rush of fear from his mind, and concentrated on a summer day years ago when it rained hard in Nevada, but not acid rain, and the air smelled so good afterward, the plants blooming like nothing he had never seen. And that time Doc found a vacuum-sealed can of chocolate powder in a redoubt, and Mildred made a devil's food cake. It was like bread, but so dark and sweet. The taste filled his mouth.

But the searing ache in his lungs was becoming agony. His vision was cloudy, and he exhaled an explosion of bubbles to ease the pain for a split second, before the urge seized him to now inhale. His own body was turning against him now, demanding that he breathe, even though it meant death. But anything was better than this terrible suffocation. No! He wouldn't do it!

Sound violently returned as his head cleared the surface and Dean greedily drank in the fresh air. Better than chocolate cake! As the pain in his chest subsided, the boy felt strength slowly return to his feeble limbs. It was then he realized that the heavy munitions bag was still draped over his shoulder, and he cut loose a laugh. Damn near drowned, and it never once occurred to drop the bag. Maybe his father was correct, and he was part mule.

"Dean, don't move!" his father shouted from somewhere far away.

As the fog lifted from his vision, Dean saw the man standing in the dugout canoe pointing the Steyr directly at him. What was going on? There seemed to be water in his ears, everything was muffled and faint. Waving back, he started that way and felt something large brush by him, raking his side as if with sand-paper. Dean cried out in pain and saw the big dorsal fin of a shark cut the surface only yards away. Hot pipe! When that ship dropped, it cleared the pass, letting the man-eater into the harbor at last.

IN THE DUGOUT, Ryan saw the shark brush past his son on an inspection pass and reacted instantly. Draw-ing the panga, Ryan slashed his palm and thrust it into the ocean, splashing the water. Doc knew fish and had said a shark could smell fresh blood from a mile away.

"Come on," he growled, flexing his hand to make it bleed more. "Over here!"

In response, the shark abruptly shifted direction and charged straight for the canoe. Dropping the knife, Ryan grabbed Doc's stick and pulled out the full yard of Toledo steel. He'd get only one chance at this. When it found no food, the shark would go right back after Dean. Dripping blood into the water, Ryan braced himself for the strike. Just a little bit closer.

He yanked out his hand as the jaws of the great white reached for the food, its huge body slamming into the canoe, nearly spilling the man. Shouting a curse, Ryan slashed down with all of his might, and blood exploded from the water as he completely re-moved the dorsal fin of the beast.

Surfacing in mindless rage, the great white snapped

insanely in an automatic response to pain, then it tried to turn and attack, but rotated helplessly around and around. Without the stiff dorsal to rudder its swim, the deadly killer was completely out of control. Spiraling away, the shark bucked and thrashed, thin blood pumped from the wound into the clear harbor waters. Turning end over end, beating its tail wildly, the great white wove a random path through the water, its motions gradually slowing until it stopped moving and limply rose to the surface, turning over to expose its pale belly to the bright sunlight.

Panting for breath, Ryan pumped a couple of rounds into its guts with the SIG-Sauer just to be sure. From the shore, the locals cheered, then stopped and ran pell-mell toward the ville gate, dropping their belongings along the beach.

"Hey," Dean wheezed, appearing over the gunwale.

Lowering the sword, Ryan helped the boy on board, then removed his jacket to drape over his greasy shoulders.

"Are you hurt?" the one-eyed man asked, checking his son for any wounds.

Dean simply shook his head, too tired to speak, and with a trembling hand he held out the munitions bag.

"A-anything else to get?" he croaked in a hoarse whisper.

Taking the soaked bag, Ryan felt a sudden rush of pride for his son. "No, we're leaving now."

A wan smile. "Okay by me."

Placing the munitions bag in the stern alongside the

med kit, bedrolls, backpacks and wire-rimmed glasses, Ryan went to the middle of the canoe, took the single oar and started paddling toward the trawler.

They had only traveled a short distance when he heard a dull metallic clanging and recognized it as the ville warning bell. That was when he noticed the people were gone from the beach, the gate closed. Glancing quickly about, Ryan saw the other companions standing on the deck of the fishing trawler, then glanced at the waterfall flowing into the lagoon that in turn fed the harbor. The dock was empty, no smoke visible from a fire. Everything seemed fine. Even the sky was clear.

Then from around the point of the island, a squat boat came steaming into view, its deck covered with men and weapons.

"Fireblast," he cursed, and started stroking faster. "We're not going to make it, son."

"Pirates?" Dean asked weakly, looking around.

"Worse," his father replied, as another PT boat cleared the point, closely followed by several more. "It's the lord baron, and he brought the whole bastard fleet."

Chapter Sixteen

Out beyond the breakers, the PT boats came steadily around the sandy point and toward the island harbor, thick smoke pouring from their aft funnels, forming a black cloud that lay over the ocean like a death shroud.

"Nine...ten," Dean counted grimly, forcing himself to sit upright. "Hot pipe, that's a lot."

"Too many," Ryan agreed, paddling fast. Out in the open, they were easy pickings. They had to reach shore, or they didn't have a chance. Looking straight ahead at the fishing trawler, Ryan saw Krysty and the others standing still, watching and waiting. There was nothing else they could do for the moment. Then the alarm gong from the ville abruptly stopped, and he realized it was so the incoming boats wouldn't hear.

Glancing over a shoulder, Ryan saw the Peteys spreading out from a tight formation, some slowing, others heading for the pass in the breakers, the water churning behind them from the spinning props. Damn things might be steam-powered, but they had real speed and were armed to the teeth. He had seen PT boats many times before, mostly just wrecks on the garage level of waterfront redoubts, but these were in

fighting trim. The hulls were shiny with paint, the
windshield sparkling clean.

Plus, a low wall of sandbags ringed the top deck,
offering protection from snipers and shrapnel. They
had to weigh a lot, but the additional tonnage didn't
seem to affect the speed of the gunboats. Fat black
tubes for predark torpedoes rested on either side of
the stubby killers, the usual quad-.50-caliber assembly
removed for a single .50-caliber machine gun. The
depth charge racks were gone, replaced with small
black-powder cannons, and in the middle of the ship
was a honeycomb arrangement of short pipes stuffed
full of sleek rockets.

"Those must be the Firebirds Jones mentioned,"
Dean grunted, pulling on his clothes. His skin was
raw on the right side of his chest, the rest of his body
greasy, and the cloth kept sticking in place and had
to be pulled loose again and again. Hopefully at the
next redoubt, there would be a working shower.

"If those were LAW rockets," his father said,
never slowing in his work, "one ship would have
enough to level the whole ville."

"Look homemade," the boy said, buttoning his
shirt closed.

"Doesn't mean they aren't as deadly as a shitter
full of muties," Ryan added grimly. Five of the boats
were staying outside the breakers, while the rest
steamed into the harbor. Point advance guard and
cover guard. These sailors weren't fools.

"Want me to help row?" the boy asked.

"Hell, no. Toss a line over the side," Ryan

growled, his hand slipping off the oar from the slippery blood. "Make it look like we're fishing, not trying to get away."

"Yes, sir," Dean said, and fumbled with some twine, tossing a loose strand over the side and gazing expectantly into the calm water.

Not far away, the chilled shark floated belly up, schools of tiny fish and the big eel taking bites from the fresh carcass.

THREE OF THE Peteys cut their motors in the middle of the harbor, as PT 264 and its escort went straight for the dock.

The wind ruffling his hair, Lieutenant Brandon stood in the wheelhouse of PT 264 and studied the harbor. Everything looked peaceful enough, father and son fishing to the right, couple of windjammer trawlers at the dock, maybe a dozen canoes on the shore. There were a lot of sec men on the brick wall of the ville, but nobody was waving, and the gate was closed. At least the alarm gong wasn't sounding, so there couldn't be anything really wrong.

"Look there, sir," Sergeant Thor said, pointing. "At the end of the dock."

Brandon did, and frowned. As always, a couple of lanterns were hung at the end of the pier, to light the arrival of ships and give them sufficient warning not to crash into the dock. But one was draped with kelp. At night the light would be a bright green, visible for miles.

"Another bastard traitor," Brandon muttered,

clenching a fist. "Kinnison only wanted the flash, nothing more."

"And now, sir?" the sergeant asked, trying not to move his face too much. On the long trip here, he had received his tattoo of rank, and the hundreds of needle stabs across his features still hurt, throbbing painfully through the night. Only the nimble tongue and young flesh of the silent slave helped him get to sleep at night. Brandon had already agreed to sell her to him. The price was high, ten blasters, but well worth it. She was the hottest slut he had ever had. Just amazing.

"This the second time we've been here and found traitors," the lieutenant said through clenched teeth. "The children go into chains, and we chill everybody else."

"Even the local baron?"

"Him first."

"Yes, sir." Thor grinned, checking the longblaster at his side.

STANDING QUIETLY in the hatchway leading to the lower deck, the slave said nothing and turned away so she could smile. Excellent. Let the norms chill one another. The fewer the better. As soon as the Peteys reached shore, she would dive overboard and swim for the jungle. She knew the formula for black powder, plus a lot of other weapons tech, and when the people faced norm soldiers again, they would be on equal footing.

"HALF REVERSE," the pilot said into the speaking tube, and the boat noticeably slowed its approach to the dock. "Quarter speed…full reverse! All stop." The motors cut, and the Petey drifted into the slip like fingers into a glove. It bumped once against the wag tires edging the wood pylons and stopped as the bow softly crunched against the clean sandy beach.

While the crew attached the mooring lines, Thor worked the bolt on his longblaster and Brandon strode onto the dock. His clothing was amazingly clean, the white shirt and pants almost spotless, and had no patches. The shirt was unbuttoned halfway down, exposing a hairy muscular chest covered with ritual scars in a graduated delta pattern. A black leather belt was draped loosely across his wide chest in the manner of a bandolier, the loops full of shiny brass cartridges, and a huge revolver jutted from the holster.

Tucking his thumbs into the belt, Brandon checked the derringer hidden behind the buckle and bumped his left boot against the sandbags to make sure his stiletto was in place. Fine.

"Ahoy, Cold Harbor ville!" he shouted through cupped hands. "Open your gate and bring me Baron Langford at once! By order of the lord baron!"

There was no response from the people moving on the brick wall. Were they loading cannons? Impossible. Nobody would dare to shoot at the sec chief from Maturo Island!

"Last chance!" the lieutenant shouted.

Again, nothing.

"Master gunner!" he said over a shoulder. "Launch a Firebird. That'll get their attention."

Puffing a green cigar, the grizzled man removed it to blow a smoke ring. "Into?" he asked.

"Over. This time."

"Aye, aye, skipper."

Going to the launch pod, a sailor touched a loose fuse with the glowing tip of the seaweed stogie. It sizzled briefly, then the Firebird in the nest shook and leaped away on a spray of flame and smoke. The people on the wall gasped, and went out of sight. Only a few remained.

"Langford is dead!" a ville sec man shouted back.

"Bullshit!" Brandon shouted over the waves on the beach. "Bring him to me right now, or I'll blast that wall apart. Ya got ten seconds!"

Hastily a dozen voices shouted it was the truth, more pleading for clemency.

"What do you know, some stud aced the monster of Cold Harbor," Brandon said, addressing the crew of both PT boats at the dock. "Must be one big son of a bitch. Thor, ace the man as soon as we know who he is. Don't want to have to fight anything that sent Langford into the ground."

"Consider it done, sir," the sergeant said, wrapping the shoulder strap of the Weatherby .30-06 around his forearm to help steady his aim. The antique was cumbersome, heavy to carry and slow to shoot. But when one of its soft lead rounds hit, it was as if they had been struck by lightning. It didn't matter how big and strong the baron was. One shot and it was all over.

"Now open that gate!" Brandon ordered, placing his fists on his hips and radiating supreme confidence.

Suddenly a frightened face appeared on the wall. "Mercy, sir!" the sec man begged. "We had no idea the crazy bitch was making black powder! She said gunpowder. We didn't know what it was until too late!"

"Shut up, fool!" another sec man snapped, and cuffed the first across the mouth. "You on the beach! Leave, or die!"

"We're not going into chains!" another added fiercely.

Walking back a step, Brandon felt a chill run along his spine. Make. The first man said make, not try, or experiment. And now open rebellion? Shitfire, it had finally happened. Some brainboy figured out the formula. Or at least, a formula. If the proportions were wrong, it would only sizzle and not send a cannonball more than a few feet. Only one way of finding out if it worked, or was just black dirt.

"Open that bastard gate right now!" Brandon bellowed at the top of his lungs, drawing his revolver. "Or I'll level the whole ville!"

"Fuck you, spud. Death to the Lord Bastard!" a sec man shouted from the wall, pointing a flintlock and firing.

There was a hum past his head and Brandon dived for cover, as both of the .50-machine guns on the PT boats cut loose, the heavy-duty rounds raking the wall. Bricks shattered under the impact of the massive rounds, and sec men toppled from view.

Thor fired, and the sniper reeled with most of his head gone. In reply, a cannon in the wall roared, and a rain of shots harmlessly peppered the beach, churning the sand. But more sec men replaced the fallen, and a dozen longblasters started shooting, gray smoke masking the gunmen on top of the wall. The pilot of the escort boat cried out as his chest erupted in blood, and he staggered along the deck from the wheelhouse, trying to hold in his guts.

"Attack!" Brandon shouted, running for PT 264 and wildly firing his blaster at the rebels above.

"Cold Harbor free forever!" the people on the wall shouted, as a flurry of arrows hit the PTs, doing no real damage, and then another cannon stridently spoke, the water between the dock and a boat rising in a tall geyser from a near miss.

"LAND HO!" a pirate in the crow's nest shouted. "Cold Harbor due west!"

The smoky peak of the volcano came into view over the horizon as the huge windjammers raced onward, sails bursting with the wind. Quickly the rest of the jungle island rose from below the horizon. Some sort of mist was covering the ville, maybe a fog bank, but it hid the pirate fleet from the helpless landlubbers. There would be no need to wait until night. This was the perfect time to attack.

"Catch them with their pants down," Giles said eagerly, limping to the railing with the aid of a crude crutch made from a tree branch. His left leg was gone from the knee down, the stump too tender yet to strap on a wooden pegleg.

It hadn't taken Bachman long to acquire seven other ships to stage a raid on as big a prize as a full shipload of black powder. And even if the captains and crews of their sister vessels weren't seasoned fighters, eight windjammers was an armada. All counted, the fleet carried more than a hundred cannons of assorted sizes. That was almost as much as the ill-fated *flotilla* that had attacked Maturo Island a hundred moons ago. But this was no predark fortress armed with Firebirds and rapidfires. Just some fat fisherman with a bunch of old cannons, half of which probably didn't work.

Standing at the wheel, Captain Bachman removed his wicker hat as he sniffed the air. ''Is that Petey smoke I smell?'' he asked the crew at large.

''Look!'' a bosun shouted, leaning far over the gunwale to point. ''Must be a dozen of the things in the harbor, skipper!''

''That many?'' a pirate asked, surprised. ''Are they attacking the ville?''

''Looks like,'' another pirate growled, loosening the sword at his side. ''What's going on, skipper?''

''Nuked if I know,'' Bachman said, studying the island through his glass. ''Mebbe they didn't pay for all that black powder the *Constellation* was carrying and now the lord bastard wants it back, with interest.''

''Or maybe Kinnison is finally building a second fortress,'' Red Blade growled, advancing to the railing of the quarterdeck and gripping the wood hard. "Not going to rule in secret anymore, just gonna take over, island by island."

"Always knew he'd try some day," Giles said gruffly, shifting to the motion of the vessel.

"Yeah," another pirate added. "But we found him first."

The bosun scratched his chest. "If it's war the fat pussball wants, then let's give him some!"

"What about the other ships?"

"They'll do as they're told," Bachman stated, tucking the lens into his vest. "If they want a piece of the booty."

"Ready all blasters for a broadside!" Red Blade shouted through cupped hands. "Solid shot and chain. We'll sink them before they even know we're here!"

"Bo, what about the Firebirds?" a pirate asked, scratching his cheek with the iron hook at the end of his wrist.

"Can't hit what they can't see. The smoke from their own blasters will let us slip in and chill them all."

"Bosun, full sails!" Captain Bachman ordered. "Tack on every yard of canvas the masts will hold! We'll charge right down their throats with guns blazing!"

"Our thirty-pounders give twice the range of any other pirate!" Red Blade boasted proudly. "Blow them out of the water, we will!"

"Just as long as the outlanders are mine," Giles stated, drawing a dagger and stabbing it into the wooden railing. "Got plans for that one-eyed fucker and his bitch.

"Gonna take them a long time to die," the pirate muttered, his mind filled with demented visions of flame, blood and knives. "Oh yeah, a real long time."

IN A SPRAY of sparks, a Firebird rustled from its nest on PT 264 and streaked across the beach to slam into the ville gate. The stout barrier was blown apart in a thunderclap, a dozen voices shrieking on the other side.

A .50-caliber machine gun stuttered at the palisades of the wall, while another flight of arrows arced high into the sky and plummeted downward, hitting water and deck, but no flesh.

"Another rocket!" Brandon ordered, reloading his blaster when there was an odd whistling noise in the air. He realized what it was just in time to drop and cover his head with both arms before the barrage of cannonballs hit.

Sand jumped on the beach, geysers rose from the water, bricks exploded outward from the Cold Harbor wall, and the dock violently shattered, spraying pieces of wood in every direction. On PT 144, sec men screamed as the hail of splinters tore them apart like a shotgun blast.

"Get moving!" Brandon commanded, scrambling aboard his own vessel. "That's the *Gibraltar* out there! Her thirties can tear us apart!"

Staggering along the deck, the crew was alive and undamaged, merely shaken from the terrible near miss. The hull bristled with splinters, and one man had a sliver sticking out of his arm that went completely through. Shock had him numb, and the sailor didn't even know he was wounded yet.

"Thirty-pound cannons?" the pilot gasped, even as he slipped the gears into reverse. "Davey save our ass if those hit!"

In agonizing slowness, the thumping of the engines increased and the ship started to back away from the decimated beach.

On the wall, the ville sec men cheered, and their fifteen pounders boomed again, a line of splashes dotting the water around the three vessels in the middle of the harbor. A sec man was slammed overboard. Two of the Peteys launched Firebirds that streaked past the ville and disappeared into the jungle beyond.

"They missed?" the pilot of PT 264 cried out aghast, struggling with the wheel. The rudder was stiff, something obviously damaged underwater. "How can that be?"

"It's the smoke." Brandon cursed bitterly. "The warheads can't see clearly." This was bad. Without the rockets for protection, the battle was going to get bloody fast. Speed was their only hope now. The ville had no range, the pirates were large but slow, while the Peteys could move like crazy once they got up full steam. "Pilot, give me a zigzag pattern! Don't let them track us for another hit!"

"Aye, sir!"

"Bastard pirates," Thor growled, and fired his longblaster twice at the distant windjammers. They were definitely in his range, but all of the exhaust fumes from their own engines, mixed with the discharges of the ville's cannons, made it damn near impossible to target anything. Their forces divided, looking in the wrong direction, it was a perfect time for the coldhearts to stage an ambush. The Peteys were trapped between two enemies, and the cross fire had already claimed one of their crafts. PT 144 was listing to starboard, clearly taking on water. Stationary, it was good as sunk.

Beyond the breakers, the five Peteys were already moving in a defensive pattern, crossing one another's wakes and circling back to confuse the enemy gunners. Then the pirate cannons thundered again, one ship a lot louder than the others combined. Splashes announced all misses, except for the ville. Cannonballs brutally impacted the weakening wall, smashing out chunks of masonry, men and debris flying everywhere.

An arm landed on the beach, and a brick shattered on the boiler of the tilting PT 144, putting a deep dent into the metal. Instantly steam whistled out of a tiny hole. Stumbling from the wheelhouse, the engineer walked around a leaking torpedo and shuffled across the bloody deck, trying to take in the sheer scope of the destruction. The rest of the crew was chopped into mincemeat, the hull broken wide open, the keel already resting on the sand at the bottom of the shallows. At least she couldn't sink any deeper. Then a whistle caught the engineer's attention, and he bitterly cursed at the fact the 144 didn't even have engine power anymore. It didn't make any real difference. The wreck was never going into battle again, but somehow it seemed to finalize her demise. The victor in a hundred fights, the deadly PT 144 had been reduced to a pile of timber in a heartbeat. Glancing around for the sister boat, the engineer saw Brandon and the crew of PT 264 racing away from shore.

"Hey, Lieutenant!" he shouted, waving an arm. "Over here! I'm still alive! Come back, sir!"

In response, a hail of miniballs hit the deck from the flintlocks of the ville sec men, and he dived behind the tattered remnant of the sandbag wall, reaching for his own blaster only to find the holster empty. Nuking hell, he had to have dropped it somewhere. Alone and unarmed, the man knew his chances for survival were zero. In a rush of blind anger, the engineer insanely stood and went to the Firebird nest. The flintlocks fired again, but the ball ammo only tugged his clothing in near misses, but never found flesh.

Bracing a boot on the smashed .50-caliber blaster, he managed to swivel the launch pod so that it faced the pirate ships. Fuck the ville. He wanted revenge on the men who had killed his ship! However, when he released the pod to light a match, it swiveled away, following the pull of gravity.

In the harbor, more harmless splashes dotted the ocean, then a hit slammed the Firebird pod of PT 75 overboard, taking six men with it into the drink. In response, PT 264 launched a lone Firebird that gracefully curved through the sky and punched through the hull of a pirate ship, detonating inside the vessel. Il-luminated from within, the windjammer burst into a million pieces, flames licking upward to ignite the mainsail, even as the craft slipped into water.

"One for us!" the engineer cried, a humming mini-ball ruffling his hair in its passage. Grabbing a moor-ing line, the man lashed the rope around the pod, looped it over a cleat, then around his own waist. Lighting the main fuse with his match as it burst into sparkling action, he ducked low, holding on to the rope tightly.

He laughed in triumph as the pod jerked to the multiple launches, Firebirds erupting from the pod on a second. But then PT 144 rocked from the impact of another cannonball and the rope slipped from his hands. Fast and furious, the Firebirds continued to launch, now heading randomly for new targets.

"No!" the engineer raged, reaching for the pod, when it swung about, the hot exhaust washing over the deck. He was caught full in the face and promptly burst into flames.

Waving his arms and screaming, the man raced for the water, but tripped over the wreckage and the dead, again and again, until he was completely disoriented and began to crawl blindly for the edge of the ship, his flesh black and peeling away from his bones. The snipers on the ville wall ignored the burning man and turned their attentions to living targets.

Spiraling crazily through the air, the full salvo of rockets from PT 144 went in every possible direction.

A rocket zoomed past PT 264 in the harbor, but

PT 53 took a direct hit in the wheelhouse, the captain and pilot volatilized by the blast, the rest of the crew on deck blown off the ship. Out of the control, the vessel continued on its last heading and charged straight for the shore.

Out beyond the breakers, the captain of PT 286 could only stare as a Firebird from shore streaked by through the smoke-filled air, heading toward the pirate vessels, then swept back across the lord baron's armada. PT 67 was hit amidships and lifted from the water by the sheer force of the blast. PT 99 was struck in the Firebird pod, the resulting detonation seeming to shatter the world.

The rest of the Firebirds streaked on to the pirate fleet, punching holes in the sails, detonating in the air, diving into the sea. Only one hit a vessel straight down from the sky, disappearing into the hold. A fireball welled from the guts of the ship, flame shooting out the gunports and hatches. The rigging caught like fuses, spreading the blaze, until the ship was burning on every deck. Dozens of pirates leaped into the ocean, only to begin splashing madly as they found the water filled with sharks.

Across the harbor, Brandon couldn't believe what he was seeing. Four of his ten gunboats annihilated by one of their own, only two enemy ships sunk. It was a disaster! Kinnison would have his balls for this. Or worse.

Shouting commands, the lieutenant rallied his crew and they began waving colored flags at the ville and specific ships, assigning targets to the other gunboats. As the ville and pirate cannons roared, the remaining PT boats changed their courses while grim sec men dashed about preparing weapons.

Chapter Seventeen

Billowing smoke covered the sea, lances of flame stabbing into the murky clouds as the giant windjammers thundered volley after volley, Cold Harbor ville doing the same.

Frantically dodging the cross fire, PT boats darted about spraying the ships with machine guns, dropping the occasional torpedo or launching another Firebird, all the while being extremely careful not to hit any of their own ships again. Two of the Peteys nearly collided in the chaos, and another just missed being crushed under the foamy bow of the *Gibraltar* when it zigged instead of zagged.

Midway between the breakers and the dock, the old fishing trawler was moored to the stump of an old gnarled tree lying on the silvery beach.

Kneeling behind the gunwale, a sec man clutched his flintlock and watched the combat with a worried expression. "Baron Wroth, we should join the other defenders in the ville."

"We stay and wait," Krysty replied, the S&W .38 in her fist. "Should be here any second now."

"What, a cannonball to blow us to hell?" another guard asked. "We must retreat to safety inside the ville while we still can."

"Try, and you'd never get this boat ten yards from shore," Krysty snapped over the explosions of the battle. "And stop shooting at the pirates. You're only wasting ammo."

The sec men did as they were ordered, but unhappily, and shared angry glances with each other.

"This is bullshit," one man whispered. "Lord bastard's ships are getting slaughtered. Pirates, too. No way of telling who's gonna come out on top."

"Doesn't matter," the other softly replied. "Long as we have the tech that made the black powder. Both sides will pay big for that. Our lives, slaves, anything we want. What do you think?"

The first guard nervously glanced at Krysty and didn't respond, his pensive face racked with indecision.

Creeping to the bow, Mildred risked a quick look at the noisy battlefield. The dead were everywhere, wrecks burning as they sank, the sharks going berserk in a feeding frenzy, and worse, a glow was rising from the jungle behind Cold Harbor. The Firebirds that missed the ville had set the jungle on fire, even more smoke thickening the sky and lowering visibility. It also neatly removed the possibility of running into the greenery to wait out the fight and steal a boat after it was settled. They were trapped, with the fire and the enemy ships forcing them toward the cannon of the ville. Classic rock and a hard place.

"Cannons to the left of them, cannon to the right," Doc rumbled, worrying his blaster.

"Poem," Jak said in disdain.

"Based on a very real battle," J.B. said, squinting at the turmoil on the ocean. He could barely see it.

The albino raised an eyebrow. "Yeah? Anybody survive?"

"No," Krysty said.

A sudden thump sounded from the side of the trawler, and Dean rose into view tossing a soggy backpack onto the deck.

"Somebody give me a hand," the boy said, holding on to the gunwale while he tossed another on board.

While the companions rushed to assist, Ryan climbed onto the craft and knelt behind the gunwale. "We've got to get off this thing," he stated gruffly. "Sooner or later somebody is going to spot movement and blow it out of the water,"

"Just been waiting for you, lover," Krysty replied, staying low.

The munitions bag back where it belonged, J.B. hit the deck alongside the man and woman. "Find them?" he asked hopefully.

"Dean did," Ryan said, reaching into a pocket and passing over the glasses.

Wiping them clean on a shirt cuff, J.B. slid on the spectacles, blinking a few times to focus his vision. Back in business.

Exchanging weapons with Mildred, the Armorer checked the Uzi, then finally looked at the fight to see how it was going. Smoke obscured most of the action, but the cannons of the ville roared defiantly, the shots hitting the large windjammers but missing every one of the darting Peteys. Another torpedo leaped from the little gunboats, but this time it struck wood. The watery blast ripped open a hole in a pirate ship large enough to drive a Hummer through. The sea poured into the vessel, men scrambling to reach the lifeboats, the cannons on the slanting deck still thundering as the pirate ship quickly began to sink.

More torpedoes plowed right by the moving pirate ships, never altering their course by a hair. Yet the much smaller rockets would swing across the harbor to impact directly onto a cannon emplacement hidden in the brick wall.

"How the hell can they do that?" J.B. demanded softly. "Just isn't possible that the lord baron was working computer guidance systems."

"For black-powder rockets?" Mildred scoffed, sliding her med kit over a shoulder and tightening the strap. "No way."

"Mebbe alive," Jak said, ripping open a damp cardboard box and pouring the shells into a pocket of his jacket. Cracking the cylinder, he yanked out a few spent shells and reloaded every chamber. The rounds from Langford's Magnum worked fine, but gave off tremendous smoke, making it hard for him to see to shoot again, and making him a perfect target, a small ball of smoke standing all by itself. Fuck that.

J.B. scrunched his face in thought, then shook his head. No. It couldn't be.

"Whoever wins," Ryan said, opening the bolt of the Steyr to check its mag, "we better be long gone when the smoke clears."

"How?" Mildred demanded. "This tub is slower than hell. They don't have to sink us. They could pull alongside and throw rocks."

"The scope okay?" Ryan asked.

J.B. patted his bag. "Sure."

"Find the damaged PT, the one without the wheelhouse. Should be on the opposite shore somewhere."

Digging the Navy brass from his backpack, J.B. swept the distant shore until locating the vessel. Straight across the harbor, the damaged PT had finally reached shore, going straight along the short runoff from the lagoon near the waterfall and plowing into the soft sand. The boat stopped traveling, but rocked back and forth as the spinning props still tried to force the vessel onward.

"Bingo," he reported, compacting the brass down and tucking it away. "She's in the lagoon, motors still running."

"There's our ride home," Ryan said, draping the Steyr across his back. "And the boiler will provide the copper tubing we need. Grab your stuff, we have to run for it through the trees."

"In front of the ville?" Dean asked, wiping his face clean on a rag. His hair was still slicked down, making the boy seem years older.

"Not going anywhere, outlander," a sec man said, cocking back the hammer on his flintlock. "Everybody freeze."

"Nobody moves, nobody gets chilled," the other man said, doing the same to his blaster.

"Sorry, Baron, but we need you to barter for our

lives,'' the first man explained, aiming the weapon at the woman. ''You die, or we do. No choice there.''

''There's always a choice,'' Krysty said, then the woman dived for the deck.

As she got out of the way, the rest of the companions cut loose with their blasters. The sec men were torn apart by the fusillade of rounds, their flintlocks discharging wildly into the sky as they fell.

''Let's go,'' Ryan urged, grabbing his backpack from the deck.

Hopping over the side of the craft, they splashed into the water and waded to the shore, using the trawler as cover. Sprinting along the dead tree, the companions made it into the bushes just as the fishing boat broke in two, a cannonball punching straight through its old hull and disappearing into the beach.

''Glad we didn't shoot at anybody while aboard,'' Mildred said, clutching the med kit.

''It was those damn black-powder blasters.'' J.B. scowled. ''The two of them going off must have resembled a cannon firing.''

''So how are we going to do this?'' Krysty asked, spreading the leaves of a flowering bush to see the ville. ''We sure as hell can't run across the front—we'll be mowed down by both sides.''

''That fire is coming mighty close,'' Doc rumbled, studying the growing conflagration on the mountainside.

''Will it burn down the ville?'' Dean asked.

Jak snorted. ''Wall too thick.''

''We go around the back,'' Ryan said, switching

the SIG-Sauer from his right hand to the left. Just the short run from the boat had opened the shallow knife wound, and he nearly dropped the blaster in the slick blood. "Around the ville, there are fields cleared for planting crops. We'll move a lot faster on flat ground and should be able to outdistance the flames. At least nobody is going to be shooting at us in that direction."

"Let's get going," Krysty said, and the companions raced deeper into the thick growth.

Moving parallel to the beach, they used knives to cut and hack a path through the dense foliage. Monkeys screamed at the intrusion, and something large thumped out of their way, never to be seen. Masked by the vines and banyan trees, the companions could hear the thunder of the cannons mixed with the whoosh of Firebirds streaking by overhead, and the occasional crash of a direct hit. As the plants thinned, the ville came into sight and they could now hear the civilians screaming and blasters firing nonstop. Rioting had to have seized the ville, old scores being settled permanently while there was no baron to level justice.

"Stupes," Jak panted, wiping the sweat from his face with a sleeve. "Doing pirates' work for them."

For the usually taciturn Cajun, it was quite a speech, and nobody disagreed with the statement. The greatest danger to man had always been humankind.

Following along the base of the brick wall, they went behind the ville and started to run across the smooth fields. In passing, Ryan noted there were only a few cannons sticking out of the wall on this side, and nobody was walking the palisades. All eyes were on the big fight in the harbor.

Sinking up to their knees in a muddy irrigation ditch, the companions half expected to hear the whip-crack report of a flintlock firing, but they reached the other side and took refuge behind a bamboo toolshed in the middle of the open expanse without incidence.

They paused to catch their breath, and canteens were passed around.

"Thought jungles were wet," Dean said, scowling at the dark smoke rising on the horizon. "So what's burning?"

"Moist on top. Underneath it's all dead leaves," Krysty replied. "And once it gets hot enough, everything will burn, even the green wood and moss."

"We must be wary of a stampede," Doc rumbled. "The fire will chase out all the animals. It could be very bad indeed."

"For the locals," J.B. said roughly, patting the Uzi. "Not us."

Walking over, Mildred took Ryan by the hand and poured water on the cut to clean it for inspection. His cheek twitched, but the man said nothing.

"Got to bandage that now," the physician said, opening her kit. "Deeper than it looks."

"Once we're at sea," he said. "No time now. J.B., Doc, cover me. We should check the toolshed."

With the others flanking him for support, Ryan clumsily drew the weapon with his left hand and kicked open the door, ready to shoot. But there were no sec men on duty inside, only some chained slaves dressed in tattered rags. The skinny prisoners cried out in terror at the sight of the armed people, and huddled together whimpering. After making sure no sec man was hiding in their midst, Ryan started to leave, then turned and fired, the 9 mm slug blowing the lock off the long chain looping through their ankle cuffs.

"Head to the north!" he barked, and the prisoners dashed away, going in every direction. Some headed straight toward the approaching jungle fire.

With a somber expression, Dean asked his father a silent question.

"They'll confuse our trail," he explained.

"Right," the boy answered.

A minute later, they started across the fields once more when a slave stumbled back from the greenery, his face split in two, eyes and brains sluggishly flowing from his ghastly head wound. Then swarms of the tentacled muties came shambling out of the trees hooting madly.

"Stickies!" Krysty cursed, firing her blaster.

In his whole life, Ryan had never seen anything like this before. Each stickie was armed with a stone ax, the shaft attached to the right arm with layers of vines tied in place. Across each of their chests was a crude shield of bamboo wrapped with leather straps. A new group had joined the battle for Cold Harbor ville, and their bizarre army was coming straight for the norms.

"Aim for their heads!" Ryan shouted, switching to

his right hand and wincing every time he fired. Blood dribbled from his hand, but the man didn't slow or stop.

More stickies boiled out of the bushes, and J.B. flipped the switch on the Uzi to full-auto. The chattering little machine gun sprayed a halo of hot lead death at the scampering creatures.

Lowering the LeMat, Doc held down the trigger and fanned the hammer. The Civil War hand cannon repeatedly thundered in discharge, blowing a foot-long lance of flame from the barrel, followed by a dense blast of black smoke. Stickies fell, but more replaced them.

"Shit. There's too many," J.B. cursed, working the bolt on the Uzi to clear a jammed round.

The booming .357 penetrated the crude armor, chilling with every hit. Ryan fired nonstop, chilling with every round, but the man was becoming pale, his sleeve red with blood.

"Use the grens," Ryan panted, dropping a clip from the SIG-Sauer, and needing two tries to insert a fresh magazine.

While J.B. and Mildred maintained fire, the rest of the companions dug the black-powder grens from their pockets, pulled the pins and threw. Then they wisely ducked, not knowing how well the reloads would work.

Two of the charges exploded in the air, showering everybody with hot steel. Doc felt a tug on his frock coat from passing shrapnel, Jak jerked as a piece of the shattered casing hit his jacket but failed to penetrate the razor blades hidden inside the lapels. He muttered something and threw the other repaired gren as far as possible—without pulling the pin first. Damn things were worse than useless.

Bleeding from a hundred wounds, the stickies broke their charge and stood dumbly picking at the wounds. Two more grens hit the ground and did nothing, but the last three finally detonated, sending pieces of muties skyward. Startled and frightened, the stickies started attacking one another, and the chaos soon spread until the fields were filled with the creatures hacking each other to bits with the stone axes.

Rummaging in his munitions bag, J.B. unearthed two real grens and used them to clear a gory path through the in-fighting. Running and shooting, the companions reached the trees again, and stopped to chill some stickies coming after them. When it was clear, they continued for the lagoon, leaping over the exposed roots and ducking under low-hanging limbs. Cannonfire from the harbor could still be heard, but it was more sporadic. The battle was being won by somebody. Not good news.

Finally reaching the beach, they dashed for the trembling PT boat and hoisted one another onto the deck. Ryan went straight for the big .50-caliber machine gun and needed both hands to work the arming bolt. A lone stickie appeared from the trees, appearing mostly confused and he tore it apart with a short burst.

"Get this crate moving!" he shouted, gritting his teeth against the pain. The SIG-Sauer had been uncomfortable, but operating the fifty was like shoving his hand into acid.

J.B. stood at the ruin of the wheelhouse, the broken remains of the walls rising no higher than a foot. The captain's chair was gone, as were the control board and the steering wheel. A few wires were sticking from the deck. Walking halfway down the short flight of steps that led to the lower level, he twisted two of the wires together and nothing happened. Shit, no electric gears. They had to be manual.

"Mildred, flashlight! Find the transmission and put this thing into neutral before we blow a gear!" J.B. shouted, prying away boards with his hands.

The woman darted below, flashlight in hand. A few seconds later, the craft stopped trembling as the propellers were disengaged.

Finding a yoke with taut cables attached, J.B. tried to shift its position, and there was some reaction at the stern of the boat. But not enough. No time for repairs. "Doc, I need your sword!"

The scholar tossed over the ebony stick. J.B. made the catch and unsheathed the blade to plunge it into the wooden yoke. Grabbing the lion's-head handle, he now had some leverage and the yoke moved much easier.

"How's the boiler?" he shouted, flipping switches.

"Seems undamaged!" Krysty answered, checking the pipes and valves.

"Keep me posted on the readings!" J.B. ordered, experimenting with the yoke.

"Dean, in the hold with Millie. Stoke the boiler and keep up the pressure."

"Check," the boy cried, and disappeared down the stairs.

"Haul ass!" Ryan shouted, burping the fifty again. The hail of bullets tore apart something in the trees overhead that screamed and thrashed about before plummeting into the lagoon and sinking without a trace.

Suddenly, Krysty and Jak started firing at the shore. Sec men from the ville dived for cover, and shot back with their long flintlocks. The muzzle loaders booming loudly, the .75 miniballs slammed into the boat with sledgehammer blows. Then one of the sec men screamed as a stickie wrapped its tentacles around his face and dragged the man off into the bushes. Caught reloading, the other pulled a knife, but the stickies pounded the norm with their axes until the screaming stopped.

Ryan wasted no bullets until the creatures started shambling for the boat. He'd been hoping they would be content with the guards. There was only one belt of ammo for the fifty anywhere about; the rest had probably blown overboard when the Firebird hit. Unfortunately stickies were attracted to noise and fire like moths to flame. The more the companions fought, the more the muties wanted them.

The scent of the fire was beginning to taint the air as Ryan cut the abominations apart. The waterfall was making it impossible to hear any movements, so the man followed his instincts and sprayed half of the remaining ammo around them in a full circle. Startled cries announced numerous hits on men and muties.

"Reverse gear!" J.B. shouted, pulling on the sword. The props spun wildly behind the gunboat, churning the water into froth. Then the craft jerked backward, scraping its hull loudly on the sand, and started chugging across the lagoon.

Switching gears, the PT headed along the shallow runoff water until reaching the harbor and then leaping ahead with renewed speed. More stickies rushed from the bushes, chasing after the departing vessel, only to flounder in the deep water and drown as they tried to reach the norms on board.

Ahead of the companions, the sea battle raged on. Four Peteys were darting around the last two pirate ships, weapons chattering steadily. The cannons from the ville sounded now and then, but the fighting crafts were beyond their limited range.

Taking a piece of shirt from a torso of dead sailor jammed under the port cannon, Ryan wrapped the cloth around his aching palm. It slowed the flow of blood. Good enough for now.

"Now what?" J.B. shouted. "We're mobile, but in a bottleneck. Use the pass, and we're sitting ducks for those wall cannons!"

"Fuck the pass," Ryan growled, digging in a pocket with his uninjured hand and extracting his butane lighter. He flicked it once to check the flame, then headed for the undamaged Firebird pod. "We're going straight through the coral reef breakers, and at full speed!"

Chapter Eighteen

Muttering curses, Giles stumped along the smoky deck of the *Gibraltar*, trying not to trip over the bodies. Only two ships of the pirate fleet were still floating; the rest were sinking or burning. The other vessel, whatever its name was, had ceased firing its cannons once the mainsail caught fire and fell to the deck, smothering the crew. Many had tried to cut their way free, but nobody escaped from the burning canvas.

Now there was only Giles, and the *Gibraltar*. The rest of the swabs on board the flagship had been aced by a Firebird that flew over and exploded in the air, the shrapnel chilling everybody on deck. Only he had survived, the mast shielding him from the deadly blast. Now Giles was alone, the last pirate on the last ship.

The Peteys were still circling the dead ships, firing bursts from those big rapidfires, but soon even those idiots would realize nobody was shooting back, and they'd start coming on board for a recce. With blasters in one hand and slave chains in the other. No way Giles would ever let others do to him what he did so often to his prisoners. Death first.

Moving among the corpses, the pirate took a knife

from a dead man, a gourd of wine and water, a machete and finally a revolver and three live rounds from the still hands of Red Blade. Or he thought it was Red Blade. It was hard to tell without a head on the body.

Well armed, Giles headed for the hatchway. He'd grab some food in the galley, then go hide in the bilge with the rats. Back on the *Delta Blue,* there had been secret places on the ship where a man could hide from the most ruthless search. Even used the cubbyhole once to smuggle out the daughter of a baron. Before the vessel had left the dock, Giles had been enjoying the girl while her frantic parents and an army of sec men searched the streets for the lost child.

Awkwardly thumping down the companionway with his cane, Giles knew it would be the same again here. He'd stay out of sight, for weeks if necessary, feeding off the rats until the time was right, then escape from under the very nose of the lord bastard himself. Afterward, he'd steal a ship and find those bastard outlanders again to finally get his revenge. This was far from over.

As THE COMPANIONS raced across the harbor in the damaged PT boat, their speed steadily increased until the craft was skimming across the water, going from wave to wave, practically flying.

Standing near the Firebird pod, Ryan noted that the pirate ships were oddly quiet, the ville, too. Only the Peteys were still darting about, shooting their machine guns and launching Firebirds. The Deathlands warrior watched as a tall man shouted orders while he fired a hand cannon into the sea, wounding the pirates being eaten by the sharks. He had to be the commander of the lord baron's armada. There would be no mercy or deals with a coldheart like that. Best to chill the man first chance he came under the crosshairs of the Steyr.

"Fifty yards!" Krysty shouted from the bow.

Quickly lighting the main fuse, Ryan aimed the pod at the water ahead of the bouncing vessel, threw a handle to lock it in position and stood clear. This worked, or it didn't. There was nothing more he could do.

Joining Ryan by the port cannon, Krysty felt a strange crawling sensation in her mind, and turned fast, staring at the rockets. She could have sworn somebody whispered to her, asking a question too soft to hear. Her skin crawled at the memory of the unnatural feeling, and her animated hair coiled tightly in reaction to her agitated state.

"Hold her steady!" Ryan shouted, keeping a firm grip on the cannon with his good hand. The other was tucked into his shirt, the throbbing almost too painful to ignore. He had been wrong; he should have let Mildred stitch it shut in the fields.

J.B. yelled an answer, but it was lost in the rustling launch of the first rocket. The Firebird shot ahead of the craft and knifed into the ocean, detonating underwater. Another launched, then a third, the blasts churning the sea with their detonations as the boat raced for the coral reef.

"Slow!" Jak bellowed, as another Firebird launched, the supply rapidly dwindling.

"Only four left," Krysty warned. "Too fast!"

"I know!" J.B. answered, wiggling the sword back and forth, making the speeding boat fishtail, its velocity decreasing imperceptibly.

But that was enough. The next-to-last Firebird slammed directly into the coral reef, violently blowing it apart, chunks of pink material flying into the air. The last rocket missed the reef completely as the boat shot through the boiling opening. There was a hard slam as they hit something, then the vessel was in the open sea and moving without hindrance.

"Damage report!" Ryan shouted down an air hole on the deck.

"We're okay," Mildred said, walking up the stairs. "No leaks in the hull. Dean got a bad knock, but nothing serious."

"Dark night, it worked!" J.B. cried in triumph and immediately angled the boat to put as much land between them and the fighting as possible. The point was only a hundred yards away. In less than a minute, they would be out of the line of blasterfire and safe.

"LOOK, SIR!" a sailor shouted, brandishing a fist. "PT 53 is running away!"

"Cowards!" Thor growled, levering a fresh round into his Weatherby. "We'll find them soon as this is done."

"I saw the crew get chilled, fool," Brandon retorted hotly, reloading his own blaster. "Must be some locals who stole the boat when it crashed on the shore.''

"Fisherman who can operate a steam engine?" the sergeant asked, pointing his longblaster at the departing boat. He tried to target the crew, but the two vessels were jostling too much for him to get a clear view. He fired twice, with no results.

"Well, it's not locals, sir," he reported. "I saw that much. They have rapidfire, and revolvers like us. But not the kind we carry."

"New blasters?" Brandon frowned. "Shitfire, it might be Langford. Always thought he had some good blasters hidden away someplace. Either way, we can't let them escape. Pilot, full speed."

"Aye, sir!" Abruptly PT 264 changed course and headed after the runaway vessel.

Feeding a fresh belt of ammo into fifty, a sec man asked, "What about the pirates?" His face was smudged with black soot from the dirty exhaust of the black powder weapon.

"They're dead. Signal the other boats to recce the pirates, make sure they're anchored securely against the tide, then follow after us. Don't like going into any battle without reserve troops."

"Aye, aye, skipper." Grabbing two flags, the corporal began stiffly moving his arms, relaying the orders to the other Peteys. Their flagman responded with an acknowledgment as the boats headed for the quiet pirate vessels.

"Already at the point, eh?" Brandon said in annoyance. "This boy is smart, all right. Best to not take any chances. How many left, Sergeant?"

"None in the pod, sir," Thor replied. "But we can reload a full salvo."

"Do it, and fast," the officer snapped. "I want this bastard blown to Davey. Faster, pilot! Use the coal oil, if necessary. Lose them, and I'll whip the flesh off your back myself. Move this crate!"

Skimming along the water at top speed, the pilot shouted orders down the tube, and soon the engine surged with power, its bow rising from the water as the craft hurtled along, smashing through the assorted wreckage and bobbing corpses blocking in its path.

ONCE PAST THE POINT, J.B. checked his pocket compass and headed due north, hoping for a break. If there was an undersea river running south, maybe there was another on this side of the island going north. They had to travel this direction anyway, so it couldn't hurt. But there was no sign of fast water.

A canteen was shoved into Ryan's face.

"Drink," Mildred ordered, taking his hand and splashing some of the vodka on his palm.

Ryan's eye went wide at the pain. "Don't waste this," he growled, pulling away. "Need every drop to leave here."

"Not anymore," the physician replied, hauling his hand back. "Dean found a pile of cans filled with coal oil."

"Must be emergency fuel for the engine," he

grunted as her needle plunged into his skin, sewing the cut closed.

"But J.B. says it will work fine in that turbine generator. We have gallons of fuel now. More than enough." Finishing a knot, Mildred paused to bite off the excess thread.

"Still got those empty bottles from the trunk?" he asked as she wrapped it tight with strips of boiled Army bedsheets.

"Sure," Mildred answered, packing away her supplies. Then she looked up and smiled. "Damn good idea. They hate fire."

"Slow it down, at least," Ryan stated, flexing the hand. "Better. Thanks."

"No problem."

A sharp whistle cut the air.

"Incoming!" Jak shouted, firing behind them.

Just rounding the point was a PT boat, stuttering flame from its .50-caliber blaster, showing it was already throwing lead their way.

Ryan went to their own fifty, and worked the massive bolt on the huge rapidfire. There was only half a belt dangling from the breech, and no spare coils of ammo anywhere in sight. Bracing himself against the recoil, Ryan fired a short burst at the approaching Petey while Krysty and Jak placed carefully shots with the handblasters. Shouldering the med kit, Mildred crouched low and started feeding cartridges into the S&W M-4000.

Pausing to let the wind clear away the acrid smoke from the fifty, Ryan cursed as he saw something with a smoky contrail arcing through the sky. Then another appeared right behind it.

"Missiles!" Doc cried, fanning his mammoth blaster at the moving target.

The companions cut loose with their blasters, while Ryan pulled the trigger of the fifty and held it down as he made concentric circles in the air, trying to zero in on the Firebird.

He got a hit as the lead rocket detonated into an aerial fireball. The second went right through and came out dripping flames only to explode one heartbeat later. Shrapnel peppered the stern of PT 53, bouncing off the side cannons, but the sandbag wall stopped most of the killer debris.

"Everybody okay back there?" J.B. asked from the helm. Both hands were white from holding the sword in place against the bucking yoke.

"Go faster," Jak replied, reloading his Magnum pistol.

"Doc, Krysty," Ryan snapped, grabbing some of the damp sandbags from the side and placing them on the aft wall. The others helped until the stern wall was three feet high and double thick. Now they had some protection against the rockets, and the extra weight forced the rear end of the boat into the water and kept the nose high. That would boost their speed. As long as another Petey didn't attack from their sides, this would work.

The Steyr resting on his shoulder, Ryan knelt behind the sandbag wall and tracked the enemy ship through the scope of the longblaster. The machine was in excellent shape, with not a single sign of rust or wear. Behind the windshield of the short wheelhouse were three men. A redhead was pointing a bigbore longblaster their way, a short guy was at the wheel and a handsome man with slicked-back hair and a fancy shoulder rig seemed to be shouting orders. Ryan assumed him to be the captain.

The enemy .50-caliber stuttered again, then a flurry of arrows lifted into the sky and fell pitifully short.

Working the bolt on the Steyr, Ryan delicately adjusted the focus and mentally calculated the sheer factor of the wind, trying to take the roll and pitch of the ships into account. The Deathlands warrior had done long shots before, but this was a pure bastard, on a moving platform aiming at another moving platform. Sea spray fogged the view, while the men on the other ship moved back, getting ready to launch another attack. The distance was closing.

Holding his breath, Ryan squeezed the trigger. A sec men on the deck threw his arms high and tumbled into the sea. He fired again, and another went overboard, but then the rest hit the deck, safe behind their own sandbag wall.

Standing, Krysty pulled a gren from her bearskin coat, pulled the pin and threw the bomb. Even with the converging vectors of the two vessels, it fell short and exploded underwater just as PT 264 went over the spot.

"Too far," she cursed, her hair moving wildly.

Giving an extra inch of wind sheer, Ryan fired once again, and the windshield of the Petey shattered, the three men clutching their faces and reeling about. With nobody at the helm, the boat veered off into the open sea, just as the pod gushed flame and a salvo of Firebirds was launched. The companions opened fire, but the rockets were pointing in the wrong direction and streaked off to the horizon to splash harmlessly into the sea.

"They seem to be out of rockets!" Doc reported, his hands busily reloading the LeMat.

"But they're still with us!" J.B. added from the smashed wheelhouse.

The Petey was struggling back on course, its side cannons booming while the fifty chattered steadily. Bullets hit the sandbag wall and one spanged off the flue of the boiler, just before a five-pound cannonball hit the water only yards behind them.

"They got our range!" Mildred cursed, going into marksman stance and quickly firing her ZKR. It was too far away to tell if the .38 rounds hit anything, but the Petey neither slowed nor swerved.

Levering in a fresh 7.62 mm round, Ryan swept the enemy deck with his scope, but the sec men had learned their lesson and were constantly moving about, even the pilot. Fireblast! No way he could hit any of them under these conditions, and the Steyr simply lacked the raw power to do any damage to the big boat itself. Wait, that wasn't true.

"Change direction!" Ryan ordered, standing and sliding the longblaster over a shoulder. "Keep the bastards right behind us!"

"Do my best!" the Armorer answered, fighting the

vibrating helm. "But this thing doesn't like going straight!"

"How's it going up there?" Dean shouted through the speaking tube. "We're low on wood. Should I stop feeding the boiler?"

"Throw in every scrap!" J.B. shouted at the tube, forcing the sword to tilt. The engraved steel bent under his harsh ministrations, but the yoke slowly followed and straightened out the Spanish blade. "Chairs, blankets, anything you can find that burns!"

"Done!" the boy's voice answered.

Going to the port cannon, Ryan found only wadding and shot, the kegs of black powder gone. The starboard cannon was out of wadding, but still had three small kegs of powder. Kinnison kept his troops well armed. Good.

Prying off a lid, Ryan drew the SIG-Sauer and shot a hole in the flat wood, then wiggled it back into place and pounded it tight with his fist. He did the same to the next two, and Jak handed him the munitions bags. Ryan rummaged around and pulled out a thick coil of plastic yellow rope. He held out a good yard length of the primacord, and Jak cut it with a leaf-shaped knife. Ryan then stuffed the fuse into the hole. The second keg got a two-foot fuse, the third even shorter.

Krysty and Doc maintained cover fire while the men hauled the kegs to the side of the boat where the sandbags had been removed.

Mildred was already there with her butane lighter ready.

"On my signal," Ryan said, going to the stern and

placing the barrel of the Steyr on the wet sandbags. Through the scope, he found the Petey easy enough and mentally marked his targets.

"Now!" he shouted, placing a finger on the trigger.

Quickly Mildred lit the long fuse, and Jak heaved the keg overboard. As it bobbed away on the wash of their vessel, the primacord sizzled brightly, then slowed, started to burn really fast, then abruptly slowed to only glow, before sizzling again.

"That not norm," Jak growled.

"Being submerged for a day must have ruined its composition," Mildred added, raising a forearm to hold off her wild tangle of beaded plaits. "Damn things might explode at any time!"

"Even better!" Ryan grunted. "Give them the rest!"

The next two were lit and tossed into the sea.

"What purpose does this serve?" Doc rumbled. "Those will never damage our pursuers. They are much too easy to avoid."

Krysty tensed her lips in understanding. "Yes, they are easy to avoid," she said, going to her knees behind the sandbags to reload. "Easy as going to hell."

Ryan said nothing, the crosshairs of the scope flicking from sec man to captain, as he waited for his real target to present itself.

Chapter Nineteen

"What did they just put overboard?" Brandon asked, his once handsome face slashed with a dozen bleeding wounds. The outlanders would pay for the mutilation in ways even the lord baron didn't like to use, except for kin turned traitors. They'd be starved until they willingly ate their own feces, and that would only be the beginning. They had scarred his face! Brandon would torture them forever, and never let them die. Under any circumstances.

"Who cares?" the pilot snarled. His right eye was gone, clear fluid oozing down his cheek, his hands a maze of shallow cuts that nearly obliterated his tattoo of rank. "Kill them all!"

In horror, Thor lowered the Weatherby scope. "Claymore!" he shouted, that being the only word he knew for a mine of any type.

Sticking his head around the wheelhouse, Brandon stared in the direction indicated. Floating on the surface were three small black-powder kegs, sizzling fuses sticking out of the lids.

"Fucking pitiful." The officer laughed. "They must be out of ammo to try something this desperate."

"Excellent," the pilot muttered hatefully, throttling down the engine.

"Maintain speed," the lieutenant snapped. "Just go around the things without letting them come close. When we reach PT 53, shoot for their legs. I want the bastards alive."

"Yes, sir!" the pilot shouted, and PT 264 banked away from the floating bombs.

Contemptuously Thor drew a bead on the other boat with the Weatherby. "I'll get rid of it," he snarled, and fired. There was an explosion, wisps of smoke rising from the bubbling water.

The sergeant neatly eliminated the second charge when something hard ricocheted off the boiler of PT 264, and a moment later there came the rolling report of a longblaster.

"The bombs were a trick!" Brandon screamed, and grabbed for the wheel from the pilot. "Angle back! Don't expose the boiler!"

But it was too late. Another slug hit the boiler, and the metal shell burst, a vent of live steam screaming across the deck, scalding most of the crew as it knocked them into the sea and boiling the rest alive. The noise was deafening, and Brandon pulled the pilot in front as a human shield in case of a full rupture. Slowly the steam eased down, exposing the partially cooked corpses littering the deck.

"Thor, do the same to their boiler!" Brandon roared, as the speed of their boat quickly dropped to nothing from lack of engine pressure.

Without a word, the sec man dropped his longblaster and slumped to the deck, a crimson stain spreading across his shirt from several pieces of twisted black metal jutting from his flesh. Furious, Brandon grabbed the Weatherby and started shooting wildly at the departing PT 53, but they were too far away, and even as he watched, the outlanders were piling sandbags around the vulnerable boiler.

"Nuking hell!" the lieutenant raged, spittle flying from his mouth, throwing the longblaster aside. "Pilot, fix that boiler and get our pressure back up, right fucking now!"

"Aye, sir," the man said sullenly, a hot rage filling his mind over being used as a shield for the cowardly officer. First an eye, and now this. He would make sure that the limp-dick bastard got his some day. Soon.

Stumbling past the moaning sec men twitching feebly on the deck, the half-blind pilot went to the hot boiler to inspect the damage. "Split a seam, sir," he reported. "Gotta let it cool more and patch her from the inside. Gonna take a couple of hours."

"Bullshit! Get it fixed in thirty minutes, or I'll remove the other eye!" Brandon stormed, then turned about looking over his wrecked gunboat. "Where's Bosun Jarvers?"

"Got aced, sir," a corporal said, holding a hand to a wound on his arm, blood trickling through his fingers.

"Then you're the bosun. Launch the torpedo."

"B-but we only got one left," the new officer

warned. "And those other guys are so far away already."

"Do it!" Brandon muttered hatefully. "I want them sent to Davey before reaching the horizon!"

"Aye, sir!" he said with a salute, and rushed over to the controls of the long fat tube. A single lever released the predark machine, and hopefully it would activate upon hitting the water. Sometimes they sank, often exploded; there was no way of telling. With his heart pounding, the sec man pulled the lever and the giant rolled off the vessel and into the ocean with a huge splash.

"ANYTHING IN SIGHT?" Krysty asked, stacking the last sandbag around the steaming boiler. The heat from the machine was intense, and the wet canvas of the bags was smoking already.

"Nothing yet," Doc reported, the LeMat cradled in his arms. "No, wait, there is something in the water. Could be somebody swimming…sweet Jesus, it is a torpedo!"

"Going too fast! Can't outrace it!" J.B. shouted, sweat dripping off his face from the exertion of controlling the boat. He didn't know which would break first, his arms or the sword.

Frowning deeply, Ryan fired the Steyr at the foaming crest coming their way. This was real trouble. The gunboat was fast, but torpedoes were a lot faster than any surface ship. Even if they had more black powder, the cannons couldn't track the aquatic missile, and bullets couldn't penetrate deep enough to set off the antique until it was dangerously close. Even at a hundred feet away, the blast would flip over their craft, leaving the companions floundering helplessly until the sec men arrived. And the trip-blasted thing would hit; it was only a question of when.

"Any more grens?" he demanded, firing the Steyr and the SIG-Sauer together.

"Not me!" Jak answered, doing the same with his Colt Python and the Webley.

"All out!" Mildred added, squeezing off shots with the ZKR. The spread pattern of the shotgun that made it so effective against the Firebirds made it useless against a torp. Unfortunately the physician didn't know where the warhead of the device was located, and so wasted seconds and precious rounds shooting randomly yards ahead of the crest, and yards behind.

Rushing to the front of the boat, Krysty snatched the Uzi away from J.B.'s outstretched hand and, going to the stern again, emptied a full clip of 9 mm rounds at the unseen war machine.

"Gaia save us!" she cried, slapping in a fresh clip. "Is the damn thing armored?"

"Maybe it doesn't have a warhead," Mildred suggested, "but is only going to punch a hole through us."

"Just as bad," Ryan answered, dropping the SIG-Sauer to reload a fresh mag into the breech of the Steyr. This job required a big-punch blaster, but the Steyr was the best they owned. Might be .75 flintlocks belowdecks, but there was no time to search for them.

Suddenly the powerful booming of the LeMat

stopped. "Why are we shooting?" Doc rumbled, holstering the mammoth pistol. "The machine only wants a target to hit."

"Yeah, us!" Jak retorted.

"No, my friend. Anything will serve that purpose fine." As loath as he was to do it, Doc grabbed the tattered corpse of a dead sec man from the deck and heaved it overboard. The headless torso hit their wake and was quickly left behind. "Flotsam meet jetsam!" the scholar cried out in grim gallows humor.

Immediately the rest of the companions started clearing the decks of anything that could float, bodies, cannon swabs, broken pieces of the wheelhouse, the wheel, captain's chair. They were still at it when the ocean thunderously erupted into a steaming geyser, the boiling spout climbing fifty yards into the stormy sky, then arching down to rain hot saltwater across the speeding gunboat.

"Any more torps?" Jak demanded, wiping the water off his face. Somehow, he looked even paler than usual.

"Only saw that one," Ryan stated, watching the enemy Petey disappear over the horizon. But that was only seven miles away, about ten minutes in a PT boat. These babies were fast.

"Then we're safe." Mildred sighed in relief.

"Until they patch that boiler," Krysty added, working the bolt on the Uzi to clear a jam. She wasn't surprised when it happened. Caked with salt residue from the ocean spray, the rapidfire needed a thorough cleaning before it would operate smoothly again.

"Speed is our best chance," Ryan said, removing the clear plastic mag from the Steyr. Just one round remained inside. Grimly he pocketed the partial and slid in the last full mag. "Got to lighten the boat. Jak, Doc, dump those side cannons. We don't have ammo for them anyway."

The men rushed to the weapons and used their belt knives to start hacking them loose from the deck.

"Mildred, stand guard," he directed, lifting a five-pound lead ball and casting it overboard. "Krysty, leave the fifty and dump the sandbags."

"Those are the only defense we got," she said, hoisting one in each hand. "You sure?"

"Too damn risky," he said, a second cannonball following the first into the drink. "Everything goes. Strip the ship!"

"I'd suggest we use that coal oil," J.B. grunted, sweat dripping off the man from his endless fight to keep the rudder straight. The cramps in his arms and shoulder were getting worse, but he stubbornly kept control of the yoke.

"It'll kill the engine in a few hours," he added. "But we're only a few hours away from Spider Island."

"You sure?" Jak asked, looking up from the destruction of the deck.

"Hell, no," J.B. replied honestly. "But I think so."

"Okay, go for it," Ryan said, brushing back his soaked hair. "We gotta reach land before those sec men find us again."

"Mayhap with reinforcements," Doc added, tumbling the small cannon off the craft. "Most undesirable."

J.B. relayed the order down to Dean, and soon the black smoke from the twin funnels shifted to a grayish color, then went almost white as the thumping of the pistons took on a more powerful sound and the PT boat lurched forward. The brine misted over the bow as the battered vessel knifed through the tropical waters.

NIGHT RULED the world, as the three Petey boats chugged softly toward the burning wreck of PT 53. A full moon was rising into the starry sky, the black horizon dotted with silhouettes of a few small islands and several sandy atolls.

Longblaster at the ready, Brandon surveyed the crippled vessel while trying not to scratch at the dozens of badly healing cuts on his face. The itching was driving him insane, and the salt spray wasn't helping any.

Behind the officer stood the launching pod completely restocked with Firebirds from his escort vessels; two spare torpedoes were primed and ready on either side of the gunboat. Even the smashed windshield had been replaced with the one from PT 77. The crew of the three vessels had been spread around so that all were short-handed, but none was too poorly manned to operate properly in a fight.

Lolling in the water, the hull of PT 53 was almost gutted to the keel, the boiler only scraps of twisted metal rising from the charred deck. The sandbags were missing, but that was something Brandon would have done himself to increase speed. However, the .50-caliber was still in place, and who would leave a blaster like that behind?

Carrying an alcohol lantern, a figure rose from the remains of the smashed wheelhouse and walked to the edge of the derelict vessel.

"They're not on board, sir," the bosun reported loudly. "Looks like the boiler blew."

"Could be the sarge hit it before getting aced," the pilot suggested, a rag wrapped around his head to hide the gaping socket of his missing eye. "Just took it a while to finally let go."

"Sometimes that happens," a sec man said, rocking to the motion of the waves. "Ya gets hit here, but blow miles away."

"Makes sense," Brandon agreed hesitantly, tightening his grip on the longblaster in an effort to not touch his face. Scratching would only make the scars worse.

"Then again," he muttered, "I wonder if these tricky bastards are trying to fool us again."

HACKING THEIR WAY through the thick bushes and vines, the companions reached the predark paved road on the hillside overlooking the fishing ville.

"Any sign of pursuit?" Ryan asked, squinting into the darkness.

J.B. already had the telescope out and was scanning the ocean back and forth. "I see some lights far to sea," he reported. "North by northeast. But nothing coming this way."

"Good," Dean said, drinking in the cool night air. The hold of the Petey had been worse than the noon desert of the western Deathlands. Many times the boy had wanted to ask for assistance, but stubbornly refused to admit any weakness. His father wouldn't have, and neither would he.

After landing the PT boat on the lee side of the forested island, the companions had off-loaded their gear, then set a bomb in the boiler and let the gunboat sail away by itself, stout ropes holding the yoke in place.

Ryan and the others went directly into the bushes, then climbed the sloping hillside to easily locate the predark road. They were only a few hours' walk away from the gateway and a fast jump out of the Marshall Islands. Hopefully their next location would be better, a nice quiet redoubt full of ammo and food. Such things had happened before, although very rarely.

Taking the point position, Ryan followed the cracked asphalt and led the group directly to the rusted iron bridge. Staying in the bushes, they waited for a few moments, but there was no sign of the cougars or the giant spider, the only sounds coming from some crickets in the grass and the waves cresting on the rocky beach far below. High overhead, a flock of condors flew by, each carrying irregular pieces of a fresh kill.

"Careful," Mildred warned in a hoarse whisper.

"Some species hide underground for weeks waiting for prey to return."

Grunting acknowledgment, Ryan drew the SIG-Sauer and pumped a few rounds into the loose soil, probing for an ambush. As the slugs hit, the ground broke part and the spider scrambled into view. Shaking off the excess dirt, the insect charged at the iron bridge, snapping its deadly mandibles. Ryan easily moved out of its reach, and the mutie slammed into the trestle, making the entire length of girders and concrete shake.

"Where brain?" Jak asked, aiming the .357 Colt Python.

"Try between the octemporal lobes," Doc said, cocking back the hammer of the LeMat.

"Don't waste the lead," J.B. said, and pulled a glass bottle from his munitions bag. It was filled with a pale tan fluid, with a greasy rag tied about the neck. "Thought we might have trouble with this thing again, so I made a few Molotov cocktails."

Krysty understood. There had been plenty of empty whiskey bottles in Langford's trunks, and the PT boat had carried more coal oil than they could ever need for the turbine. Then a new sound caught her attention, and she strained to hear it again, but there was nothing audible above the cries of the struggling mutie.

"Use it!" Ryan ordered, pumping in a few rounds with the 9 mm SIG-Sauer. No wonder the locals had leashed cougars to the bridge to hold off the insect. Axes and flintlocks were useless against this monster.

Lighting the rag, J.B. tossed the Molotov overhand and it hit the ground in front of the spider. As the bug retreated from the pool of fire, the Armorer withdrew another from his bag.

"Let it die," Mildred said, touching his arm. "There could be a lot more of these on the island. We might need every Molotov to reach the mesa."

J.B. lit another rag and threw the bottle. It crashed on the upper girders of the bridge, raining liquid fire onto the spider. Squealing in agony, the insect rammed the trestle, trying to squeeze inside. Black blood mixed with the flames as the colossal bug extended its head on a segmented neck, the mandibles snapping at the tiny humans.

The SIG-Sauer coughed in response as Ryan put a slug into its head. Squealing, the huge spider fought free of the narrow opening to now climb on top of the trestle, stabbing at the norms with its clawed legs. The light of the burning mutie illuminated the entire expanse of the ancient bridge, casting nightmarish shadows on both of the island cliffs.

"Son of a bitch!" J.B. growled, craning his neck. "Can't use a Molotov with it up there!"

Having no other choice, the companions cut loose with their blasters, the barrage of slugs tearing chunks from its mottled flesh. Hissing in unbridled fury, the giant shook the entire length of the bridge as it strove to break the steel girders and reach the defiant food.

Nearly falling into a pothole, Mildred shot a leg as it stabbed toward her, and it quickly withdrew. But another reached for Doc, and he hacked it off with his sword. Pouring forth blood, the stump withdrew and a different leg reached between the girders to slam the whitehair from behind. With a cry, he fell onto the cracked pavement and lay very still.

Searching for loose rounds in her bearskin coat, Krysty heard the odd sound again, clearer and closer this time. Some sort of a mechanical noise. Another PT boat?

The woman shouted a warning, just as the far end of the bridge violently detonated, the support girders screeching in protest as the bridge tilted to the side, the concrete cracking into a million pieces. The companions were thrown from their feet and hit the side girders hard. As they clung for dear life to keep from falling, the burning spider plummeted into the dark waters below, and Ryan cursed as he saw a Petey steaming through the moonlit waters, numerous flashes coming from its rocket pod.

"They found us!" he snarled, trying to reach the Steyr, tangled in the straps of his backpack and canteen.

"DO IT AGAIN!" Brandon shouted, leaning forward over the controls. "Launch them all! Everything we got!"

Fuses were lit, and the rest of the Firebirds rustled out of the pod spraying smoke and hot sparks in their wake. Fiery explosions dotted the entire length of the bridge as the rockets hit, tearing the rusty structure apart. The twisting metal screeching, the trestle fell away from the opposite cliffs, breaking apart as it hurtled into the choppy waves. The assorted tons of predark steel crashed down on top of each other for what seemed an eternity.

"They're aced," the pilot stated with a grin when peace and quiet finally returned. "Ain't nobody coulda lived through that!"

The crew cheered in victory.

"Mebbe, but they have escaped us before," Brandon growled, and the jubilation raggedly stopped. "Bosun, launch a torpedo at the wreckage. No, launch both of them. Afterwards we hit the island."

"The island, sir?" a sec man asked, confused.

"The bastards were fighting a mutie to get to the other side of that bridge," the lieutenant stated. "Not running away from us, but headed toward something. Hell, there might be more of them hidden in the jungle. I want half of the remaining Firebirds launched at anything in sight."

"Ain't nothing there but some ruins," the pilot offered.

"We'll start with those, then hit that tall mesa," Brandon said, pointing at one surrounded by a flock of condors. "It'll make a good base camp for a recce. Then at dawn, we'll land and see exactly what those people were running toward."

"Who knows? It could even be something the lord baron might have a use for," the lieutenant added thoughtfully.

Epilogue

"Here they come again!" a sec man cried, firing his flintlock.

The rest of the sec men and civilians hacked at the muties scrambling through the smashed gate of Cold Harbor ville, but without any black powder for their blaster, the clubs and axes did little to stem the invading horde.

Once inside the ville, the stickies spread out, hooting wildly and attacking anything that moved with their stone clubs: horses, dogs, children, it made no difference. Red blood flowed along the muddy streets of the ville as the slaughter became absolute.

A small group of norms had taken refuge behind the sandbag wall surrounding the locked armory. While a blacksmith pounded on the lock with a sledgehammer, the rest valiantly fought off the stickies with crossbows, knives and crude spears. As the dead piled at the wall, a sec man cried out and plucked a sliver of bamboo from his hand. Trying to toss it away, the sec man discovered that he couldn't open his numb fingers. Then a terrible cold flowed up his veins and into his chest. Breathing became labored, then impossible, and the ville guard fell with his mouth flapping, as if trying to chew air into his dead lungs.

More bamboo darts hit the last defenders and, as they fell, the stickies swarmed over the people in savage abandonment, their writhing tentacles tearing the norms into bloody gobbets.

Strolling among the carnage were a dozen barefoot girls in loose clothing. Oddly, aside from some scars and length of hair, the strange females looked almost identical, an unnatural similarity far beyond that of sisters, or even twins.

"Bitches!" a sec man cried, wielding an ax as he ran at them, swinging his dire weapon. "You did this to us!"

Casually, one of the girls shot him in the throat with a blowpipe. He stopped instantly, then tumbled to the filthy ground, his ax still clenched in a paralyzed fist.

"No, human," she whispered. "Your race did it to yourselves."

As the strange females turned a corner, a stickie blindly charged at the two-legs until it got close, then the creature darted away, hooting in terror. Amused, they continued walking, watching the norms and muties battle to the death, then stopped to observe the stickies rip skin off the human and mutie corpses alike to reach the tender organs inside. The feeding was very noisy, almost bestial in manner.

"How disgusting," a girl sniffed in disdain, stepping over the bodies of the slain. "Look at the mess they're making!"

"Oh, let them feed," Silver chuckled, tucking her blowpipe away. "The extra food will nicely fatten the mindless ones for when they go into our cooking pots."

"No wonder the Maker created us," she hissed in amusement. "Norms are completely helpless without their weapons."

"Most, but not all, sister," Silver corrected, remembering the fight at sea between the two PT boats.

"Some might even be as dangerous as us," she added grimly.

A forked tongue dangling from lush lips, one of the clones shrugged in response, while another knelt to knife a wounded man trying to crawl under a toppled wheelbarrow. He feebly tried to fight back, and so the chuckling mutie took her time finishing the gory job.

EVENTUALLY a bloodred dawn rose over the Pacific islands, the dim sunlight revealing six bodies sprawled on a distant shore, the only movement coming from the gentle swells cresting over the deathly still forms.

Don't miss JUDAS STRIKE,
the second exciting episode of the
SKYDARK CHRONICLES,
available in June.

Take
2 explosive books
plus a
mystery bonus
FREE

James Axler
OUTLANDERS®
PURGATORY ROAD

The fate of humanity remains ever uncertain, dictated by the obscure forces that have commandeered mankind's destiny for thousands of years. The plenipotentiaries of these ancient oppressors—the nine barons who have controlled America in the two hundred years since the nukecaust—are now falling prey to their own rabid desire for power.

Book #3 of *The Imperator Wars* saga, a trilogy chronicling the introduction of a new child imperator—launching the baronies into war!